Y0-AQT-065

BISSELL POINT

MISSOURI SMITH

JAN,
cut down on
the burgers!

Missouri
Smith

Illustrated by
Dan Patterson

Reading Lamp Publications • Saint Louis, MO

Editor: Florence Achenbach
Design: Gail Morey Hudson
Illustrations: Dan Patterson

This book is a work of fiction. Names, characters, places,
incidents, and dialogues are either the products of the author's
imagination or are used fictitiously. Any resemblance to
actual events or locales or persons, living or dead, is
entirely coincidental.

Copyright © 2002 by Michael J. Smith

All rights reserved. No part of this publication may be reproduced,
stored in a retrieval system, or transmitted, in any form or by any
means, electronic, mechanical, photocopying, recording, or otherwise, without prior written permission from the author.

Manufactured in the United States of America

Printing/Binding
Walsworth Press, Inc.
306 North Kansas Avenue
Marceline, MO 64658

Publisher
Reading Lamp Publications
9433 Marlowe Avenue
St. Louis, Missouri 63114

International Standard Book Number 0-615-12066-0

02   03   04   05

Acknowledgments

Several years ago, Jon Lilienkamp and I wrote our first murder mystery for the Bissell Mansion. It was set in St. Louis during the Civil War. Jon, a Civil War buff, introduced me to a fascinating book, *The Civil War in St. Louis* written by William C. Winter for the Civil War Round Table of St. Louis, a valuable resource in the writing of this book.

The Bissell Mansion provides dinner guests with a brief outline of the Mansion's history, starting with its construction by Lewis Bissell and proceeding through today. Dinner guests invariably want to know more about the mansion and its history. The most frequently asked question is, "Where can we find more information about Captain Lewis Bissell?"

I asked Bissell Mansion shareholder Jakob Schepker if he knew more about Lewis Bissell. He told me there is very little information available. Jake suggested I write a book about Captain Bissell and the Mansion. He provided invaluable historical works: *A Brief History of the Bremen-Hyde Park Area* by Norbury L Wayman; the *Mallinckrodt 125th Year Anniversary* book written and produced by The History Factory, Washington, D.C.; and a booklet published by the Archdiocesan Council of the Laity called *Historic Churches in St. Louis.*

Combined with leaflets and historical pamphlets about other local businesses, I had the groundwork to begin this book.

My first trip to the Missouri Historical Society in St. Louis provided invaluable information. The efficient and courteous staff guided me to a book, *Daniel Bissell* by Edith Newbold Jessop, another valuable resource.

The Missouri Historical Society also provided maps and surveys done by the St. Louis County Parks Department, which provided me with invaluable geographical information. I also want to thank the St. Louis Public Library System's Historical Reference section and Science and Business section for providing me with the answers to a multitude of questions.

At the Indian Trails branch of the St. Louis County Public Library I found a book that helped me immensely, *Missouri and Missourians* by Floyd Calvin Shoemaker, L.L.D. I also made use of the *Dictionary of American Biographies* by the American Council of Learned Societies, Webster's *New Biographical Dictionary*, and the *Dictionary of Missouri Biography* by Christensen, Foley, Kremer, and Winn. *Great North American Indians* by Frederick J. Dockstader was also extremely helpful.

A visit to the General Daniel Bissell Home in north St. Louis County further enlightened me. The St. Louis County Parks Department owns and preserves the Bissell House in Bellefontaine Neighbors. A trip to the St. Louis Science Center was very informative as well.

Through my involvement with the Missouri Playwrights Association, I met Robert Friedman. Mr. Friedman asked me to direct a play he had written about the assassination of President Lincoln, *A Simple Assassination,* another enlightening and significant source of information.

While searching for a locale to perform this unique play, a friend, Noel Stasiak, suggested I visit the Blow School in Carondelet, the site of the Carondelet Historical Society. He recommended a book that provided a wealth of information, the *History of Carondelet* by NiNi Harris.

I visited the Bissell family plot in Bellefontaine cemetery. The friendly cemetery staff provided invaluable source material.

Florence Achenbach, my editor and agent, is a Senior Production Editor for C.V. Mosby. Whenever The Captain got too blustery, she cut the wind from his sails.

Gail Morey Hudson designed the interior and the cover of the book. Her expertise is appreciated.

With the luck of the Irish on my side, Dan Patterson agreed to illustrate this book. Dan has my heartfelt gratitude.

I also thank Mario and Linda Ierardi for reading the manuscript and giving encouragement.

Bissell Point is a tale about real people and actual events and settings. However, the character depictions and interaction between characters are purely the result of deduction and my imagination.

Missouri Smith

TO FREE THINKERS

Contents

BISSELL POINT

Captain Lewis Bissell

A Family of Soldiers

I am Captain Lewis Bissell, an old soldier. I would like to tell you the story of my tour of this mortal sphere. I must warn you. Every tale an old soldier tells is a "war" story. So bear with me if I embellish a bit.

My Norse ancestors were Protestants who fled to France *(called Huguenots by the French),* then to Somerset, England, finally to America. They settled in Windsor, Connecticut, in Hartford County. John Bissell, my great great-grandfather, operated a ferryboat on the Windsor River in the mid-1600s.

The family mottoes, "In rectitude, honor" and "Honor is to be found on the straight road" were emblazoned in ancient Norse on our family coat of arms. Believe me, folks, the American branch of the Bissell family did not disappoint their ancestors when it came to upholding these principles.

I was born in 1789 in Windsor, Connecticut, while my father, Russell Bissell, was off soldiering somewhere. George Washington was chosen the first President of the United States that year. During my early years, I remember that my father and Uncle Daniel never referred to George Washington as "The President." They always called him "General Washington." I came to understand why as I got older.

I was an army brat. I'm proud to say I achieved the rank of Captain in the United States Army. I have a special place in my heart for veterans. The bond of brotherhood is strong.

(I was also a keelboat skipper on the Mississippi River for many years. Some people called me Captain until the day I died.)

Ozias Bissell, my grandfather and a general hell-raiser, raised the first company of soldiers in the Revolutionary War. In 1775, he marched his men to Boston to meet up with George Washington. General Washington now had the vanguard of the Revolutionary Army. It was basically the beginning of the U.S. Army.

Old Ozias was hard to kill. He was wounded three times in the war, captured twice, and spent two years as a prisoner of war.

Six of Ozias' sons served in the Revolutionary Army. Daniel, my uncle, and Russell, my father, started out as fifers in the 8th regiment. They were very young, 12 and 11 years old, respectively. Daniel and Russell were the most renowned of Ozias' sons. It wasn't easy following in their footsteps. They left deep prints.

During the Revolutionary War, my father was also taken prisoner and spent over a year as a guest of the British. After the war, Dad and Grandpa Bissell told my brother George and me war stories about their adventures as revolutionaries, but they wouldn't talk about their experiences as prisoners of war.

Uncle Daniel carried a secret dispatch from Philadelphia to Pittsburgh. That's a distance of 308 miles. Daniel made the journey on foot. He had to avoid Indians, go without food, endure bitter cold and extreme heat, and cross the many rivers and streams coursing through Pennsylvania at that time. The officer receiving the dispatch had trouble believing Uncle Dan survived that journey.

Daniel and Russell served with Major General Arthur Sinclair and his troops during the Indian wars. I loved hearing my father's war story about how they were ambushed by Indians on a branch of the Wabash River, one day's march from the site of Fort Wayne in Indiana.

It was November 4, 1791. When the smoke cleared, my father and uncle were the only ones left of their company. A piece of shot from a British cannon creased my father's skull, rendering him unconscious. Dad ended the tale by claiming that, when he awoke three days later, Uncle Dan said, "If that was a beauty rest, it failed miserably!"

Dad received stitches and a nasty headache, while Uncle Dan was promoted to Ensign for courage displayed in that battle. If Uncle Dan was in earshot of the telling of this story, Dad would always add, "As usual, I did all the work and he got all the credit." Uncle Dan countered with, "That's what big brothers are for."

Grandpa Ozias and his six sons were in for the duration of the Revolutionary War, eight years. Between them, the Bissell men served a grand total of 120 years military service. That's a claim no other American family of that time could make. Bissell is the English version of an Old Norse name that translates "to strive vehemently." Our family certainly lived up to their name!

• • •

In 1804, President Thomas Jefferson sent Lewis and Clark to explore the recently purchased Louisiana Territory, a huge land mass stretching from the Mississippi River to the Rocky Mountains and bounded by Canada and the Gulf of Mexico. James Monroe was the chief negotiator for the Louisiana Purchase.

Lewis and Clark chose a site near the confluence of the Mississippi and the Missouri rivers for the Army to build Fort Bellefontaine. My father, Russell Bissell, was assigned that task. William Clark gave dad one of the "peace" medals they presented to tribal leaders on their journey to the northwest. Dad sent it to my mother who was an avid collector of artifacts she thought might be of historical significance and of possible value in the future. Mom was filled with weird ideas. I don't know what happened to that medal after mom died. Never asked.

The army built the new fort and trading post to keep the British from traveling up the Missouri River to enlist the aid of Native American tribes to the northwest. They already had enough Native American allies.

In 1805, my father and his men built log cabins and a trading post just below a bluff near Bellefontaine Creek, not far from swamp water caused by periodic flooding of the two mighty rivers. Many soldiers took sick and died. The troops called it "the fever." Some soldiers thought gases from the sickly water were poisoning the air. Others surmised that the victims died from bites from the hordes of insects. A few suggested that maybe an Indian medicine man laid a curse on them. By Easter, a fifth of dad's troops were dead from the fever.

My dad died in late 1807 from the fever. Uncle Daniel, upon hearing of his death, rode 200 miles from Fort Massac, Illinois, for his burial. It was too far to take dad to Connecticut to bury him in the Rockwell family plot *(my mother, Eunice, was a Rockwell),* so he was buried in the little cemetery plot behind the trading post at Fort Bellefontaine alongside other victims of the fever.

Captain John Miller took command of this post after my father's death. Lieutenant Zebulon Pike and his men were involved in several skirmishes with the Sioux, Fox, and Sauk (Sac) tribes.

Tecumseh and The Prophet were stirring things up on the east side of the Mississippi, saying their federation of tribes would "eliminate all white men who crossed The Great River." Pike led his "rascals" from Fort Bellefontaine on an expedition west in 1809, long before Tecumseh convinced half the Indians in Missouri to attack the fort in 1811—but, that's another story.

In 1808, Uncle Dan took leave to return to Connecticut to get dad's papers in order. I joined the U.S. Army after working on the Windsor River ferryboat for a couple of summers. *(In 1663, the ferry was moved to Scantuck, Connecticut.)* I was 18 years old and an Ensign in the 1st Infantry Division.

Uncle Daniel needed a soldier with riverboat experience to operate the Army boat at Fort Bellefontaine. The riverboat would intercept boats going upriver to search them for British spies. It would also be used to carry supplies out to the fort from a warehouse in downtown St. Louis. He said I was the man he needed. He got permission from the War Department to transfer me to his command. It was no cushy transfer. Believe me, poling up the Mississippi is hard on the back!

In late 1808, Uncle Daniel, now a Colonel, received orders to take command of Fort Bellefontaine, but he took ill and we didn't get to Fort Bellefontaine until early 1809. *(His enemies used circumstances like this to discredit him with the War Department.)*

He was laid low by the fever. It was a strange malady. Uncle Dan felt weak and drained during the day, but had no fever. As soon as the sun went down, his temperature shot up. He became delirious and his body shook. When the sun came up, his temperature went back down.

He was beset by dark and terrifying dreams. Sometimes his heart beat so hard, it sounded like a great drum was pounding in his head. He would awaken with a ringing in his ears so loud that he became dizzy. Nausea followed.

One night, while floating just below consciousness, Uncle Dan heard my mother and me in the next room. We were talking in conversational tones. To him, the sound of our voices grew until it was like that of the roar of a waterfall. Visions of demons assailed him and the sound of our voices became the screeching of banshees. He awoke, staggered into the dining room, and screamed at us, "Shut up! For the love of God, please just shut up!"

The next day, he apologized. We told him we understood. Seeing him suffer like that reminded me that my father died from the same sickness that was tormenting Uncle Dan. What a ghastly way for a warrior to die!

In the last week of February 1809, we left Connecticut by sleigh. The snow was thick and well packed, and we enjoyed the ride. We made good time to Philadelphia. From there, we took the mail stage to Pittsburgh.

Warmer temperatures melted the snow and the roads were extremely muddy. We traveled day and night. The mountain passes were treacherous, and on moonless and rainy nights each passenger had to take a turn walking with a lantern beside the stage. Unfortunately, this didn't keep us from having an upset. After much struggling, we got the stage righted and on its way again. I don't remember how long it took us to reach Pittsburgh, but after all the jostling on that nerve-wracking road we were worn out from fatigue and lack of sleep.

In Pittsburgh, we bought a deep hull to make a keelboat

and we fitted a makeshift cabin on the stern. We enlisted some "volunteers" from Fort Pitt to help add a deck, a couple of gun ports on each side, and running boards for leverage to pole the boat. We needed the running boards because we laid the deck lower than normal to take advantage of the gun ports. We needed the gun ports because we would use this vessel for the risky task of intercepting boats suspected of carrying British spies. We added a mast for a small sail to take advantage of the wind when it was right. We accomplished the outfitting in 10 days. We christened her *Belle Fontaine.*

Outside the post, I ran into my old nemesis, Mike Fink. Drunk as usual, he challenged me to a fight. I reminded him that Army regs forbid fighting with civilians. I walked away to sounds of derision.

We set sail down the Ohio River, at times poling, at times drifting with the current. Often, strong winds and heavy debris forced us ashore. At last, we reached Isaiah Bird's plantation at the mouth of the Ohio.

Uncle Dan paid Isaiah for the use of several of his strongest Negroes to assist us in ascending to the Mississippi River on the shallow end of the Ohio. This was backbreaking labor from dawn to dusk. We had to cordell the boat at times *(pull the boat by rope while walking along the riverbank through the thick brush and trees).*

Mr. Bird sent a couple of slave-hands along to ride herd on his "property." The overseers didn't do a lick of work. They just followed along and kept an eye on the slaves. They wanted to get back home and complained every time we called for a rest break.

During one such break, I said to Uncle Dan, "This isn't right." I indicated the slaves, "Those poor fellows are busting a gut, while Mr. Bird's sitting in his house counting his money."

He replied, "Bird served with me at Fort Wayne. He's no saint, but he treats his slaves better than most. He feeds them regular and he doesn't beat them unless they get out of line."

"It still isn't right."

We finally reached the Mississippi River and arrived in St.

Louis on 10 May 1809. The riverfront was a perpendicular ledge of rock, not a good spot for landing. The city was smaller than I expected. The western boundary was 3rd Street and the northwest boundary was a few buildings on the end of 2nd Street. Where the courthouse now stands was a mix of forest and plains, and there wasn't a brick building in the village.

We stayed the night. The next day, we visited the Army warehouse so I could get my bearings and meet the soldiers guarding the place, since I would run the supply boat. We reached Fort Bellefontaine on the following day.

• • •

On the journey to St. Louis, I told Uncle Dan a war story of my own. The 1st Infantry Division was sent to pursue renegades raiding farms near the ruins of Fort Edward on the Hudson River. While on patrol, I got to see Robert Fulton's steamship, *The Clermont,* steam by on the first successful steamboat voyage in America. In 1803, Fulton's first attempt in Paris met with disaster when his boat sank. "Fulton's Folly," people called it. I read about it in the newspaper and kept track thereafter. In 1806, Fulton commissioned an English company to build him a steam engine, which he had shipped to America and placed in a steamboat. He had his life savings invested in the venture.

I told Uncle Dan, *"The Clermont* was heading upstream against a heavy current, cutting through the water like it was butter. It was astonishing."

In 1817, the first steamboat arrived in St. Louis. The steamboat changed the lives of people who worked on the river, people like Mike Fink, the so-called "King of Keelboatmen." Old Mike Fink, another military brat, was born at Fort Pitt, Pennsylvania.

Old time rivermen were forced to acquire steam engines and convert their keelboats into paddle wheelers. Otherwise, they couldn't compete with the swifter boats and they'd lose business.

• • •

Uncle Daniel thought Fort Bellefontaine should be up on the bluff above the original site, like Fort Edward. The new site would afford a better view and be an easier position to defend. Besides, it was further away from that sickly bottomland. The steady breeze would help keep insects away.

Most of the walls for the fort were up by 1810. The interior buildings, mostly logs on a rock bed, weren't finished until 1812. Uncle Daniel used nails from Philadelphia to construct these buildings, an unnecessary expense according to The War Department. Uncle Dan kept records that showed the entire project cost the Army only $1,000. At his court martial in 1816, he challenged, "I defy any man present to build a fort of that size for a lesser price."

We kept supplies for other forts. Fort Osage, near what is now Kansas City, and Fort Madison, on the Des Moines River in Iowa, relied on us for supplies. At Tippecanoe, in November 1811, General William Henry Harrison and his troops defeated The Prophet and a large band of Indians aided by British artillery. In December 1811, the British convinced several Missouri tribes to besiege Fort Osage and Fort Madison. Our troops abandoned these forts, which were quickly burned. Both forts were eventually restored to working order.

The troops retreated to Fort Bellefontaine, which was soon overflowing with soldiers. Some pitched tents outside the fort, so a pair of lookout towers were built. The Army also built a lookout tower and stone gun port at Portage Des Sioux *(commanded by Captain Charles Lucas)* and a cellar and stone gun port at Fort Zumwalt *(engineered by Colonel John Shaw)*.

It was standard operating procedure to dig a ditch around a fort. Uncle Dan had the newly arrived troops widen this ditch and fill it with sharp wooden spikes braced and half-buried in the ground, an old Roman trick. Uncle Dan said he never regretted reading *Caesar in Gaul*.

Uncle Daniel warned the troops, "We stop them here or die trying."

The troops were apprehensive, but they respected this crafty veteran of the Revolutionary War and early Indian Wars.

War stories about him spoke volumes and most of us had our own Indian war story to tell. Hell! Indians would sometimes pop up out of the brush and shoot at our supply boat when we were on runs to downtown St. Louis. I had a nice collection of arrows.

• • •

In 1804, the Army cleared a road from the fort to what would someday be called Bremen *(eventually Hyde Park),* a settlement just west of the St. Louis city limits. The Military Road, or Bellefontaine Road, was impassible when it rained. The mud and deep ruts just wouldn't accommodate a wagon laden with supplies. During my tour there, 1810-1814, I had to pole or sail Fort Bellefontaine's boat downriver to get supplies from the warehouse in St. Louis and take them back upriver to the fort. Sometimes, the river would be so high, rough, and filled with debris, it was too risky to travel.

We also needed the boat to carry out our main assignment —intercept river craft that might be carrying British envoys to the Indians. There was an early thaw in 1810. In late February, we caught two British soldiers posing as traders. One almost shot me in the face! On 12 March 1810, I was promoted to 2nd Lieutenant.

Out of necessity, the troops grew their own food. Uncle Daniel noticed that the men spent more time growing crops to produce alcoholic drinks instead of food. He looked the other way.

Uncle Dan knew a soldier's life was not easy. Soldiers throughout history suffer from the same psychological disorders. Loneliness, boredom, and battle fatigue are their worst enemies. Although Fort Bellefontaine had it's own "black hole" for the solitary confinement of soldiers who warranted it, Uncle Dan rarely used it. He was lenient about allowing drinking and gambling in the barracks. Gaming was one of the few ways for the soldiers to let off steam.

Uncle Dan loved playing the game of cribbage. He owned a beautiful ivory cribbage board adorned with Aleut scrimshaw.

Uncle Dan's laxity came with a price tag. The local Baptist

minister, John Mason Peck, complained that drunken U.S. soldiers and their French drinking buddies taunted his parishioners, making them afraid to attend church *(I wish I had thought of that one)*. With an assist from Captain Robert Lucas, the minister wrote a letter to the War Department to complain about the situation at Fort Bellefontaine. Robert Lucas also wrote his brother, Captain Charles Lucas, about Uncle Daniel's laxity and complete disregard of military discipline.

Both Robert and Charles Lucas decided to write letters to the War Department. In his letter, Robert Lucas said that Uncle Daniel himself gambled and drank with the troops, that there wasn't a game of chance he didn't like. Charles Lucas insisted that Uncle Daniel be relieved of his command. This feud between the Bissell family and the Lucas family was triggered by a field report written by Uncle Daniel in which Captain Robert Lucas was placed in a bad light.

As I said earlier, in December 1811, the British gave weapons and ammunition to the Fox and Sauk, the Kickapoos, and Iowas to induce these tribes to band together and go on the warpath against us. These Indians were averse to fighting in winter so the British used Tecumseh to convince his Missouri allies now was the best time to attack Fort Bellefontaine. An early cold snap froze the rivers, rendering our boat useless. Crossing the river on foot or horseback was now possible. Since our troops fled Fort Osage and Fort Madison, these Indians didn't have any trophies to crow about. They wanted our heads!

Uncle Dan knew that to the Native Americans making one "lose face" was more of a victory than killing one's enemy. When Tecumseh asked for a meeting with the "blue coat" leader of this post, Uncle Dan knew Tecumseh wanted to take his measure, to test his resolve.

Near sunset, Uncle Daniel, Captain Lucas, Auguste

Chouteau the younger, and I rode out under a white flag to meet Tecumseh's emissary, Yellow Dog, another legendary warrior. As Ensign, I was the flag bearer. Uncle Dan warned us to "show no fear."

Yellow Dog spoke excellent English and I was surprised at the similarities between the old Norseman and this sturdy Native American. Each had a harsh countenance, a look to them that defined the term "warrior." The sharp light in their eyes bespoke fierce spirits that would not be denied. They sized each other up and neither found the other lacking. Other than color, the main physical difference was size, Uncle Dan being the much larger of the two. No matter. Neither man would back down from this fight.

By comparison, Captain Lucas and his cherubic face looked out of place, his demeanor suggesting a more civilized nature. He was wary and his unsettled nature spooked his horse. It whinnied several times. I just hoped it wouldn't bolt, as unnerved horses are wont to do. Later, Uncle Daniel berated him in a report for almost getting us killed.

Yellow Dog's message was simple and familiar, "The white man has come far enough. You will not steal any more of our land. The bluecoats and the settlers must go back across the Great River and not cross to this side again."

He gave us until the sun is high on the next day to leave. Yellow Dog raised his spear to the sky. "Our people are not alone. The spirits of our ancestors ride with us."

Uncle Daniel's message was also brief. "The Great Chief in Washington will not permit me to leave. The few soldiers you will fight here are just an advance force for an army that will cover the plains."

Uncle Dan knew that Indians were superstitious and he played on it. He warned Yellow Dog, "The white man is also protected by a Great Spirit, a powerful God whose wrath is terrible to behold."

We rode back to the fort, Indian eyes boring into our backs. I wondered if we would survive the moment. However, Tecumseh's emissary, Yellow Dog, was true to his word. We reached the post unscathed.

That night, I had a strange experience. I was slipping off my boots when I felt a tingling on the back of my neck. For an instance my hair rose and then flopped back down again. I was really spooked.

I plopped down on my bunk and pulled the covers over me. I thought I'd have trouble getting to sleep but I nodded off immediately. It was like I closed my eyes and instantly found myself in a dream.

I was a small boy standing in a dry creek bed. My mother was yelling at me to get out before it was too late. Suddenly, a thundering wall of water rushed toward me. Seconds before it struck me, a great eagle grabbed me by the shoulders with its huge talons and lifted me out of the way of the torrent. It set me down next to my mother. I watched in amazement as claws gave way to fingers and talons to hands. The eagle changed into a man in front of my eyes.

My father stood before me. "Family always looks out for family, Lewis. Don't ever forget that."

My mother was crying. With a mighty screech, dad leapt into the air, instantly an eagle again. I yelled at him to come back as he flew away. I screamed until my lungs burned. Someone shook my shoulder. I opened my eyes and John Fredericks stood over me, telling me to stop my screeching before I woke everyone in the barracks. Chagrined, I apologized. I lay awake the rest of the night wondering what my dream meant. Just as I started to drift back to sleep, someone blew reveille.

The sun rose on what I thought was to be the last day of my life, 16 December 1811. I was 22 years old and way too young to die. Through the leafless trees to the west, all we could see were Indians and British artillery. Uncle Daniel called all the troops, even the tower lookouts, into the fort and assigned them places. We had eight cannons primed and loaded. We waited.

Just before noon, Mother Nature intervened. An earthquake of such intense magnitude struck that you could hear the river ice crack. The horizon tilted and re-tilted. I felt as if I was

on the supply boat in rough waters. The "hole" used for
punishing soldiers caved in. Luckily, no one was in it at the
time. The empty lookout towers crashed to the earth. The
timbers holding the fort together groaned in protest but held.
Those Philadelphia nails paid for themselves!

After what seemed an interminable length of time, the
ground stopped shaking. I climbed the wall and looked to the
west. Yellow Dog and his Indians were breaking camp. I guess
they wanted no part of our God! The tribes went their separate
ways and never banded together again.

My breath caught as I scanned the horizon. In the distance
where there had been nothing but blue skies, there were now
huge humps of trees. The forest had taken on a new shape.
Later, we rode west as far as caution permitted and discovered
rolling hills where once the forest had been fairly flat. A
gigantic hand had reshaped the landscape.

On 12 January 1812, a second earthquake hit, almost the
equal of the first. A similar earthquake struck on 12 February
1812. Miraculously, the fort suffered only minor damage each
time. The landscape was again changed. Bellefontaine Creek,
after which the fort was named, completely disappeared! In
time, a new creek emerged about a half mile south of the old
creek. We named this new rivulet, Coldwater Creek, since it
was born in winter. After the third earthquake, I kidded Uncle
Dan, "You might want to think twice before you threaten with
the wrath of God again!"

1814 rolled around. Uncle Dan and I were ordered to
Canada to join the fight against the British. Uncle Dan was
down with the fever again and was too weak to travel. He
reported late, another act the War Department used against
Uncle Dan to revoke his commission.

Daniel Bissell, now a colonel, was given the rank of
Brevet General, a temporary rank given to soldiers during

times of war. He caught up with his regiment at Lake Erie.
After a stint in Canada, his regiment was sent to Mobile,
Alabama. Later, they fought at New Orleans and Baton Rouge,
Louisiana. He commanded the last battle of the War of 1812 at
Lyon's Creek. It was one of the few battles of that war in
which the U.S. Army won a decisive victory on American soil.

I fought under General Winfield Scott at The Battle of
Lundy's Lane, named for a road that ran due west from the
Chippawa River. The Chippawa River runs from Lake Ontario
to Lake Erie, with the state of New York to the east and the
province of Ontario on the western side.

Although a 2nd Lieutenant, I was given the "honor" of
carrying the regimental flag into every battle. This honor is
risky business and is usually rotated among the Ensigns. After
all, capturing the other side's flag is what it's all about. The
flag bearer may as well wear a bulls-eye on his back. I made a
big target and was in the thick of it, but I survived.

The Battle of Lundy's Lane was a decisive victory for our
side. General Scott and General Jakob Brown, a Quaker,
received high praise for their actions in this campaign.
Outflanking the enemy from both the side and the rear, our
regiment captured a British General and the British artillery
battery.

General Eleazor Ripley received poor marks for his part in
this campaign, not because of his actions, but because of his
attitude. He thought fighting on Canadian soil was pointless
and said so.

After the war, Uncle Daniel and I returned to Fort
Bellefontaine. I was promoted to 1st Lieutenant on 30 March
1814. I was assigned to the 3rd Infantry on 17 May 1815. I
was commissioned a Captain on 30 June 1815, a couple of
weeks after Napoleon was defeated in Belgium at Waterloo.

Upon Napoleon's defeat, Pope Pius VII was released from
his imprisonment in France. One of the Pope's first acts was to
revoke the suppression order that would have disbanded the
Society of Jesus. The Jesuits played an important role in St.
Louis history, making major contributions to education and the
development of medical facilities.

Then I was transferred to the 8th Infantry on 2 December 1815. I left my recently acquired lands at Bissell Point under the care of my friend, Captain John O'Fallon *(Crazy John).* Crazy John also took fine care of his land. He turned it into a prosperous farm and orchard.

Land

*U*ncle Daniel, a Captain in 1804, was ordered by President Jefferson to accompany Captain Stoddard to New Madrid, Missouri, the seat of Spanish authority. Captain Stoddard was to assume the post of military governor of upper Louisiana. The Spaniards ruled an area half the size of Europe and were reluctant to give it up. They still had a considerable force in the area.

Not trusting the local Spanish government, the crafty Captain Stoddard didn't commit all of his forces at once. He sent Uncle Dan, with about one half of his command, to oversee the changing of the guard. If there was going to be any trouble, Captain Stoddard wanted to keep enough troops in reserve to counterattack any military move made by the Spaniards. Fortunately, he didn't need to use these troops. At New Madrid, Don Juan Vallee, the Spanish governor, officially surrendered the post and district to my uncle.

The Spanish secretly sold the Louisiana Territory to the French earlier in the year. However, they were still the official caretakers of the territory in March. The Louisiana Purchase was also known as the Treaty of Ildefonso, and Three Flags Day.

Don Juan Vallee was not well liked by the locals and by his senior military officers. He had commandeered nearly 8,000 acres of land, practically all of New Madrid.

In a gesture of goodwill and hope of protection, he gave Uncle Daniel a gift of 1,000 acres of this land. How did this affect me? Major earthquakes destroyed much of New Madrid.

In 1815, an act of Congress awarded equal tracts of land elsewhere in Missouri to landowners victimized by the quake.

Uncle Daniel bequeathed 150 acres to me, land he originally promised to my father. He sold 50 acres to our friend, Captain John B. O'Fallon *(Crazy John)* and kept 800 acres for himself. *(Another event enemies would use to discredit my uncle.)* Captain O'Fallon purchased an additional 100 acres north and west of my land.

I claimed 150 acres of prime land on the military road. My land stretched north across what is now Grand Avenue, west to the fairgrounds, south to what would become Ferry Street, and east to the Mississippi River. This house is built on what is called "Bissell Point" by river pilots, a landmark that lets them know St. Louis is just around the bend.

Doctor Bernard Farrar, the only American-born physician in St. Louis, did just as well. It was rumored Doctor Farrar went to New Madrid and bought 250 acres of destroyed land for pennies on the dollar. Supposedly, the Lucas brothers did the same thing. Doctor Farrar claimed land in several areas just outside the city limits. As the city grew, he sold these tracts of land to businessmen, developers, warehousemen, and others. He made out like a bandit.

• • •

1816 arrived and was quite a year. Uncle Daniel was court-martialed. Several charges were leveled against him. General Andy Jackson was the presiding judge. I was called to Nashville, Tennessee, to testify on his behalf.

Oddly, they asked me what I knew about Uncle Daniel's tour of duty at Fort Massac. Fort Massac was in Illinois on the north bank of the Ohio about 38 miles from its convergence with the Mississippi, a mile southeast of Metropolis, Illinois.

I advised the court I had only secondhand knowledge. I testified that all I could tell them was a war story my uncle told me on our trip from Connecticut to St. Louis. They wanted to hear it.

Uncle Daniel was the commandant of Fort Massac. President Thomas Jefferson charged him with the duty of Port

Authority Officer, a tedious job inspecting ships moving up
and down the Ohio to and from the Mississippi. There was still
bad blood between England and America.

In early 1807, Aaron Burr was tried for treason. Even
though acquitted, Burr knew he was no longer welcome in
America. He took to the waterways. A message was sent to
Uncle Daniel to watch for Burr's traveling party, which was
suspected of smuggling arms to foment rebellion.

Aaron Burr did show up. However, Uncle Daniel found no
arms or anything at all suspicious on any of the boats of his
traveling party. Aaron Burr stayed for one night, and even had
dinner with Uncle Daniel. The last he saw of Burr's party it
was moving downriver to the Mississippi.

Uncle Daniel told me, "Mister Burr was just a worn out
old man, hardly a danger to anyone."

Robert Lucas accused Uncle Dan of promoting illegal
gambling on government property. Charles Lucas charged that
Uncle Dan used soldiers to build his house. The soldiers
testified they were paid for their labor. The Lucas brothers'
father, Judge J.B. Lucas, was also present. During a recess,
Uncle Daniel hinted a threat to the Lucas brothers, saying that
his contacts at the Spanish Land Bureau had kept very good
records of all New Madrid property transactions. Unwilling to
call his bluff, they withdrew their charges and left.

When asked why he used Philadelphia nails to build Fort
Bellefontaine against the wishes of the War Department, Uncle
Daniel told them he built that fort for half the cost of building
forts that size—$1,000. Those nails held that fort together
during three earthquakes.

The only court martial charge that stuck was that of
"conduct unbecoming an officer," brought by Colonel Robert
C. Nicholas. The court asked me my knowledge of the
incident. Uncle Daniel had told me Colonel Nicholas made
unwanted overtures to his daughter Mary. When confronted,
Nicholas denied the accusations, calling Mary a liar. Uncle
Daniel used foul language to dress him down. He told
Nicholas that, if it were legal under military law, he'd

challenge him to a duel. All other charges were dropped because they fell outside a 2-year statute of limitations.

• • •

In 1817, the U.S. Army assigned my Uncle Daniel the task of building and commanding a fort in central Illinois, Fort Clark. *(Today, it is the site of the city of Peoria.)* Uncle Daniel was in ill health, once again in the grip of the fever. Plus, he was building slave quarters on his property. I had resigned my commission on 31 March 1817 to take care of my property at Bissell Point.

Uncle Daniel convinced me to retake my commission. He commandeered me, Crazy John, and a company of soldiers to build Fort Clark for him. He promised to send men to clear our land. *(Another act that would get him into trouble with the War Department.)*

I was commandant at Fort Clark until mid-1818 when I was ordered to take a contingent of soldiers to protect a group of explorers led by James Johnson on the Yellowstone Expedition up the Missouri River. Crazy John said, "no way," and resigned his commission. In early 1819, while I was on the Yellowstone Expedition, Fort Clark was overrun and destroyed by Indians. The Expedition founded a small fort on a site in Nebraska. Briefly, I was the first commandant of Fort Omaha.

When I returned from the Yellowstone Expedition in 1820, Uncle Daniel filled me in on local events. In 1816, the 1st Bank of St. Louis opened. Uncle Daniel was a stockholder. In 1818, a bank clerk, John B.N. Smith, issued notes that had only one bank official's signature on them. Though invalid, the board of directors voted to honor them, but there was no guarantee the loans would be repaid.

Unhappy with the decision, Uncle Daniel, Thomas Hart Benton, Lieutenant James McGunnegle, and Jeremiah Connor held a meeting of shareholders and voted to take action. They entered the bank, locked the doors, and demanded the keys to the safe. The bank director called their bluff and refused. In the meantime, John B.N. Smith fled to Kentucky, where he made more large real estate loans. Such land speculation led to a money panic in 1819 and the bank almost folded. Uncle Daniel and a contingent of his troops helped head off a run on the bank.

Bishop DuBourg, a Roman Catholic clergyman, established The St. Louis Academy in 1818. It was the first high school west of the Mississippi. It was located at 9th and Washington. Bishop DuBourg put the educational reins in the hands of Jesuit priests.

The streets of St. Louis looked different; the city government paved them with pitch over gravel. The streets turned gooey on hot days. The pitch stuck to shoes, wheels, and hooves. Winter freezes cracked and broke the pavement, leaving huge holes. The city had to re-tar the streets every spring.

Bissell Point

1821, another good year. I became a minor partner in a ferryboat business operated by Samuel Wiggins. He knew I was the boat commander from Fort Bellefontaine and owned the land at Bissell Point. The road into St. Louis started at the southern edge of my property *(now Ferry Street)*.

I apportioned Sam some of my land and I sweet-talked some Army buddies to help us build small shacks for shelter at the ferry landings on both sides of the river, the one on the Illinois side slightly upriver. As Sam said, "A ferryboat can get to reeking!"

Wiggins owned two flatboats, team-ferries, *Sea Serpent* and *Antelope.* Each was equipped with a horse-drawn treadmill that turned a stern wheel.

We hauled some rough characters across the river; some argued about paying in advance. We needed a deterrent. That's why we hired my old army buddy, ex-gunnery sergeant Tom Miller, and an ex-Missouri Ranger, Gustav Hesse, to "ride shotgun."

Jean Leguerre operated *Sea Serpent* from the east bank and Samuel worked the *Antelope* from the west bank of the river. We fenced the landings and erected gates so people couldn't just bolt without paying.

John O'Fallon helped me build temporary living quarters, bunk houses, at the foot of the dirt track that later became Bissell Street. We used wood from trees we cleared to the west of our lands. Weary travelers could bed down there until ready to push on. Crazy John brokered a deal with the U.S. Army to

supply food, simple fare like beans and bread. He got me the
same low rate as the Army. We were outside city limits, not
subject to licensing fees.

1821 was a rough year for my Uncle Dan. One of his old
enemies resurfaced. Major Winfield Scott had the ear of
President James Monroe. Earlier, Major Scott was passed over
when Daniel Bissell was promoted to colonel. Scott was livid.
Uncle Dan had written a stinging report of Scott's treatment of
me while I was under Scott's command during the War of
1812. Scott was passed over repeatedly for promotion.

Scott enlisted the aid of Major Henry Atkinson. They
convinced President Monroe that the U.S. Army needed
realignment. Scott claimed there were too many regiments and
too many colonels, several of which were getting long in the
tooth.

Monroe agreed and ordered the realignment. Monroe said,
"to reduce and fix the military peace establishment of the
United States, supernumerary officers would be released." He
discharged four colonels, my uncle among them. However, the
U.S. Army didn't actually reduce its number of regiments.
They simply reassigned roles. They transformed the Army's
one light artillery regiment, one ordnance regiment, one
rifleman regiment, and eight regiments of infantry into four
artillery regiments and seven infantry regiments. So they had
to promote four new officers to the rank of colonel to
command them, Majors Scott and Atkinson among them.

Uncle Dan had friends in high places. His old banking
buddy, Senator Thomas Hart Benton, took up his cause. The
Senate challenged the President's authority to make such a
decision and passed a resolution reinstating Uncle Daniel and
the other three colonels who had been dismissed. President
Monroe stood his ground.

Uncle Dan was caught between a rock and a hard place.
The President said he was out; the Senate said he was in.
Finally, after pleas from several prominent Missourians, Henry
Dodge and Rufus Easton among them, the President agreed to
reinstate Uncle Dan but said he would lose all of his time in

grade. Uncle Dan refused to report. He fought for full
replacement of his military rights until the day he died.

• • •

It was now 1822. James Monroe was still President. He
acquired Florida, much to the sorrow of the Native Americans
living there.

I resigned my commission. The military road was
improved and downtown St. Louis could be reached by wagon.
The war with Britain was over, so I was able to convince the
Army to sell me the keelboat. It held a lot of cargo but took
muscle to handle. I scraped off *Belle Fontaine* and re-chris-
tened her *Pole Cat*. I convinced Sergeant Pat Keegan to quit
the Army and work the other side of the boat for me. I hired
Henri Picot as helmsman *(no relation to Louis G. Picot)*.

Grandpa Ozias Bissell died. He was 93 years old at the
time of his death.

• • •

In 1823, I built my mansion on the bluff overlooking the
river. The surrounding trees provided shade for my house.
From the widow's walk I built on my roof, you could see that
St. Louis was a city built in a forest. The view from my roof
was magnificent, as well as strategic. I could see someone
coming from a long way off. As I got older, I spent more and
more time up there.

*(Many homes on the East Coast had a widow's walk, a flat
surface at the peak of the roof with a small fence around it, a
place to watch for returning ships.)*

With trees and water, come birds. We enjoyed watching
bluejays, bluebirds, redbirds, cardinals, sparrows, mocking-
birds, robins, hummingbirds, magpies, and pigeons. From our
high vantage point, we could see hawks and the occasional
eagle glide over the river and up the creek in search of prey.
Flocks of wild geese, ducks, eagles, and pelicans migrated
through our area. If they decided to land and visit, the mess
they left was disgusting.

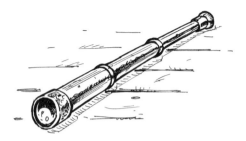

Carrion birds such as crow and raven came calling as well. I once saw a pair of buzzards eating something on Pelican Island on the Missouri River. *(Never saw a flock of vultures until my trip to California.)*

I'm glad I built our house of brick, because there were also plenty of woodpeckers in the area. I sat on the widow's walk with my spyglass, especially at sunup and sundown, listening to the chatter and music of the bird kingdom.

Uncle Dan gave me some peach tree saplings to plant. Soon, I had trees producing sweeter tasting peaches than the trees in his orchard.

I always had a fascination with brick structures. I enlisted the aid of John Leitensdorfer of Carondelet, a soldier of fortune and a magician. Carondelet was a settlement just south of St. Louis. John would help me procure some bricks.

After a stint in Canada, my unit was sent to Louisiana toward the end of the War of 1812. That's where I met Leitensdorfer. He fought under Napoleon and was part of the French National Guard that Lafayette formed in 1791. He also served in the Turkish army. He was an inspector general in the U.S. services in the war against the Barbary pirates.

The U.S. Government gave Jean Lafitte and his men pardons for their help in defeating the British. John knew Lafitte and introduced him to me. Lafitte took one look at my size and said, "Grand soldat, you are in the wrong line of work. You should be a pirate."

Dorf, as I called him, could talk the fleas off a dog. He got me a great deal on some bricks. He was a friend of John Lee, a brick-maker. John was one of the few brick-makers west of the Mississippi to make high-quality brick.

Lee needed a secure way to get his brick up to Alton, a settlement being developed by Rufus Easton. Poor Rufus! In 1818, he received a big loan from the 1st Bank of St. Louis but he defaulted in 1820, losing everything.

(Alton became a city in 1831. Rufus recovered financially and became quite wealthy.)

Navigating the river to Alton was tricky. The second earthquake in 1812 raised stone shelves in the river, creating what rivermen called the Chain of Rocks. Anyway, John Lee needed my boat and I needed bricks, a nice trade-off. Lee introduced me to the Mueller brothers, a pair of newly arrived German immigrants, topnotch bricklayers who were delighted to work for room and board.

I built my home with brick. I'd seen more than my fair share of burned-out forts and homes. The woods were full of Indians, and there was no fire department or public water system out here. I wanted to make my home as fireproof as possible and easy to rebuild. At the Mueller's suggestion, we also built a brick pit for burning brush and trash. We called it an "ash pit," like they did in Germany. Years later, just about every home had one.

(Stretching to the south from what would become Forest Park, there were over 70 miles of caves under the area Italian settlers would call "The Hill." High-quality fire clay was abundant. It would be used for paving brick, terra cotta, fire protection, sewer pipe, and refractory tiles. Missouri would become the largest producer of fire clay in the world.)

• • •

1824 was a good year. I returned to Connecticut to marry Mary Woodbridge. Mary's family was from Manchester, Connecticut. I met Mary in church.

When I was about twelve years old, my mother decided that living on military posts was having a bad influence on me. I was drinking and cursing like a sailor. Besides, she missed our home back in Windsor. She also worried that my older brother, George, wasn't taking good care of the place in our absence. So, my mother, my sisters Eunice and Nancy, and I came home.

My mother sent me to an all-boys school in nearby Hartford. I hated it. It was a Catholic school run by Jesuits. In one class, I was required to learn the Catholic Catechism, a tedious chore even for good Catholic boys. *(I come from good Protestant stock, by God!)*

I spent this hour daydreaming about heroes like the strong-willed Thor and the humble Balder the Brave, which often landed me in the doghouse. The Jebbies made us study English grammar and learn Latin *(ugh!)* but had us write in French. I wished they'd just make up their minds!

The Jesuits were an "order of clerks," specialists at the art of bureaucracy. Many called them "the political arm of the Pope." In 1773, Pope Clement XIV, under pressure from other Catholic orders that were jealous of the Jesuit's success, issued a suppression order. The society was to be dissolved and its members flouted.

The Jesuits in America were luckier than their counterparts in other parts of the world. Spain, France, and Portugal obeyed the suppression edict. They evicted or imprisoned Jesuit missionaries in their respective empires. In order for full suppression to take place, all countries would have to follow the directive.

Catherine II of Russia respected the Jesuits' ability to educate. When 200 Jesuit priests fled to Russia from Poland, she decided to ignore the edict, in effect saving the order. I guess that meant I would have to keep going to school.

During the week, I stayed with my Aunt Eugenia. Most of the boys boarded at the school but my mother couldn't afford it. I don't know who was luckier.

Aunt Eugenia thought I needed a good dose of religion, especially after so much exposure to Catholics. So she took me to her church every chance she got.

Mary's father was the minister. Even at the tender age of twelve, I was smitten with Mary. After all, at fourteen, she was practically a "full-growed" woman. I didn't mind going to

church after setting eyes on her. She thought I was a "wild child" and said as much. Secretly, I think that's what attracted her to me. Anyway, we became sweethearts and then mates for life.

Our wedding was supposed to be a simple church ceremony with just family in attendance. However, word got out and several of my old Army buddies showed up to see me tie the knot. They made a lot of noise and were generally rowdy. This upset Mary, and didn't make my mother too happy, either.

For a wedding present, my mother gave me the ancient Norse battle-axe my father had displayed on the wall over the fireplace. She couldn't have given me a better gift. I put it on the wall in my study.

Mary wasn't too keen on the idea of traveling halfway across the country to live on the frontier. I had to promise her

that I would never again take up the mantle of soldier, a
decision that also made my mother very happy.

"Mother" Bissell, as Mary called her, didn't want Mary to
spend her life "wandering from post to post" or "waiting at
home wondering when bad news would come."

We returned to my mansion near St. Louis and mother
came with us because she wanted to visit dad's grave and see
my house and property. Homesick after a few months, my
mother returned to Connecticut.

Uncle Daniel challenged Winfield Scott to a duel on
Christmas Eve. Scott declined and lived to become
Commander-in-Chief of the Army during the Mexican War.

The General

*I*n 1825, General Lafayette, the legendary Revolutionary War hero, accepted an invitation to come to St. Louis. Because they thought Uncle Dan knew Lafayette, a group of St. Louis businessmen asked him to write the invitation. The whole city was excited. Competition for the opportunity to entertain Lafayette in one's home was heated. I found it all very amusing.

Uncle Daniel was in charge of the reception committee. The day before Lafayette's arrival, a final meeting of the committee was held. The membership had the nerve to insist that Uncle Dan pay the cost of Lafayette's visit. Some of the more affluent citizens of the city struck down the notion that Lafayette would be housed at Uncle Dan's home *(Franklinville Farm)*. Why, his home wasn't even inside the city limits! After a heated argument, Uncle Daniel stormed out of the hall.

Uncle Daniel went hunting and stayed away during Lafayette's visit. How unfortunate! Events and coincidences made it a visit to be remembered. In the end, the Bissell family had the last laugh.

Lafayette arrived by steamboat. The riverfront was packed with people. Politicians, reporters, soldiers, farmers, and families rubbed elbows on the landing. I was standing at the back of the crowd with John Leitensdorfer *(Dorf)* and John O'Fallon *(Crazy John)*.

When the famous Frenchman arrived, the crowd pushed forward. The old general practically had to force his way through the throng. Lafayette spotted Dorf and headed toward

29

us. We moved forward to meet him. The old man was smiling and tears were at the corners of his eyes. Dorf saluted his old commanding officer and said, in French, "General, I am at your service as always."

The General laughed heartily and hugged him. He replied in kind, "As I am ever in your debt, guardsman."

The crowd looked on, amazed. After a moment's silence, everyone started speaking at once. The general took the high ground and turned to address the crowd, "Good citizens of St. Louis, I greet you. French people and French tradition have played a huge role in shaping the destiny of your city and your young nation. I may be far from my native France but I know I will feel at home here in your city."

People started clapping. The General held up his hands to quell the applause. "I will tour your city tomorrow but, for now, I need to rest."

He looked around expectantly. Auguste Chouteau, Sr, started to speak but was quickly shouted down by dozens of others in the crowd offering their hospitality to Lafayette. The General turned to Dorf and whispered, "How do I get out of this?"

Dorf looked at me, inspired. He introduced Crazy John and me to General Lafayette. The General sized me up and then asked if I was in any way related to Ozias Bissell's clan. When I told him he was my grandfather, he grabbed me by the arms and kissed me on both cheeks. Before I regained my wits, Dorf whispered something to the General and pointed in the direction of my house.

Now, in 1825, not many structures stood on the edge of the city where the steamboats docked. My house was just a dot on its perch on the bluff. The general whispered something back to Dorf and then addressed the crowd. "I thank you for your kind offers but I choose to stay with young Mr. Bissell here."

The crowd buzzed with objections but the General held firm. "Please, I am very tired. I have made my choice."

Fortunately, I rode to the riverfront with Crazy John in the fancy French racing carriage he won from Pierre Chouteau, Jr, in a poker game. Otherwise, we'd be hauling this great man up to my house in Dorf's stock wagon.

Two baggage handlers from the steamboat hauled Lafayette's belongings to Crazy John's carriage. We made sure The General was comfortable and stuffed his luggage where we could. I stood on the running board on the passenger side. Crazy John had to snap his whip twice before The Prophet responded.

(Crazy John and his wry sense of humor, naming that slowpoke nag The Prophet and putting it in front of a racing carriage.)

We headed for home, Dorf in his stock wagon right behind us, the crowd behind him. On the way back, Crazy John surmised that the barracks would be full tonight. *(Crazy John never got over calling things by military names.)* He'd bring extra beans down to the barracks and add them to my bill. Crazy John sometimes even pitched in and cooked one of his "specials."

The General gave me a quizzical look. I explained about my ferryboat and bread and bed venture. He smiled, nodded, and then yawned. He sat back and, shortly, we could hear him snore. As we neared the house, I remembered Mary. Oh boy, was she in for a shock. I didn't want to think about what I was in for. Springing a surprise guest on Mary could be detrimental to my health.

I jumped off the running board and raced up the hill ahead of the carriage. I was a swift runner and in better health than The Prophet.

(Crazy John loved that old nag. He was a gift from Cloud Bank, the Shawnee medicine man. Cloud Bank was the tribal name-giver. He gave Crazy John his Shawnee name, He Who Talks Tall.)

I burst into the house and startled Mary. I quickly explained the situation. Mary, who was at the stove, shook her head and said, "Lewis, I figured you might bring some friends back with you but this. . .," her voice trailed off. She sprang into action, "I need to put out the good linen and freshen up. Watch my stew."

She removed her apron and headed upstairs, shouting, "And get rid of the Mueller boys."

The brothers had no work so I hired them to break up stone and haul it from the riverfront to set in the dirt pathways to and from the river. I was tired of scraping mud off my shoes. The Mueller brothers had a very off-color sense of humor. I didn't have the time or the patience to explain to Mary that Lafayette was a soldier and had heard it all. So I went out and explained apologetically that they'd be eating down in the bunkhouse. Maybe Crazy John would cook. They smiled, grunted something in German, probably a flatulence joke, and headed down the hill. They liked Crazy John's "mystery" meat and bean combinations. I wouldn't put it past old Crazy John to cook up some wild dog.

I heard The Prophet snort as Crazy John halted his new carriage outside our front door. Next, I heard Dorf calling halt to his big old Missouri mule. Mary was already coming back down the steps so I went out into the yard to help. As Lafayette stepped from the wagon, Crazy John grabbed his bags and carried them to my porch. Dorf called my name. I looked over and he pointed down the hill toward St. Louis. A long procession of people was making its way toward my house on foot and in every kind of conveyance.

General Lafayette put his hand on my shoulder. He pointed toward the river. "What an elegant view," he said in a tone so low it was more a breath. "One should always appreciate beauty."

Then he looked toward the crowd making its way from the city and shook his head. He told me, "Of all the things I have acquired in my lifetime, the one thing I'd give back is my fame. All I desire now is a good night's sleep."

Mary stood nervously in the doorway. I quickly introduced her to The General and she ushered him into the house. I said, "I'll be in directly."

As both Johns walked over to me, I couldn't help noticing the similarities between them. Ramrod straight, they were both close to six feet tall. *(The average person at that time was 5'6".)* Their skin was rough and weathered and their scars revealed both men had been in their fair share of fights. The most startling resemblance was in the eyes—gray, with a brightness to them that bespoke a keen intelligence. They even smiled alike. Big men, like me. Soldiers. Warriors. My friends. Thank God!

As I looked down at them, I realized that I was cut from the same mold, only bigger. I laughed. Crazy John asked, "What's so funny?"

I said, "We are."

He chuckled, shaking his head.

Someone called my name and the voice had an edge to it. I turned my attention to the crowd at my doorstep. Some of the richest men in the territory, the Chouteaus, Judge J.B. Lucas and his sons, and Rufus Easton, were standing on my front lawn and they were all in a bad mood.

The Chouteaus weren't happy. They had arranged a big reception at their mansion on the city's south side.

• • •

The Chouteaus were prominent St. Louis citizens and slave owners. Auguste the elder and Pierre, Sr, engineered the construction of Fort Osage while the territory was still under Spanish rule. They turned the fort over to the Spanish authorities, who renamed it Fort Carondelet after the Spanish governor. In return, the Chouteaus were given exclusive fur trading rights with the Osage tribe. In 1804, the fort would be renamed Fort Osage when it became the property of the United States as part of the Louisiana Purchase.

Back in February 1754, Auguste the elder, under orders from Pierre Laclede, directed thirty workers to begin clearing the site for the new city of St. Louis. Auguste became a rich but fair man. He served as Judge of the Court of Common Pleas, the Justice of the Peace, and the 1st President of the Board of Trustees of the City of St. Louis.

In 1804, his half brother, (Jean) Pierre Chouteau, son of Pierre Laclede, was named the U.S. Agent of Indian Affairs for all tribes west of the Mississippi. It was a position that Pierre and his brother used to great advantage, as previously noted. Pierre became the president of the St. Louis Missouri Fur Company. He was a Captain, then a Major, in the St. Louis Militia and a Justice of the Peace. Pierre was also a straight shooter who was noted for willingness to meet his enemies head on.

Auguste Pierre Chouteau, the eldest son of Pierre Chouteau, graduated from the United States Military Academy in 1806, but he resigned his commission to take the position of Indian Treaty Commissioner for all tribes west of the Mississippi. He negotiated treaties with the Wichita and other Southwest Indian tribes. I had no quarrel with this man. Oh, there's no denying he used his influence with the Indians to help the family fur trading business, but so what. Helping one's family prosper is an American tradition.

It was Auguste who warned us of the impending arrival of Tecumseh and his Indian army. He could have left, but he stayed to try and negotiate with Tecumseh's envoy, all the while knowing there was little chance. He spent most of his life working diligently, a brave man who died at Fort Gibson, Oklahoma, on 25 December 1838.

• • •

Pierre Chouteau, Jr, was a different story. Now, every family has its black sheep and the Chouteau family was no exception. Pierre's family called him "Cadet," but we called him Junior because we knew he hated it. He was very smart, probably spoiled, and like many a misguided youth resentful of his father's standing in the community. Junior feared people would attribute his successes a result of being the son of such a great man.

Junior made the mistake of surrounding himself with people of disreputable character, "friends," who were really freeloaders. They pandered to him, making him the center of attention, boosting his ego. They dared him to partake in dangerous and, often, illicit activities. Before he knew it, he was the leader of a gang. To add to his fall into infamy, wanton women claimed to find his "dark" side attractive and yielded to him. The fool thought himself quite the Lothario. When his father took him to task for his iniquities and attempted to point out to him that these men and women were using him, it made Junior more determined to continue on his wayward path.

Junior seemed to live two lives. He got involved in the fur trade in 1805 and eventually became the head of the American Fur Company and a fixture on the board of directors of several banks and railroads. Elitists held him in high esteem.

People who frequented the back alleys and docks of the city saw him in a different light. It was whispered that he sold liquor to the Indians and used his crew of "bodyguards" to intimidate people into paying "protection" money to him. There was talk he used his political clout to keep his favorite cutthroats out of jail when they got caught doing something unsavory, say, like collecting "phantom" docking fees from riverboat pilots.

His reputation as a shrewd businessman and political motivator helped squelch rumors that he might be a crime lord. Junior was undecided if he liked this development. He loved being the center of attention and relished the air of mystery that hung about him.

An Alton bricklayer told me Junior operated a bordello in Alton and that he was blackmailing men of affluence. Now I don't know if any of this hearsay was true, nor was it my job to do anything about it. It was up to Marshall Dodge and his Rangers to uphold the law around here. I was just a riverboat captain.

Every war story needs a villain and I applaud Pierre for a job well done. In Norse mythology, attaining heaven isn't a matter of whether one's good or evil; it's how fervently you play the role in life that's been assigned to you.

Star-crossed, we were both born in 1789. Small of stature, I suspected Junior suffered from a "Napoleon complex" and my being a big man made me his natural enemy. My reputation as a straight shooter made me the butt of many of his jokes.

Junior married his cousin, Emilie Gratiot, in 1814. *(It was common practice to marry relatives. It insured the business stayed in the family.)*

Junior and Emilie had five children. Some people said he was a devoted husband and father. Others claimed he had paramours. Who knows? The rumor mill has ground many a reputation into dust. I say let it be. A man's personal life belongs to him and his conscience.

• • •

Junior barked commands. He kept his bodyguards close at hand, a half dozen river rats who would cut your throat for a dime. Most of his men went to the top of the hill. They admitted one last carriage and then blocked the path up the hill to those on foot. I didn't like the looks of this.

My partner, Sam Wiggins, was hustling up the path with Tom Miller and Gustav Hesse, his ferryboat guards. Sam had a short fuse. I'm glad I had my service revolver strapped to my hip. Though not an accurate weapon, it would at least make my enemies duck. I noted Dorf had his usual mix of guns and knives attached in strategic spots to his body. Crazy John never went anywhere unarmed, even after he became a banker. He was keenly aware that only a few thousand yards separated civilization from the savage wilderness. Catching my eye, he patted his Allen pepper pot pistol.

Junior didn't waste any time. He accused me of conspiring with my Uncle Dan to get General Lafayette to my house. He demanded that I call my uncle out. The crowd erupted, yelling and screaming. Crazy John went to the porch and picked up my hunting rifle.

Embarrassed, Auguste, Sr, yelled at his nephew to calm down. Junior didn't hear him or just ignored him. He pushed past his uncle and started toward us. Like good soldiers, we took the high ground and joined Crazy John on the steps of my porch.

Jean Daniel Levi, a Jewish convert of Bishop DuBourg, stood near my horseshoe pit with Father Saulnier, his friend, who was also the pastor of Our Lady of Mount Carmel Church in Carondelet.

Levi quickly sized up the situation. Horse sense told him there wouldn't be any gunplay with such an important man in the house. However, he knew Junior was quick on the trigger. He cut Junior off, grabbing him by the sleeve of his gun arm.

In a booming voice, which he developed as a young actor on the London stage, he demanded "Silence!"

Miracle of miracles, he got it. He asked Junior, "Are you out of your mind?"

Before Junior could answer, another voice rang out. It was General Lafayette. Propriety keeps me from repeating The General's first words. After Lafayette had their attention, he said, "Stop this nonsense, all of you! I am here of my own volition."

He pointed at the house and continued, "You think Daniel Bissell is hiding in this man's home. Com me sot!" He raised both fists. "That is an insult!"

Most of the unwanted guests looked mortified and bowed their heads like children getting caught in a naughty deed. The General took a deep breath and declared, "You will get your fill of me on the morrow," and with a wave of dismissal, "so please just leave me in peace so I can get some rest!"

A moment of silence ensued; then a familiar voice broke the spell. Thomas Hart Benton *(T.H.),* who just arrived in that last carriage, was standing on a running board. He shouted, "Sorry I'm late. Hello and goodbye. All right, people. You heard the man. Let's go!"

T.H. got back into his carriage and drove off. Shuffling their feet while mumbling an assortment of apologies, the crowd followed the senator's example and got back into their carriages.

Junior realized Jean Levi still had a hand on his sleeve so he pulled his arm away. He was seething. Levi backed away from him. Lafayette pushed past us, stepped off the porch, and confronted Junior. The General towered over him. Through clenched teeth, Lafayette warned him to calm down before he knocked some sense into him, himself. Junior retreated a few steps. He glared at me.

His father stepped past him and offered his family's apologies to The General and to me, the other Chouteaus chiming in. Angrily, Junior spun on his heel and left. He yelled to his gang, "Mount up."

As they did so, they looked daggers at us.

The General retook the porch. He apologized for putting my family in harm's way. I shrugged. On the frontier, we are always in harm's way. Then he asked me if I had room at the table for Jean Levi. I nodded yes and invited Mr. Levi to dine with us. Haltingly, Levi explained that Father Saulnier was his guest today. I looked at Mary, who just smiled and waved them both in.

As General Lafayette passed, I realized I was a head taller than he. He remarked, "Napoleon. That angry young man. They don't understand. It's not their size that makes them small men. It's their exaggerated sense of self importance."

The throng of pedestrians impeded by Chouteau's henchmen parted and let the carriages pass. I marched down to speak to the newspapermen in the crowd to give them an accurate account of what just occurred. I extended The General's apologies, emphasizing that he badly needed his rest. Several members of the press corps traveled a long distance to record this historic event for the City of St. Louis so I invited them to spend the night at the bunkhouse —first come, first served.

As they raced down the hill, I yelled, "Crazy John'll be down later. For a small fee, I'm sure he'll let you try some of his home-made Irish whiskey."

John's training at Fort Bellefontaine finally paid off. He had captured a fair share of the local whiskey market.

Sam Wiggins tapped me on the shoulder. Caught off guard,

I spun around, my fists raised in defense. Sam leapt back, yelping, "Take it easy, Lewis! Don't you know who your friends are?"

Chagrined, I dropped my fists. Tom Miller *(Sarge)* and Gustav Hesse *(Ranger)* were beside him, armed to the teeth and laughing. I asked if they wanted to join us for dinner but Sam begged off, "We need to get back to the ferryboats." He was ecstatic. "It's been a near record day—and easy."

Usually, we hauled families who had everything they owned with them, and it was backbreaking labor. Today, it was mostly people coming to see General Lafayette.

The three men thought we might need help when they saw Chouteau's hired guns blocking the hill. Sam asked, "What was Junior up in arms about this time?"

When I told him he thought Uncle Dan and I had conspired to steal his thunder, Sam laughed. He knew about Junior's other "activities" and muttered, "Now there's the pot calling the kettle black."

(I suspected Sam dabbled in the black market himself and paid occasional visits to that Alton bordello.)

I appreciated just how lucky I was. I thanked these faithful friends and watched them return to the ferry. I saw a big crowd of people gathering at the ferry landing.

War Stories

*D*inner was excellent. Everyone wolfed down Mary's beef stew and hot bread. The conversation was even better. Our war stories enthralled Jean Levi and Father Saulnier.

General Lafayette told us he first became a soldier in France in 1771. In 1776, The General withdrew from the French army to seize the opportunity to fight the British in America. In 1777, he joined the Continental Army and soon gained the confidence of George Washington. He regaled us with tales of the war and, several times, praised the battle savvy of my grandfather, Ozias.

After the war, he returned to France. In July 1791, he became the first commander of the newly formed French National Guard. At this time, most of France was starving while the rich lavished themselves with food and drink. He gradually realized there needed to be a transfer of power from the aristocracy to the bourgeois.

It was a compromising situation for him. His duty as a soldier put him in direct conflict with his new-found beliefs. He knew it would be just a matter of time before there was open rebellion.

Things came to a boil in October 1791. People were rioting all over France. The Guard was called to the Champ de Mars, where armed civilians barricaded the street. After talk failed to persuade these rebels to withdraw, Lafayette was compelled to order his men to remove them by force. Sick at heart, he stood in the open, watching the carnage.

Suddenly someone pushed him down. The General looked back and saw young John Leitensdorfer stretched out on the ground behind him, blood pouring from an ugly chest wound, a wound from which few recover. Dorf had taken a bullet meant for The General.

We all looked at Dorf, who was just grinning from ear to ear. The General raised his glass and toasted him. We did likewise. Dorf, still grinning like a monkey, chanted, "Merci, Merci!"

When we quieted the General added, "I resigned my commission the next day."

● ● ●

Lafayette asked John O'Fallon, "Why do they call you Crazy John?"

I entreated, "Let me tell this story"

I explained, "You might find this hard to believe, but John's an accountant. He can do math in his head that I can't do on paper."

Dorf said, "He's an adder all right!"

After the moaning from that terrible pun subsided, I continued, "That reminds me. For some unknown reason, Mr. O'Fallon here thinks the moniker 'Crazy John' casts him in a bit of a strange light and puts a crimp in his reputation as a wheeler dealer."

Crazy John put his right hand in his vest ala Napoleon and said, "Hi! I'm Crazy John. Will you lend me $10,000?"

"So can we all agree to call him just John in public?"

Everyone agreed.

In a conspiratorial whisper, I added, "But not to fear. He says his innermost circle of friends can still call him Crazy John. Correct, Just John?'

Crazy John burst into laughter and we all followed suit. That's one of the things I loved about the man. He always laughed at my jokes, no matter how bad they were. When everyone settled down, I told the story how Crazy John got his nickname.

    With the Missouri forests saturated with Indians, the safest place to be was inside Fort Bellefontaine. Uncle Daniel sent out patrols regularly to check on local settlers—the last thing any soldier wanted to do—any soldier except John O'Fallon, that is. John pulled bookkeeper duty. Because he found it "so boring," he volunteered to lead all the patrols and Uncle Daniel let him, but that's not how he got his name.

    John O'Fallon's regard for the safety of the pioneers endeared him with more settlers than anybody in Missouri. He did the same thing in Illinois while up at Fort Clark. He didn't know it at the time, but he was insuring a successful business future.

    Late in 1811, shortly after Crazy John arrived fresh from being wounded at Tippecanoe, but before Fort Bellefontaine came under siege, a family of settlers was murdered and their home burned by a band of Indians up near Portage Des Sioux. The smoke could be seen from Fort Bellefontaine and Fort Zumwalt.

    Colonel John Shaw and Lieutenant John McNair, two officers overseeing the installation of gun ports at Fort Zumwalt, rode out to meet the local militia at a pre-selected rallying point, standard operating procedure *(S.O.P.)* in such a situation. These officers knew that Fort Bellefontaine would send a troop of soldiers out to investigate as well. Crazy John convinced my uncle he was almost completely recovered from his wounds and could handle the job.

    Twelve members of the militia met Shaw and McNair at the rallying point. They set out in the direction of the smoke and reached a burned-out farm. The settlers—a man, two women, and three small children—had been burned as well. The Indians left tracks and the militia members wanted to give chase. McNair and Shaw thought it better to wait for reinforce-

ments from Fort Bellefontaine. The militia members didn't
wait.

The officers reluctantly followed. The tracks led them
along the northern bank of the Missouri River to a wooded
area across from Pelican Island. The nearby woods erupted
with gunfire and Lieutenant McNair saw men toppling from
their horses. Colonel Shaw was killed instantly. A flight of
arrows followed. McNair ordered the survivors to head for the
river. They fled for their lives with the Indians in pursuit.

Crazy John and a troop of thirty men were following the
Missouri River up to Musick's Ferry. They were on the south
bank near Pelican Island when they heard gunfire, about a half
a mile ahead from the sound of it. Crazy John and his men
looked across the river and saw a single soldier riding hell-bent
for leather along the riverside, twenty Indians hot on his trail.

An arrow struck the fleeing rider *(Lieutenant McNair)* in
the back and he fell off his horse and rolled into the Missouri,
snapping off the shaft of the arrow. He grabbed a piece of
floating debris before it could take his head off and hung on
for his life. Crazy John turned his attention to the Indians. He
ordered his men to set up a picket line and fire. After two
volleys, the pursuing Indians fled.

The water was high for this time of year and the current
mighty swift. The water was freezing cold. Crazy John could
see the wounded man struggling to maintain his grip. Without
hesitation he flung off his weapons and waded into the river.
He took three more steps and was swept away. He shouted,
"Get the boat!"

He took a deep breath and went under. His head popped up
about a minute later. This time he kept his head above water
and used the current to his advantage. McNair and the floating
debris were almost upon him. Crazy John struck out toward
him and snagged a limb as it went by. He pulled his way
around to McNair, grabbed him around the waist, and heaved
him higher on the debris. By then, Sergeant Tom Miller was
racing headlong back to the fort.

Crazy John was blessed with the luck of the Irish. It was
late in the year, and we just happened to be on the dock,

stockpiling for winter. Soon the river would freeze and we'd
have to struggle overland to get supplies. A ferocious storm up
north deposited a ton of debris in the river. With the Indians on
the warpath, the river route was the lesser of two evils. Still, it
was tricky going. Corporal Patrick Keegan and I had just
finished unloading supplies at the lookout tower on the
Missouri River. The tower was directly across from the east
end of Coral Island.

We had just pushed off to move down to the fort when I
saw John Miller galloping toward us. I stuck my pole into the
riverbed and Keegan did likewise, halting the boat. Miller
jumped off his horse and shouted, pointing upriver. It was hard
to hear him with the whistling wind, so I looked in the
direction he was pointing.

At first, all I saw was the usual river detritus. Then, I
spotted a head at the back of a tangle of tree branches. My
heart skipped a beat. Some crazy fool was out there in that
freezing water. Then I saw a second man lying on top of the
branches. There were two fools out there!

Their life raft was caught in the swift current, hurtling
them toward us, moving them away from Coral Island. I
quickly plotted an intercept course and we shoved off. I knew
we would get only one chance to net them. If they got past us
into the swifter Mississippi current, we'd never catch them
before they froze to death.

Stick the pole and walk the running board. Stick the pole
and walk the running board. I had done this drill hundreds of
times before but now someone's life depended on it. I thanked
God it was Corporal Keegan with me today. He was one of the
few soldiers at Fort Bellefontaine big enough and strong
enough to keep up with me.

We lifted our poles and the swift current started carrying
us. I could see we were on a good course and our speed was
just about right. The trick would be to not plow through the
two men. I manned the wheel and Keegan grabbed the
grappling hook. They got to the intercept point slightly ahead
of us and my heart sank. Crazy John grabbed McNair and
pushed the two of them away from their makeshift raft, his feet

kicking against the dead tree limbs. This slowed him just enough for Corporal Keegan to spear them with the grappling hook.

I released the wheel and moved to the side of the boat to help Keegan. Spray from the river made everything slippery and Keegan was struggling to maintain a grip on the grappling hook. I reached around him and grabbed further up the handle of the grappling hook and started walking it with my hands. Between the two of us we were able to lift them up out of the river far enough for me to grab them. Keegan stuck the pole under one arm, still clutching it with his left hand, and snagged my belt with the other. With a mighty effort, we pulled those two drowned river rats into the boat.

All four of us flopped around on the bottom of the *Belle Fontaine* like freshly caught fish. No one was steering the boat and we were heading out into the Mississippi River. I jumped up, retook the wheel, and steered us toward the Missouri shore. The Missouri River quickly shoots you to the Illinois side of the Mississippi where the channel is so deep and the current so swift we'd have been halfway to St. Louis before I could have worked us back to this side of the river.

Crazy John and McNair lay on the deck while Keegan and I poled the boat into a shallow cove about three miles by land from the fort. I tended to John while Corporal Keegan aided Lieutenant McNair. John was shivering and bleeding profusely from a huge hole near his shoulder. It was bad.

I asked him if he was shot but he shook his head "no" and pointed to the grappling hook. We had snagged him all right. I made a feeble attempt at humor to allay shock. I said, "Don't you know it's against regs for more than one soldier a day to jump into freezing water? You're crazy, John."

I hurried to the boat's medical kit and grabbed a fistful of cotton. I wrapped a piece of thick sailing canvas around it and went back and stuffed it into his wound. Crazy John contorted with pain. The thigh wound he received at Tippecanoe had reopened. I wrapped it as well. Just before he passed out, he managed to croak, "That's me. Crazy John!"

The shaft of the arrow that struck Lieutenant McNair was

broken off and the arrowhead was inside him. Both soldiers needed a doctor and soon. I sprinted to the top of the riverbank to see how far we were from the fort. I can't tell you how relieved I was to see Uncle Daniel and half the troop heading toward us. Uncle Dan always carried a surgical kit. There was a shortage of doctors in the military and it was S.O.P. for the company commander to double as doctor for his men. The supply wagon was right behind them.

Crazy John resigned his commission and worked with his uncle, William Clark, at the Bureau of Indian Affairs until the War of 1812 began in earnest. He retook his commission and served as the commander of the Canadian post at Malden, which he delivered back to the British at the end of the war. He earned the rank of Captain.

• • •

Everyone was quiet for a moment. Then Lafayette stood, raised his glass, and toasted Crazy John. We joined the toast. To my surprise, Lafayette also toasted me. I beamed as everyone toasted me as well.

Lafayette told Crazy John that he knew his uncle, George Rogers Clark, but not William. Oh, he met him once, but William Clark was just a small boy at the time of the Revolutionary War.

Crazy John told The General some of his family history. He was born near Louisville, Kentucky, in 1791. His father, James O'Fallon, died in 1793. His uncle, William Clark, became a surrogate father and in 1807 assumed formal guardianship of Crazy John. He still seeks his uncle's advice on the rare occasions he needs it.

I snorted and said, "Like everyday."

We all laughed heartily, Crazy John the loudest of all.

Jean Levi told us the Army was interested in buying land in Carondelet to build a new training post. Fort Bellefontaine was showing its age and the Army wanted to get away from the swampland.

Father Saulnier told General Lafayette that Bishop DuBourg saw the need for a high school in St. Louis and brought to pass the St. Louis Academy, a high school for boys only. One day, one of my sons would graduate from that school.

Mary, quiet to this point, asked if they wanted to hear her war story, the one about her capture of Lewis Bissell. The consensus was "yes."

During the course of her story there were several hearty rounds of laughter, especially when Mary said, "Aunt Eugenia thought Lewis needed a good dose of religion."

Cheerfully, Lafayette saluted her as well. He commented that it took a very beautiful woman to get a rogue like me into church.

It was getting late and our guests began to leave. The General bid us good night and retired.

It was a night I'll never forget.

Early the next morning, Uncle Dan's daughter, Eliza, and her husband, William, blessed us with a rare visit. They wanted to meet The General. We invited them to breakfast.

Lafayette slept well and was in a good mood. Over breakfast, it was decided that William and Eliza would haul The General into town. He enjoyed our hospitality so much that he didn't hesitate when Eliza invited him to dine with her and William that evening. Lafayette spent his second night in St. Louis at their home.

Too bad Uncle Dan was still fuming in the woods.

Friends and Enemies

*M*ary and I had our first child in 1826, a boy. We named him James. Mary had a rough go of it but pulled through. Seeing that baby for the first time was the most incredible moment of my life. While Mary recuperated, Uncle Daniel's daughter, Mary, took care of the household.

Uncle Dan wanted to send a couple of his Negroes to help as well, but I wouldn't hear of it. I thought slavery was just plain wrong and found it unfathomable that Uncle Daniel had over twenty slaves working his land. He swore that these thralls were better off with him, that there was no way they'd ever be integrated into the white society, and they didn't have the means to get back to Africa. My head said he was right. My heart knew he was wrong.

The baby kept us busy and I was driving both Marys up the wall. Every time James coughed, I wanted to run get the doctor. My wife would calm me down and hustle me out to work. I'd throw myself into whatever I was doing, anxious to get back to the little tyke. Crazy John never passed up a chance to make wisecracks about new fathers.

Anyway, busy as I was, and with Crazy John expanding his horizons, we hired Stumpy Fredericks, a one-legged ex-Army cook, to prepare food at the bread and board. *(We never could make up our minds what to call it.)*

Here's Stumpy's war story.

In 1814, Stumpy was enjoying a couple of snorts in an old lookout tower outside Fort Bellefontaine. He'd sneak up there whenever Captain Lucas was on one of his temperance crusades. To catch errant soldiers, Captain Lucas sounded the general alarm, a drill that requires all personnel to fall out and assemble. *(Uncle Dan wrote Captain Lucas up for his overzealousness.)*

Hastily climbing down, Stumpy slipped and took a mighty fall. His left leg snapped right above the knee, just a bit of flesh holding it together. Uncle Dan set it and stitched Stumpy together as best he could, but infection set in and he had to remove the leg.

Stumpy mustered out of the Army and had saved a little money. Stumpy's brother Mike owned a boat dock on the Mississippi near Herculaneum. He lived in a wood shack by the dock. Mike sold bait, fishing supplies, and, after Stumpy moved in with him, bad whiskey. Stumpy was bitter and sullen. He drank heavily.

I dropped by occasionally to see how Stumpy was doing. On one visit, I told him about Will Root.

William Root, from Sussex, England, a maker of grand-father clocks, fell on hard times during the War of 1812. An English immigrant, his thick British accent and mannerisms engendered distrust. Folks whispered as they passed him in the street, suspecting he was a British spy.

Toward the end of the war, he started making cabinets and bed furniture, but folks wouldn't buy these much-needed items from him. He was ready to look for greener pastures when fortune shined on him.

St. Louis had its fair share of returning veterans, some who lost legs. In a gesture of good will, Root took some of his finest wood and fashioned wooden legs to give to these poor fellows. Now Will was a craftsman who turned these artificial limbs into works of art.

Aramis Laybee, an Ensign in the USN, lost both legs at the

knees to cannon shot during the battle of New Orleans. His spirit broken, he came home. Lost in self-pity, he wanted to die.

Will carved two legs for Laybee that made it appear he was supported by two of the prettiest mermaids you could imagine. Machingo, a Shawnee Indian artist, painted the legs using brilliant colors.

Upon receipt, Laybee cried. He would later say, "Will Root and Machingo gave me my life back."

Root's charitable actions won over the community and his business boomed. Dorf dubbed him "Peg Leg" Root, a nickname that stuck.

Will got great pleasure from personalizing these artificial limbs. A man of books, Root would show the maimed veterans pictures of things he fancied to carve.

Stumpy Fredericks asked Will to make him a teakwood leg shaped like a Roman column. When Will delivered the leg to him, he told Stumpy what he told all the veterans, "It's my greatest artistic triumph."

Stumpy never let us forget it.

In 1826, Stumpy's brother died. Mike was a gambler and owed a bundle of money to some unsavory characters. When they came to collect, they found nothing of value except a whiskey still. They took the still, beat Stumpy, and burned the shack. Stumpy was homeless but at least they didn't get his leg. When I heard what happened, I found Stumpy and hired him to work for me.

• • •

Crazy John brokered a contract with the City of St. Louis to replace pitch streets with brick. It would be the first step in modernizing city streets. They tried wood bricks at first, then clay bricks. John also helped staff the City Street Department.

The Mueller brothers built brick roads back in Germany and knew other bricklayers who could help supply the manpower. It was backbreaking labor for the bricklayers, but at least the hod carriers would be happy. No ladders!

I learned how difficult carrying bricks and mortar was when I played hod carrier for the Muellers when they bricked my house. I also learned a little about bricklaying, just enough to let me know it was the wrong line of work for me.

Dorf introduced Crazy John to John Lee and his brick company, which was on the south edge of Carondelet. Lee needed to increase his labor force as well. An influx of German immigrants to Alton created a glut of bricklayers in that newly forming city. Crazy John figured if they could lay brick, they could make brick.

Alton became a regular stop for Sam Wiggins and the *Antelope*. He hauled a lot of Germans to St. Louis to do brick work and quite a few Italians to work in the clay mines.

The road builders had to wait for the spring thaw and soft ground to set the foundations. Heavy rains made it nearly impossible to haul brick by wagon on the muddy roads. So Crazy John subcontracted me to haul John Lee's bricks to downtown St. Louis on the *Pole Cat*.

The river was up and nasty, but the money was too good to pass up. Besides, it pays to live a little on the edge. It keeps you on your toes. Between you and me, Keegan, Picot, and I hauled a *(censored)* load of bricks.

I want to tell you the war story about Crazy John winning Junior Chouteau's fancy German carriage. It's one of my favorites. John was a gambler who couldn't resist a dare. Junior was a carriage racer. He imported a carriage from Germany built by Porsche, the finest carriage makers in Europe *(according to them)*.

Junior drove so recklessly through the streets of St. Louis the city passed an ordinance that prohibited racing a horse or driving a wheeled carriage in the street faster than necessary. Violators were fined one dollar. Junior would race through town, taunt the law, and speed back to sanctuary at Chouteau Manor.

The local constabulary had orders from City Hall to stay off Chouteau property. On the rare occasions they did catch Junior in the act, he tore up the ticket and raced off.

Crazy John persuaded his friend, Doctor Bernard Farrar *(Doc Bernie),* to lend him his buggy so he could put Junior in his place. Doc Bernie's carriage was built by the Studebaker brothers in Ohio. It was a sleek, modern carriage with wooden axles and wheels that were reinforced with metal plating.

Doc Bernie was somewhat of a daredevil himself. He was ticketed several times for speeding and was involved in several duels. He killed James A. Graham in a duel back in 1810.

Crazy John was sure he could whip Junior. Junior's carriage was larger and heavily laden with ornamentation. Junior's biggest plus was the horse he had pulling his buggy, a beautiful black stallion that was a gift to him from Blackhawk, the chief of the Fox and Sauk Indian tribe. Rumor was, Junior traded him rifles for horses.

The Porsche beat the Studebaker and Crazy John lost $1,000. $1,000! Unbelievable! John, prideful, was desperate to win his money back.

Junior could be very shrewd. He invited Crazy John to his brother's manor to play poker, knowing full well that John couldn't resist the challenge. It seems Junior wanted Crazy John's land, as well as mine. He knew the city would expand and the holders of surrounding land would be blessed with a cash windfall. He didn't need the money. He just wanted it.

Junior planned to win Crazy John's land with his straight-laced brother, Auguste, looking on. Everyone would know that the game was on the up and up. He couldn't lose.

Crazy John was a wily poker player *(his training at Fort Bellefontaine paid off again)* but he was playing against some really high rollers. Besides the Chouteaus, Rufus Easton and Thomas Hart Benton *(T.H.)* were sitting in. Doc Bernie accompanied Crazy John to watch his back and got sucked into the action as well. The stakes were high. Money passed back and forth all night.

Doc Bernie and T.H. were friends. Back in 1817, he was T.H.'s second at several duels, including both duels with Charles Lucas. In their second duel, T.H. killed Lucas. Plagued with guilt, T.H. vowed to never duel again.

T.H. knew Crazy John because of his friendship with William Clark, Crazy John's uncle and guardian.

Anyway, Lady Luck finally embraced Crazy John. He got the hand he was waiting for. He sat stone-faced as the other players folded early, all except Junior, that is. Perfect! Crazy John threw down the gauntlet. He pushed the puny pot aside and said, "Let's quit playing games."

He reached inside his jacket, took out the deed to his land, and laid it on the table. John said, "I'm sure you know what this is."

John didn't have to wait for an answer. Junior was practically salivating. John continued, "My land against your Porsche, that pretty black horse of yours, and $1,000 says I have better cards than you."

You could hear a pin drop.

Doc Bernie broke the spell. "You crazy, O'Fallon? Your land's worth more than that."

John drawled, "It ain't always about the money, Doc."

His voice turned hard, "What do you say, Junior? If you want my land, let's see what you got."

Junior didn't hesitate. He couldn't contain his glee as he turned over a queens over eights full house. Junior reached for the deed but T.H. stopped him, "Hold your horses, Chouteau. You don't touch anything until all the cards have been turned over."

Junior smiled, sat back in his chair, folded his hands behind his head, and nodded to Crazy John. When Crazy John turned over a jack high straight flush, Junior let loose a string of profanities. When it comes to cussing, the French don't have to take a back seat to anybody. He was so angry he almost drew down on Crazy John. His brother Auguste, who dealt that hand, stopped him. He probably saved his life! Crazy John told us winning that hand was one of the sweetest moments of his life.

In a related war story, Junior and three of his bilge rats rode up to my mansion one evening near sunset. I was working on my horseshoe pitch and feeling pretty good. Back to back double-ringers will do that for you. Junior cleared his throat to get my attention. I knew he was there and tossed four more ringers before I acknowledged him. I picked up a loose brick left over from building my ash pit. I asked if he was interested in a "friendly" game. He declined. My skill as a horseshoe player far exceeded his and he knew it.

Instead, he offered to buy my land, told me he'd pay top dollar for it. His offer was a joke. He knew as well as I did what my land would be worth down the road. I told him I had no interest in selling, especially to him. He warned me, "You're making a big mistake, Bissell. It's no secret how you got this land. I just might take you to court for it."

I retorted, "Fine! Go ahead. Take it up with my lawyer. He's the Attorney General of the United States."

"You're crazy."

"Junior, I'm telling you straight. You sue me and Uncle Sam will be a co-defendant. Now, take your friends and get off my property."

He was mad, so mad his voice broke. He squeaked, "I'm the wrong person to have as an enemy."

He was on horseback, but I was almost looking him in the eye. Choking back laughter, I managed to tell him, "You're mistaken. You're the wrong person to have as a friend!"

Then I did burst into laughter. Tarnation! I'd never seen him so mad, but it was a cold anger. He nodded to his henchmen and then said, "Look around, Bissell. You're out here all alone, miles from anybody. You could have a fatal accident and nobody would know."

He looked me in the eyes, "That pretty wife of yours would be a widow." He held up his hand, "But, not to worry. I'd love to take care of her!"

His cutthroats laughed and fanned out. I was caught off stride. Was this for real?

I was wearing my pistol, but my heavy armaments were in the house. My old pepper pot pistol was about as accurate as a blind navigator. I still had that brick in my hand. I figured I could hurl the brick in Junior's face and maybe toss off a couple rounds. If nothing else, it would make their horses skittish enough to occupy their attention. I would make a run for the house and my shotguns. I zeroed in on that slimy weasel and thanked God Mary and the baby were at Uncle Dan's.

Someone pulled back the hammer of a weapon. Junior and his cohorts looked to their right. I shot a peek. To my relief, Sam Wiggins stood there, the bore of his .75-caliber Brown Bess rifle looking as big and as deep as one of the caves under my house. The Sarge was a few feet to his left, one double-barreled shotgun in his hands and another slung over his shoulder. The Sarge had both hammers pulled back. Tom sure loved testing his scatterguns.

(My grandfather knew Henry Nock, whose invention in 1787 of a more efficient breech allowed shotguns to be made that were lighter and easier to handle.)

Wiggins spat on the ground and asked Junior, "Well Sonny, you gonna leave or you gonna bleed?"

Junior threw up his hands as if in surrender, repeating that Tom and Sam should take it easy. He motioned to his men to back off. After a tense moment, they withdrew their hands from the vicinity of their side arms and raised their arms as well.

Junior croaked, "I was just yanking his chain, Wiggins. No need to get all excited."

Sam motioned with his Brown Bess toward St. Louis and Junior took the hint. He spun his horse around and bolted, his squad of thugs following. Tom Miller fired into the air and Junior almost fell off his horse. We all laughed.

Sam grunted and said, "It's a good thing for you my belly got to growling, Lewis."

I walked with them to the bunkhouse and we heated some beans and ham. Sam was already embellishing on what happened. By tomorrow, Tom Miller and I wouldn't even be in the story.

Wheeling and Dealing

A group of Navy veterans wanted to get into the boat building and repair business. They had the expertise, but no land or the cash to buy materials. Crazy John thought the idea had potential. He devised a scheme to make money on both ends. He rented his new partners a portion of his land near the river and lent them the money to buy materials and equipment. Then he brokered a deal with the suppliers, making a nice commission on the sale. It was a profitable venture.

After several years of paying rent, the boat builders bought land on the river in Carondelet and moved the business there. They were forever grateful to Crazy John.

Between locusts and drought, farmers just northwest of the city had a run of bad luck. One of them had been a shipbuilder in France. John lent them money so they could build what they called prairie schooners, big wagons that would "sail" across the plains. People thought Crazy John was throwing his money away but it turned out to be another investment that paid great dividends.

He also invested in a foundry on the river in Carondelet, a place that built boilers for steam engines. John was making a $1,000 a month. I added Moneybags to his list of nicknames.

Jean Levi was right. On 8 July 1826, twelve Carondelet residents signed a deed relegating 1,700 acres of Carondelet common grounds to the United States government for a place to build Jefferson Barracks. The price tag was a measly five dollars. The sellers believed the post would be a real boon to the local economy.

Within a week, Major Stephen Kearney led four companies of the 1st Infantry to Carondelet to set up a camp. They called the temporary camp "Cantonment Adams" after President John Quincy Adams. By October, barracks were up. The camp was officially named Jefferson Barracks *(JB)* after the recently departed Thomas Jefferson. It was the first "Infantry School Of Practice" in the United States. It became the home of the 3rd and 6th Infantry. Some of the most famous soldiers in history would serve there.

Everything of use was taken from crumbling Fort Bellefontaine to JB. The Army hired me to haul 100 tons of munitions to JB in the *Pole Cat*. They stored the munitions at JB until the arsenal they were building on the river three miles south of St. Louis was completed.

Fort Bellefontaine was at the heart of a significant chapter in the book of my life. The officer in charge, Ensign Jefferson Davis, was just 20 years old. He was a decent person and a sharp soldier. He said he loved sailing, especially on the ocean. He picked a marvelous time to be on the river. The fall foliage was magnificent to behold.

On a jaunt downriver, Ensign Davis asked me, "Bissell. What kind of name is that? It sounds English."

Smiling wickedly, I answered, "A lot of people make that mistake. Once!" Jeff laughed. He looked surprised when I said, "It's Norse."

I gave him the short version of the family history. I mentioned Uncle Daniel and he drawled, "I heard you was related."

I ended with the story how my father died at Fort Bellefontaine.

Jeff was silent for a while. Then he made me a promise, "When the word comes down to torch what's left of the fort, you can do it if you like."

"Me?"

"You can consider it an honorary Viking funeral. It'd be a fitting tribute to your father."

Davis was sitting on a powder keg, smoking. I couldn't help but like him. So did Keegan and Picot.

• • •

As an afterthought, the Army decided to move the bodies
of the soldiers buried in the little cemetery behind Fort
Bellefontaine to Jefferson Barracks. They were afraid the river
would reclaim that spot. It was the most grisly cargo I ever
hauled. I delivered the coffins to JB, all except one. I took my
father's remains to Bissell Point where we buried him in a
shady spot under a big elm.

• • •

1827. John Quincy Adams was in his 3rd year as
President. We dubbed him John "Quaint" Adams. In 1811, he
declined the post of Supreme Court Justice offered to him by
James Madison. It surprised me when he accepted the nomina-
tion for President. I think it astonished him when he won. I
voted for the other fellow, whose name escapes me right now.
People rarely remember the names of the losers.

The U.S. government decided to go into the banking
business, establishing federal banks all across the country.
St. Louis was granted a charter to establish a federal bank here.
The prominent blowhards in this area and in the state capitol
put their heads together in an effort to figure out who would
make the ideal president of the 1st Federal Bank of St. Louis.
It would have to be someone everyone trusted.

I'd just finished hauling the last of the munitions from Fort
Bellefontaine to JB, a job that was interrupted by an early
winter freeze in 1826. It was early April. I spotted a twister to
the northeast, so we took shelter in the cavern under the house.
The twister was running away from us but the following
storms and high winds were fierce. Folks say the tornado set
down near Alton.

The next day, I was up on the widow's walk checking the
roof when Uncle Daniel stopped by. I almost took a tumble
when he yelled the news up to me. Crazy John was the new
president of the 1st National Bank.

The fox was in the hen house!

Family Matters

*U*ncle Daniel's yelling brought Mary out to the porch. I could hear Uncle Dan talking excitedly as I quickly climbed down from the roof. As I joined them, I motioned to them to sit down. Ensign Davis let me have the big old bench my father hauled from post to post. How my father got it was one of my mom's favorite war stories.

You see, my dad was a huge man. Mom's cousin, Joshua, made furniture and sold it. Josh's parents were killed by Iroquois while fording the Podunk River near South Windsor, so he was raised by mom's parents. Mom was like a sister to him and he wanted to do something special for her wedding.

Uncle Josh, as I called him although we were second cousins, had a dry goods and furniture store in nearby Hartford. Josh was given to practical jokes. First, he made a beautiful oak bed. On the headboard, in the fashion of an arch, he carved my mom and dad's name in ancient Norse. Sven Frissgard, a blacksmith in Windsor, had an Old Norse bible and helped him with the translation.

In the very center of the headboard, he carved the Sacred Heart of Jesus as depicted in so many religious pictures. On the heart, he inscribed "Together in Eternity." Mom said until I came along it was the best present she ever received. She told my brother George the same thing!

She said she was flabbergasted when she first saw the headboard. Uncle Josh had a couple of his friends sneak it into their house during the wedding. Then, he tricked my folks into thinking that their wedding present was that big old wooden bench he set on the front porch.

Uncle Josh made an oversized bench large enough for a man even as enormous as my father to stretch out on. He put it on the porch and it was the first thing the wedding party saw when they arrived at my parent's new home. Uncle Josh leapt from his horse and jumped up on the porch. He called to my dad, "Here you go, Russell, something every man should get on his wedding day, a place to sleep when you're in the doghouse."

Mom would always finish the story with, "You know, he was right!"

• • •

The bench was my dad's favorite present. He was bigger than any Army cot could handle. Until he got that bench, he'd wake every morning about a half an hour before his legs would. I know how he felt.

We sat on that old bench while Uncle Daniel told us the news. Crazy John was indeed the new president of the United States Bank of St. Louis. Big Jim McGunnegle's son, George, would be the bank clerk. Big Jim had been a shareholder in the 1st City Bank of St. Louis. The board of directors included William Clark, John Mullanphy, and Pierre Chouteau, Jr,

The revelation that Junior was on the board of directors of the new federal bank floored me; so much so I forgot Mary was present. I jumped up and went off on the little skunk, using language that would make a sailor blush. I stopped when I saw the look of shock on Mary's face.

Uncle Daniel was enraged. He stood up and threatened me, "I'm not too old to teach you some manners, Lewis!"

Mary just stood up and said, "Men!"

She rushed into the house. I started to follow but Uncle Dan grabbed my arm and said, "I'm not done with you yet."

I pulled my arm loose and sat back down. I knew I was in for the same old lecture.

This all started last Sunday. We took James to be baptized at Our Lady of Mount Carmel Catholic Church in Carondelet. There wouldn't be a Protestant church in St. Louis until 1848. Father Saulnier performed the baptism. Dorf, Crazy John, and Jean Levi attended the christening. To my surprise, Uncle "I'll never set foot in a Catholic Church" Daniel also attended.

I guess the baptism got Uncle Dan to thinking about life and mortality because he told me recurring bouts of the fever and his age, 65, prompted him to have a will drawn up. He told me again, "I'm leaving my slaves to my next of kin, Mary and you included."

"I already told you . . ."

"Just hear me out!"

It was the same old song. He adored Mary and he was worried about her and that baby, alone, with the wilderness practically at her back door.

"Mary's not a strong woman, Lewis. You know that. It's a hard life out here on the frontier, and if that girl doesn't get help, you'll put her into an early grave."

He bent my ears until I could take no more.

Agitated, I said, "I'm tired of hearing this same old nonsense over and over again. Uncle Dan, Mary's a lot stronger than you think. She doesn't need any help, at least not that kind!"

Uncle Daniel didn't know Mary was as opposed to slavery as I was. I didn't tell the old lunkhead because I didn't want him to sour on Mary. Besides, he wasn't "given to asking the opinion of women."

So, instead of celebrating Crazy John's good fortune, Uncle Dan and I had a long argument. He did most of the talking, while I fumed. Finally, I jumped up and said, "Shut up! I'm my own man and I don't need some broken down old warhorse to tell me what to do!"

I saw Uncle Dan's shoulders sag and I immediately regretted my words. He seemed to shrink, that gigantic bench adding to the effect. Jehosaphat, how could I do that to him? Uncle Dan had been a pillar of strength for me and I always admired his stubborn independence. He probably broke more rules and regulations than any man who ever served in the U.S. Army. He never let anyone tell him what to do, not even his commanding officers—they just thought they did. Now, he was old and in poor health, and I just voiced his greatest fear. I felt ashamed.

Then something amazing occurred. A strange energy coursed through me. Electricity danced on my neck and my scalp prickled. I felt a presence and I knew. I just knew. My father was present!

Uncle Dan sensed it, too. He stopped talking, stood up, and looked around. A tide of emotions welled up in me. I blinked back tears. Uncle Dan asked me, "You all right?"

My voice shook as I told him, "I'm fine. Just got something in my eye."

I wiped my hand across my face and looked at him. I was shocked. His eyes were bloodshot and swollen. Tears ran down his face. I stepped to him and hugged him, something I had never done before. I somehow managed to tell him, "I'm sorry, Uncle Dan. I love you."

Believe me, I never, ever, imagined myself doing that. It was something the men in my family just didn't do. I think the uniform always got in the way.

I heard a board creak. I turned around and Mary was standing there. After a moment of stunned silence, Uncle Dan, Mary, and I sat and marveled at what had just happened. I joked, "Even the dead want us to clear the air."

Uncle Dan agreed. He said, "Lewis, I'll respect your wishes if you'll respect mine."

"Uncle Dan, I'm sorry. My conscience just will not let me accept slaves, but I promise you I'll get Mary some help, and maybe do a good deed at the same time."

At Jimmy's baptism, Father Saulnier told us he took in some recently orphaned black children, two 15-year-old girls and an 8-year-old boy, all unrelated. He was looking for homes for them.

Their parents and other freemen slaves were heading west in two rickety old wagons laden with all their worldly possessions. They halted near a bluff overlooking the banks of the Big River due west of Herculaneum. The wagon master, a grizzled ex-slave they called Old Cal, sent the three oldest children down to the river to fill water skins, an act that saved their lives. While at the river, the little wagon train was attacked by an outlaw gang. Hearing gunshots, the three children ran to the nearest cover and hid.

Marshall Henry Dodge and six Rangers, on the trail of a band of renegade Indians, heard the shooting and investigated. The raiders were slaughtering everyone. Appalled by the carnage and throwing caution to the winds, Dodge and his Rangers rode down on the raiders, guns blazing even though they were out of range.

The outlaws grabbed one of the pioneer's wagons and took off. Dodge wanted to give chase but halted so he and his men could give aid to the wounded settlers. Their efforts were in vain. Dodge dispatched a Ranger with word of the attack to JB.

Dodge and his posse were surprised when the three children emerged from the brush. They told him they were down at the river when the shooting started. When the shooting stopped, the girls had to restrain the boy to keep him from breaking cover. The girls thought it best to stay hidden until they could determine if it was safe to come out. The boy looked at the bodies on the ground and said, 'My daddy's not here."

Marshall Dodge sent one of his scouts to search for tracks of a possible survivor. The posse was just finishing burying the

six dead settlers—four adults and two children—and one
outlaw when the scout came back and reported. He found
tracks of a single man that ended at the top of a bluff. He
picked up the trail below the bluff but after a mile the trail
turned cold. Marshall Dodge promised the boy they'd keep
looking. He and his men brought the survivors to Father
Saulnier in St. Louis.

Lieutenant Albert Johnson led a troop of twenty soldiers to
track the killers, accompanied by Marshall Henry Dodge and
Nahaboo, one of his Shawnee trackers. The pro-slavery clique
grumbled about the use of government troops to track the
murderers. They argued that, after all, the victims were just a
bunch of "niggers." The government could make better use of
its manpower and money.

The posse found the abandoned wagon. It had a broken
axle and was stripped of everything of value.

"Those butchers must've figured no one was going to
come looking for 'em," Dodge said. "They made no attempt to
cover their tracks."

The posse trailed Nahaboo as he followed the tracks of
between seven and eight riders. The hoofprints eventually
turned back east. After two miles, the trail became muddled
with other tracks, the prints of unshod horses.

After close inspection, Dodge and Nahaboo figured that a
band of about twenty Indians, most likely Fox and Sauk, were
about a half hour behind the raiders and about an hour ahead
of the troops. They followed and were led to a clearing on the
south bank of the Meramec, not far from High Ridge. The
bodies of the outlaws were strewn on the ground, with most of
their loot. They were badly butchered and most were unrecog-
nizable. However, Lieutenant Davis recognized Joe Lynch and
"One-eared" Martin, two of Junior's strongmen. Captain
Johnson figured they were moonlighting, but young Jeff Davis
wasn't so sure. He'd heard rumors that Junior dealt in the slave
black-market.

Realizing it wasn't healthy to stay in one place too long
with Indians on the warpath, they quickly buried the remains
of the raiders. It was probably better than those cutthroats

deserved. The troop gathered up what they could carry of the stolen property and took it back to the survivors. Henry Dodge called the event "frontier justice."

• • •

Now, my Uncle Daniel and I weren't the only people who argued over this slavery issue. Missouri was admitted to the Union in 1821 as a slave state, maintaining the balance of slave and free states. People like me were called abolitionists because we wanted to see slavery abolished. We believed "All men are created equal." I helped bury some mighty fine people who fought for that belief.

Our counterparts, the anti-abolitionists, didn't think the constitution applied to Negroes, since, as they argued, the Negroes were "sub-humans." Some called them the "devil's kin." They usually referred to blacks in derogatory terms, calling them "coloreds" or "niggers."

Only three percent of the population of the city were slave owners, but they were very vocal. They had money and the support of many people whose ignorance led them to believe that hogwash about Negroes being "unearthly" creatures.

• • •

Father Saulnier was under fire from some of his parish-ioners for taking in the black children orphaned in the raid. Some members of his flock were already disturbed because he allowed blacks to stand at the back of the church during Mass. Word had it the collection plate was going to be a lot lighter as long as those "nigger kids" were on the parish grounds.

So he was elated when I told him Mary and I would take the kids off his hands.

"It's a trade off, Father. Mary's pregnant again and those girls will help her with the household and the baby. The boy can help me with outside chores and on my boat. In return, I'll provide your orphans with a roof over their heads and food for their bellies."

"Thank you, thank you," Father Saulnier replied. "I'm sure you'll do the right thing by them, Captain."

I vouchsafed, "Father, I'll treat them like my own."

The paperwork in the property returned by the Army revealed that the children's parents were freemen, slaves granted freedom by their former owner. So, by rights, the children were also freemen. I promised Father Saulnier that these youngsters would never lose that freedom.

Mary and I took the *Pole Cat* to pick up the children. It was her second time out on the boat. When we first arrived from Connecticut, I took her and my mother out on the river. The water was rough. When they set foot on shore, they vowed to never go out again.

I decided to pick up the orphans by boat so we wouldn't have to parade them through town. It wasn't that we were embarrassed to be seen with them. They'd been badly traumatized. I thought a boat ride might help cheer them up.

Mary hadn't met the children. I first laid eyes on them the day I told Father Saulnier I would provide a home for them. He brought them into the foyer of the church and introduced me. He told them that I would take them to my home, where they would live with me and my wife and my son, James.

Both girls were tall, skinny, and courteous. I asked their names. They chimed in together, like birds trying to out chirp each other. I laughed and said, "One at a time."

One girl clamped her hand over the other's mouth and said, "I'm Sophie Jones and she's Lolanda Sneed."

Lolanda pulled Sophie's hand from her mouth and said, "Lolo. My name's Lolo."

The boy, a short chubby fellow with huge hands and feet, was more skittish than the girls. I asked him his name but he just stood silent, looking at the floor. Father Saulnier whispered that his name was Lawrence Williams and that he still hadn't come to grips with the fact that his father wasn't coming back. Unsure of what to say, I asked him, "Do you want to be called Lawrence or Larry?"

He looked up and quickly put his head back down, then mumbled, "Larry."

He was shuffling his feet. I thought he was going to run. Like a thunderbolt, it struck me that he was afraid of me. I was some strange white man he'd never seen before. I towered over him like a mountain, and my ugly old face was as scarred as a gamecock's. I tried to make him feel less vulnerable by kneeling down. I spoke in a soft voice and told him, "Larry's a fine name. My first commanding officer was named Larry."

Larry said softly, "Just like me."

"Yep, 'cepting we called him Laughing Larry because he was so jolly and always ready with a joke. He was a good man. He taught me a lot about soldiering and life, almost as much as my father."

Larry didn't say anything for a moment, then he told me, "My daddy's funny, too." Then he screwed up his courage and said, "Go away now. My daddy's gonna be comin' to take me home."

I looked up at Father Saulnier and the girls. The good priest shook his head. Then inspiration struck! Doesn't happen often for me, so I seized the moment, "Larry, everyone who comes to St. Louis lands in my back yard. More people are likely to see you at the river crossing than anywhere and the more you're seen, the more likely you are to be found. So, I think it'd be smart for you to join us, don't you?"

"No."

I added, "We can leave a message at the church for your father telling him where you are and how to get there. If need be, Father Saulnier can send word and we'll come in my boat and pick your daddy up. How about that?"

"No."

I decided to let it rest, "Well, I'll be back in a few days. You think about it."

Well, it was three days later and I'd find out shortly what he thought about it. Just before landing, I said to Mary, "I wonder if I'll have to wrestle that boy aboard."

The kids were waiting on the riverbank, their few belongings bundled up in a sackcloth. After the raiders and the Indians, all that remained were some clothes, a beat up old Bible, and, most importantly, the papers making them freemen.

I stopped at the foot of the gangplank to talk to Father Saulnier. Mary was behind me, out of view. Father Saulnier said, "Larry's still reluctant to leave. He's says it's because he's afraid his daddy won't find him if he keeps moving around, but . . ."

I finished his thought, "He's really afraid of me."

"I believe so."

I looked at Larry and he looked down at his feet. When I stepped off the gangplank, Mary was no longer hidden. Larry looked back up when she said to the girls, "Hello, ladies. I'm Mary."

Lolo said, "I'm Lolo." Sophie punched her on the arm when Lolo quickly added, "And she's Sophie."

Mary looked at Larry and smiled, "And you're Larry. I've heard a lot about you."

Mary's such a tiny person, it takes just an instant to take a shine to her. Boys of all ages fall under her spell and Larry was no exception. Mary said, "I would like you to come stay with me. Is that okay?"

Mary offered him her hand. Larry didn't hesitate. He took her hand and said, "Okay."

Father Saulnier and I stood there grinning as Mary led Larry and the girls past us and up the gangplank, a look of triumph on her face. I shook Father Saulnier's hand, picked up the sackcloth, and followed. We got back home without incident.

The girls adjusted quickly to their new home. Larry was another story. We have six bedrooms upstairs, four on the second floor and we split the attic into two bedrooms. The steps to the attic continued to the trap door in the roof. I took them to the roof and showed them the widow's walk. They loved it.

The bedrooms in the attic got extremely hot in the summer and very cold in the winter, but try telling that to people who spent most of their life roughing it outdoors and never had their own room before. We put Lolo and Sophie in one room in the attic and Larry in the other. In the morning, we'd find Larry curled up on the floor in the girls' room.

Larry was at ease with Mary, but still leery of me. After dinner one evening, Larry went outside to play. I took my

Norse battle-axe off the wall and went out to find him. He was sitting on a tree limb watching the river, his back to me.

I said, "Larry."

He turned and saw me with the battle-axe in my hands and jumped from the tree. He took a tumble when he hit the ground. I said, "Whoa, son. Take it easy. I just want to show you my pride and joy."

He scrambled to his feet. I quickly turned the handle toward him and said, "Here Larry, take it. It's all right."

Larry looked at the axe a second and then took it. He said, "What is it?"

"A Viking battle-axe."

"A Viking. What's a Viking?"

Well, that question sure got me started. I was proud of my heritage. I regaled Larry with tales of Norse legends, while he jumped around with the axe, swiping at invisible enemies. I stopped talking when his mock fighting got so serious he was no longer listening. Noting the silence, Larry stopped. He put the axe head to the ground and leaned on the handle.

"You a Viking?"

"Well, I suppose. . . yes, yes I am." With that answer I think I became Larry's hero for life. We battled imaginary foes and I talked until dark. Mary had to call us in.

We ceremoniously returned the battle-axe to the wall. After that night, Larry finally accepted rooming alone and began calling me Captain.

● ● ●

Also in 1827, war drums were beating in the Midwest. Black Hawk of the Sauk tribe and Red Bird of the Sioux were reigniting the Indian nations, goading them to war against the whites. In June, Captain William Selby Harney led two companies of infantry from JB in an attempt to apprehend these war chiefs. The trail led them all the way to the territory of Wisconsin.

Arts and Crafts

1828. We had an early thaw and a rainy spring. The Army had me haul that 100 tons of munitions from JB to the arsenal. My boat needed a major overhaul. Crazy John suggested I take it down to Carondelet to a couple of fellows he helped get started in the boat building and repair business. I was glad I took his advice. Those boat-smiths knew their business.

We winched my boat out of the river and worked on the keel, scraping away all manner of crud. Then we applied a thick coat of pitch to the seams and a lighter coat to the rest of the keel. Afterwards, we painted it a dark brown. We improved on the wheelhouse Uncle Daniel and I built in Pittsburgh back in 1810, adding a sliding window and a new pilot's wheel. We removed the running boards and raised the deck.

The boat-smiths suggested I install a small steam engine and add a paddle wheel to save my back. The steamboats made

better time and were putting men like me out of business. I was tempted but reluctant to spend the money, especially with another baby on the way. They recommended I get Machingo, the Shawnee artist, to render a depiction of a polecat on the bow of the boat.

• • •

I knew Machingo. He and I were about the same age. Machingo would come to the trading post at Fort Bellefontaine to sell or trade paintings he put on deerskin. Uncle Daniel thought he was such a fine artist, he had an easel and canvas sent from Chicago to the fort. He tried to convince Machingo to paint on canvas, but Machingo wouldn't, saying the canvas was too dead. Machingo's brother, Nahaboo, was as big as I was and the best wrestler in his tribe. *(Cloud Bank named him Man Mountain.)*

Nahaboo could beat Machingo at any game except knife throwing. Machingo the artist was deadly with a knife. *(Cloud Bank, the shaman of his tribe, named him Magic Hands.)*

One summer day several Shawnee from another tribe visited the post at the same time as Machingo's tribe. Challenges were made and a wrestling round robin ensued. Nahaboo beat all comers. He crowed to the soldiers watching the matches, bragging that no one from the Mighty River to the Great Mountains could whip him. He dared the blue coats to prove him wrong.

Crazy John stepped forward and told Nahaboo to get ready to meet his match. He took off his coat and handed it to Sergeant Miller. Sarge asked, "Have you lost your senses, you crazy fool?"

Crazy John stood straight and flexed his muscles. Nahaboo and the Shawnees laughed. Crazy John looked at Sarge and explained, "It's too hot for a coat today."

"Obviously."

Crazy John turned to me, pointed at Nahaboo, and said, "Go get him."

Now, I spent most of my early years on Army posts and did a lot of wrestling. My father, like most Army fathers,

taught me hand-to-hand combat. Life was fragile on the
frontier and protecting one's self was vital. I was big, strong,
and fast and whipped all contenders.

The only person who could hold his ground against me
was my older brother, George. George, who was slight like our
mother and quick as lightning, said I'd be unbeatable in a few
years, when he'd no longer be able to get his arms around me.
I attended an all-boys school and was the wrestling champ
there as well.

A good portion of being a soldier is enduring boredom.
During the down times, if the troops weren't playing cards or
horseshoes, we filled the hours competing against each other in
athletic events, such as foot races, pugil sticks, boxing, and
wrestling. I was the unbeaten, barely challenged, wrestling
champ of Fort Bellefontaine. Before he lost his leg, I once
wrestled and beat Stumpy Fredericks with one hand tied
behind my back.

I could tell Nahaboo was impressed by my size and
musculature. He spoke excitedly to his Shawnee brothers and
they all started whooping and clapping each other on the back.
Crazy John told Nahaboo he had good money that said I would
whip all of them, one at a time, finishing with the Man
Mountain himself.

They accepted the challenge, putting up a couple of fine
ponies against Crazy John's money. Secretly delighted, I told
Crazy John in my most deprecating tone, "Thanks a lot. You're
next."

This was fun. I had no trouble besting the other Indians
who wrestled in the round robin. Nahaboo was a different
story. He was large and had tremendous balance. As did I.
Walking on side boards on a boat in choppy waters in a swift
current will do that for you.

We struggled to get leverage, grunting like pigs. Neither
could trip the other. The few occasions one of us accomplished
a leg sweep, we'd quickly get back on our feet. Then I did
something that impressed every one in the crowd, and myself
as well. I found out how strong I really was. Nahaboo weighed
about 17 stone *(238 lbs)*. I picked him straight up and snapped

back, flipping him completely over my head. He landed flat on his back. I dropped on him and pinned him.

From that day forward, the Shawnee called me Mountain Crusher. The story of Nahaboo's defeat became part of Shawnee legend. After our wrestling match, tribes from all over the region sent their best wrestlers to test me. I was undefeated.

• • •

Later, Machingo told me my victory over his brother was a boon. Nahaboo got a dose of humility and, as a result, treated people with more respect. Machingo agreed to paint my boat but refused my offer of money. In return, he just wanted a few days room and board so he could paint a portrait of the view from Bissell Point. He wished to be free to paint from his heart. We waited up on the bluff while he worked on my boat.

The moment of unveiling came and Machingo sent Larry up to fetch us. Sophie, Larry, and Lolo, who carried little James, hurried down to the river. Mary and I followed, pushing our newborn little Mary in her baby carriage. My breath caught when I saw my boat. Machingo had painted the name *Pole Cat* on both sides of the prow, the letters themselves being a whole series of little polecats. On both sides of the boat, underneath the name, he added a gigantic pair of open hands. The hands rested against each other and held a huge mountain that covered both palms.

Mary and the kids heaped praise on Machingo, who took in the whole scene with obvious pleasure. Larry asked what the hands holding the mountain meant. I told my family the war story about my wrestling match with Man Mountain, trying not to sound too much like a braggart. I didn't need to. Machingo did that for me. Admiring the boat, I told Mary I'd have to retell this story up and down the river.

Machingo set up on my porch and worked on his painting for a few hours every morning. In the afternoon, he spent time with Larry in the woods, teaching him how to track, throw knives, and handle a tomahawk. When I was home, I joined them.

When Mary was napping, I'd take little James with us. After all, he was a member of the secret brotherhood of men. We didn't stray too far into the woods on these occasions in case I needed to get back to the house in a hurry. I don't know why I bothered. Mary always found out about it. When I asked her how she knew, she always responded, "A little bird told me."

I wondered if that "little bird" was Lolo or Sophie.

Machingo could do something that really spooked me. Now I know Native Americans are more in touch with nature and, at least according to lore, have sharper eyes and ears than we Europeans. Still, that doesn't explain how Machingo could be sitting in my den and say, "Crazy John come," or, "Marshall Dodge come with two riders."

Ten minutes later they'd be at my door. When I asked how he knew they were coming, he'd say, "A little bird told me."

One morning, Larry went down to Gingras Creek to catch some crawdads. Gingras Creek was spring fed. It started a few miles northwest of John O'Fallon's land and ran parallel with Bellefontaine Road until it veered to the river, about a half mile southeast of the ferry landing.

A short time later, Larry walked into the kitchen with a bucket full of crawdads. I asked him, "How did you catch them so fast?"

"The water in the creek's real low. I just walked in and picked 'em up."

I had stayed off the river the last two days because of high winds and thunderstorms. The same storm drove Machingo indoors. I wondered aloud, "Why is the creek low? It can't be from lack of rain."

Machingo, who was painting a cougar on the stock of my shotgun, said, "Beaver at work."

We went to investigate. We followed Gingras Creek upstream to a point about one-half mile northwest of John O'Fallon's land. I wasn't surprised to see Crazy John's fancy carriage parked by the creek. We walked down the embankment and saw Crazy John. He motioned to us to be quiet. When we got close, we could see a dam made from limbs, leaves, other debris, and mud. Beavers, a whole slough of them.

Larry, Machingo, Crazy John, and I watched the beavers swimming back and forth, adding more debris and daubing mud on the dam to reinforce it. When they went back for more foliage to add to their dam, the beavers would swim under water, a trail of bubbles giving away their positions. Larry could hardly contain his laughter when the beavers used their flat tails to pack the mud. Crazy John pointed to the bubbles and whispered, "I hope those little fellows didn't have beans for supper last night. Better hold your nose."

Larry couldn't contain his laughter and snorted, spooking the beavers. We waited for a while but the beavers stayed hidden. We left.

Larry said, "We should do something about the dam. The crawdads by our house will run out of water."

I said, "We will do something about it. We'll just let nature take its course."

Crazy John added, "Those beavers won't last long. Too many trappers in this neck of the woods."

Larry's eyes got wide and I thought he was going to cry. "Way to go, John."

• • •

Machingo told Larry the story of the first beaver. He told us about Tirawa, who went by many names: The Supreme

Creator, Father, and The Maker of All. The Maker created all the animals and a beautiful forest in which they could dwell. Then He rested.

Now, one of the first animals The Maker fashioned was the beaver. The little beaver was very smart and stood in good favor with The Maker of All Things. The other animals soon resented the beaver and puzzled over his behavior. When The Maker was asleep, he ran amok, changing things. The beaver pulled limbs from trees and pulled up bushes, leaving mounds of loose dirt. He carried it all, limbs, bushes and dirt to the middle of the forest. This angered the other animals. They told the beaver that when The Maker awoke they would tell Him that the beaver wasn't happy with Paradise. They would ask Him to banish the beaver from the forest forever. But it was too late.

The animals' disharmony awoke The Maker. This discord upset The Maker and His tears flowed freely. The Great Waterfall hit the floor of the forest with a sound like the thundering hooves of a thousand horses. All the animals gathered on a little island in the middle of the forest. Soon the island would be gone and they would all drown.

The beaver filled his tail with dirt and went to the edge of the island. He dipped his tail into the water and swiftly pulled it back out. The dirt became mud. He grabbed the bushes and limbs with his teeth and his arms. The other animals watched in awe as the beaver swiftly ducked under The Great Waterfall, his tiny figure barely visible as he ran fearlessly up The Mountain that was The Maker. Up, up, up, the beaver climbed, all the way to The Maker's eyes.

Starting at one corner and going to the other, the tiny beaver furiously dabbed the mud under The Maker's eyes and used the sticks and bushes to stop the flow of tears. When the water backed up, The Maker stopped crying. He reached up and wiped the dirt, sticks, and bushes from his eyes. When He looked at the beaver, who rested on His nose, He saw two of them.

In a voice so deep it contained it's own echo, He rumbled, "You have saved the forest and all the other animals. For that, I give you a mate. Go forth and multiply." And they did.

After hearing this story, I told Machingo, "That was the best dam story I ever heard!"

• • •

After the groaning stopped, we all went back to my house. Crazy John hadn't seen baby Mary yet. On the way home, we stopped by his place to pick up his wife, Ruth. John's first wife, Harriet Stokes, an Englishwoman he married in 1821, died from consumption two years after their marriage.

Last year, Crazy John married Ruth Caroline Sheets of Baltimore. He met her in Washington, D.C., while on business for the 1st National Bank of St. Louis. According to T.H. Benton, Crazy John was well received by the inner circle of Washington's power brokers. I didn't doubt that. He certainly had the knack for getting people to like him. Anyway, John and Ruth came over and had dinner. While the adults talked, Crazy John played with the kids.

After the children were down for the night, Crazy John and I sat out on the porch. We talked about how we'd get rich when the city expanded. People would pay a pretty price for apportions of our property. But that was in the future. He asked me how I was set financially.

I told him I was doing all right. The ferryboat business was growing and I was getting my cut. Once again, he chided me for taking such a small percentage of the earnings. I reminded him that Sam Wiggin's supplied the ferryboats. I was just a glorified extra hand. He said never mind. He had some keel-boat work for me if I wanted it. I thought, oh no, here it comes. I was right. More brick hauling! Thank you, very much, Mr. O'Fallon!

O'Fallon secured contracts with brick masons in Herculaneum, Hannibal, and Clarksville. He brokered brick orders with John Lee's company. John Lee's company made the finest bricks in the area and road tests performed by the City of St. Louis proved it. John Lee hired me to haul the bricks. He had been swindled by unscrupulous keelboat operators. Mike Fink came to mind. I don't know why. I heard he was dead.

Hauling brick was hard work. Brick deliveries are made as

close to the usage site as possible. Usually, there's no dock. I
had to get close to shore without running aground. A gangplank can be only so long. Picot would run the bricks down the
gangplank to us on a brick wagon, using a rope wrapped
around the sailing mast to control the slide. Keegan and I
sloshed through water and mud to carry the bricks ashore using
hods.

My crew and I spent most of 1828 hauling brick. We had
two brick wagons so I'd bring Larry with us. Larry had quick
hands and stacked bricks on one wagon while Henri lowered
the other. Keegan kept quiet, but I could tell he couldn't stand
Larry. Picot worried we might be asking for trouble. I said not
to worry, I carried Larry's papers wrapped in oilskin.

Mary's second hard delivery left her sickly until Thanks-
giving. The Black Hawk War was heating up and the Army
sent more soldiers from Jefferson Barracks to Wisconsin to
help capture Black Hawk.

What next?

• • •

1829 brought us a new President, Andy Jackson. He was a
rough old cuss. When he was still a general in the U.S. Army,

he got into it with Thomas Hart Benton. They almost beat each other to death. I know the feeling.

Here's a war story that took place one payday.

After John Lee settled up with me for a load of bricks we hauled to Hannibal, Pat Keegan and Henri Picot stopped by to get their pay. It was late and I was about to retire for the night. Mary and the kids were already in bed. Keegan was drunk and surly. He said, "Henri and me should be getting hazardous duty pay."

Before I could tell him I added a bonus to their regular pay, Keegan demanded, "We want extra money. I didn't hire on to work with no niggers."

That remark really stiffened my back. I warned him, "I normally don't hit drunks, but I'm real close to making an exception."

"Take your best shot. You don't scare me, Bissell." He spat on the ground. "What are you doing with those nigger kids anyway?"

"Watch your mouth!"

 "They got papers. They ain't no slaves," he slurred. "You're getting some from those pretty little fillies, aren't you?"

Time stopped.

It's hard to explain what happened next. I saw a block of red. Then we were into it, crashing punch after punch off each other, two giants slugging it out. Keegan started to give ground so he slid down to tackle me. I threw my legs back and he couldn't grab them. Then I kneed him in the face, his nose flattening as it broke. I caught him so flush I knocked him on his back.

The battle lust was upon me. I dropped on him and grabbed him by the throat. The next thing I knew, Mary was screaming at me and hitting me with a broom while little Henri Picot tried to pull me off Keegan. I had strangled Keegan into unconsciousness and didn't even know it!

I got up and stepped back. Mary was sobbing and Henri Picot was shaking. So was I. Mary looked at me and I saw fear in her eyes, something I never imagined I would ever see. I was mortified. Mary turned and went into the house.

 I helped Henri get Keegan onto my work sled. I hitched Buck to the sled and said, "Henri, take him up to Doc Bernie's place. Tell him to send me the bill."

Henri wasn't as good with mules as he was with boats and Buck knew it. That old mule gave me the funniest look when Henri took the reins. Sam Wiggins gave me Buck. Some drover gave him the mule in exchange for ferrying his herd across the river.

(Sam was often paid in trade, so much so, he eventually turned the shelters we built into trading posts.)

I realized I still had their pay. I chased after the sled to give them their money. Picot was still shaken. I apologized profusely and explained, "I haven't lost my temper like that since I was a kid. Most of my fighting experience's been while soldiering."

I went back to the house. Mary was sitting on the steps to the upstairs. All the kids were at the top of the stairs looking over the railing. She said, "Give me a few moments. I need to think."

She knew the kids would want to know what happened. So did she. I went back outside and sat on my dad's old bench. I stretched out, just for a moment, mind you, and the next thing I knew, the sun was up.

I got up and went inside. Mary and Lolo were making breakfast. Sophie was such a bad cook she was given the task of permanent dishwashing duty. Larry said, "You're up with the chickens, Cap'n."

I just grunted. Mary put a plate of eggs and grits in front of me and said, "You better eat before it gets cold."

We ate in silence.

The baby started crying, so Mary got up to take care of her. I finished my food and followed her to the crib in our bedroom. Mary was nursing the baby. I knelt down in front of her and watched. Little Mary stopped suckling, looked at me with her sparkling blue eyes, clapped her tiny little hands together, and squealed with delight. Absolution!

I took the baby from Mary, who watched as I played with the little tyke, making her squeal with laughter. Little Mary liked to touch my face, especially when it was slightly whiskered. She would rub her hand across my stubble, then look at her hand, then repeat the whole thing over and over. She tried to speak but only made funny noises. If she could talk, I'm sure she'd say, "Fuzzy!" I marveled at her.

Mary called for Lolo to take the baby. Lolo liked playing mother. She picked up little Mary and took her to the kitchen. As she went down the steps, Lolo said, "Phew! Stinky! Stinky! Stinky! Time for a bath."

When Lolo was out of earshot, Mary finally spoke, "Lewis, you are the gentlest man I know and I love you deeply. Last night was a nightmare. I thought you were possessed."

I didn't offer any excuses. I had none.

"I'm sorry, Mary. I love you more than anything on earth. I would never harm you or the kids, no matter how angry I got."

"I know that. I was just shocked to see you trying to kill that man. I never want to see you like that again. If I do, I'll pack up and take the kids back to Connecticut."

As the words sunk in, my heart skipped a beat. Life without Mary—I may as well be dead. I took her hand and fondled it. I pulled her to me and hugged her, promising over and over, "Never again."

Nahaboo

$\mathcal{I}$ needed to hire a new hand. I wanted someone as big and strong as Keegan and I got him. Machingo and Nahaboo stopped by for a visit. They heard about my altercation with Keegan. I was glad to see jolly Nahaboo. The Man Mountain was working for Territorial Marshall Henry Dodge as a tracker.

Since the War of 1812, Dodge was head of the Missouri Militia. He had four regiments of dragoons, light cavalry that fought on foot or horseback, and about 40 Shawnee under him. His dragoons and Shawnee deputies were called Rangers. The Shawnees made little money but received billeting and food at Ranger headquarters. They were proud to wear the Ranger uniform.

Machingo knew I was looking for a new man, so he suggested Nahaboo. It was a great idea. Nahaboo was strong and had terrific balance. Nahaboo thought it was a great idea, too. He could make some money, and he would no longer have to sleep in the barracks on those soft cots or wood floors. No tepees were allowed on the Ranger compound. I promised him a salary, meals, and a place to pitch his tepee. Nahaboo could lie down and sleep on the ground again. The Earth Mother would be pleased and so would he.

Henri Picot showed up just before the next jaunt upriver. I was glad to see him. He was the best helmsman I knew. He admitted I scared him the other night, but he liked the *Pole Cat* and he recognized I knew the river around here as well as any man. Navigating the Mississippi was treacherous, and I had

DAN PATTERSON

been doing it for years. Navigating the Missouri was considered suicidal by some, and I had been on it about as much as any boatman he knew. I was good at spotting snags.

(A "snag" is an underwater obstacle, usually a fallen tree. Over 400 steamboats were lost to the Missouri River, about 300 to snags.)

The key was, Henri trusted me. When I introduced our new deck hand, Picot chuckled and said, "Do you have papers for him, too?"

Nahaboo and I laughed. The Man Mountain slapped Henri on the back and said, "I like funny man."

Looking up at Nahaboo, Henri remarked, "That's the best news I've heard all day."

The *Pole Cat's* crew was now a Frenchman, a Viking, a black boy, and a giant Indian. Fate managed to land us all in the same boat.

Nahaboo was a real asset. He was a much better worker than Tom Keegan; he worked in perfect concert with me. He had a knack for making friends and was welcomed everywhere. A lot of people knew him from his days as a scout for Henry Dodge's Rangers.

He was my biggest fan. He told everyone the tale that inspired the painting on the boat. Like most war stories, it got better every time he told it. Did you know that both he and I had to wrestle and beat 50 Indians before we could wrestle each other? I guess I lost count.

Larry loved hearing the story, and we got the biggest kick out of Henri Picot. Every time Nahaboo started to tell the story, Henri threw his arms up and said, "Not again." Still, he sat and listened, occasionally taking a nip from the bottle he carried.

Larry took to staying in Nahaboo's tepee, the beginning of a lasting friendship.

Machingo gave Larry a tomahawk for his birthday. I think he liked it more than my Viking battle-axe. Larry was so proud of that tomahawk he took it everywhere with him. That practice stopped after he took it to church one Sunday. Father Saulnier halted his sermon and asked, "Will the young man in the back of the church please take his tomahawk outside?"

Mary was mortified. She lectured Larry for so long the rest of us felt we were being punished.

After that Sunday, we kept the tomahawk on the boat in the footlocker with the tools. Some tomahawks were like clubs but not this one. It was more like a hatchet and was very sharp. Larry spent a lot of time on the *Pole Cat* honing it.

Nahaboo knew the name of almost every plant we came across and how people could put them to use. The Shawnee don't have a word in their language equivalent to weed. This Native American strongman gave Larry many lessons in horticulture. Nahaboo regaled us with Native American folklore and I countered with stories from Norse mythology. Larry couldn't get enough of either.

I showed Nahaboo my collection of arrows. He identified the tribes who "gifted" me with them. He grunted, "No have Shawnee arrow," and gave me one.

When we delivered to places where bigots gave us a hard time, we unloaded as fast as we could. Seeing us carry heavy hod loads of brick with ease, these zealots realized they didn't want any part of us. We preferred a cold shoulder to hot lead.

Ragnarok

*W*e had a standing invitation for Sunday dinner at Uncle Daniel's house. Occasionally, we went. We would have visited more often except for the slave issue and Aunt Deborah's aloofness.

Larry, Lolo, and Sophie liked to go, too. They'd jump out of the wagon and run down to the slave quarters where they were received like long-lost cousins. They ate in the slave quarters while we had dinner at the main house.

After dinner, I joined Uncle Dan in his den. Puffing on a cigar, he asked me about the altercation between Tom Keegan and me. He had heard it was a dandy.

I told him, "I'm not too keen on remembering that event."

Uncle Dan said, "Well, Tom Keegan sure remembers it. Word is, he's getting loaded down at Sullivan's every night and bragging about how he's going to get even. I hear Junior recently added him to his gang of bullies."

That didn't surprise me in the least.

I didn't want to speak of it, but I knew Uncle Dan wouldn't let me leave until I did. I just said, "Keegan said something that made me mad."

"Just mad? Mary said you were more like a crazy man. Tell me exactly what happened."

"I don't know what happened. I saw a red cube in front of my eyes and my brain stopped working. I didn't come to my senses until I'd almost strangled Tom Keegan to death. It wasn't a good experience."

Uncle Dan nodded. He understood that whatever it is that separates a man from an animal left me. Uncle Dan knocked the ash off his cigar and said, "I've been there myself. Hand-to-hand combat brings out the beast in a man. Soldiers call it battle lust or blood lust. Our Norse ancestors called it the 'berserker' rage."

Uncle Dan continued, "I saw you in a 'berserker' state once, back when you were a kid. It was at Fort Pitt. Remember?"

I remembered. I must have been close to 10 years old. Uncle Dan and my dad had temporary duty postings at Fort Pitt while waiting for reassignment.

Uncle Dan said, "That Fink kid sure gave you a warm welcome to Fort Pitt."

How could I forget? Without a word, Fink had walked up and punched me smack on the chin, right on the knockout button, knocking me for a loop.

Uncle Dan said, "He hit you right in the jaw and you flew through the air and landed flat on your back."

I was momentarily unconscious, so I didn't remember that part. When I hit the ground, consciousness returned immediately. I tasted my own blood. When Fink struck me, my mouth clamped shut and my teeth bit through a part of my tongue. Tasting my own blood enraged me. I saw that red cube.

I bounced up so fast it amazed Fink. He thought I was down for the count. Fink had about five years and thirty pounds on me, but it didn't matter. I jumped up and started kicking him, one kick after another, fast and furious. Uncle Dan said I looked like one of those Russian dancers. I caught him in that place that really hurts and he went down. I jumped on top of him and started pummeling. A group of soldiers on the porch of the Post Exchange started clapping and cheering.

Fink's mother came out of the PX and screamed at us, "Stop. Stop this right now!"

My dad jumped in and pulled me off the big bully. Fink's mother grabbed her son by the ear, twisting it. As she pulled, Fink followed. She was cursing at him as she led him away.

Light Horse Harry Lee, the post commandant, was in his

last tour of duty before resigning his commission to go into politics. The crusty Virginian sidled up to us, surprising Uncle Dan and my dad. After some back thumping and hand shaking between the old friends, the old soldier turned to me. Uncle Dan told him, "This is Russell's boy."

As the Revolutionary War legend and I pumped hands, everyone in the compound clapped and cheered, soldiers and civilians alike. I was amazed. Light Horse Harry said, "Mike Fink's the biggest bully this side of the Ohio and we've been waiting for someone to come along and kick that kid's rump for years."

"I can shee why," I said with a thick tongue.

"Some of my men were waiting for him to come of age so they could knock the tar out of him. You've done the job for them."

Uncle Dan relit his cigar. It was funny he mentioned Mike Fink. For some reason, I'd been thinking of him lately. I said, "I heard Fink got killed about six years ago, shot outside of Fort Henry."

"You may be right."

There were many different stories of Mike Fink's demise told by rivermen.

According to Uncle Dan's war story, Mike Fink was outside a trading post near the ruins of Fort Henry. He put a bullet between some trapper's eyes trying to shoot a can off his head. He got into a knife fight with the victim's buddy, an 18-year-old kid. The kid drove his knife into Fink's rib cage just before Fink slit the kid's throat.

Fink bolted. Five of the kid's buddies pursued. One of them fired a shot that hit Fink in the back, knocking him to the ground. Two of them overtook Fink just as he struggled back to his feet, a pistol in his hand. He grabbed one of his attackers by the throat and held him at arm's length, while he blew the head off the other. Then he lifted the other fellow up over his head and brought him down across his knee, breaking his back, one of Fink's favorite maneuvers. The remaining three pursuers slowed and spread out, the desire for revenge yielding to caution. Fink ran onto his keelboat and started to withdraw the gangplank. His pursuers grabbed the end of the gangplank and pulled it back down.

With blood gushing from two wounds and his strength dwindling, Fink realized he couldn't win the tug-of-war, so he let go. His opponents fell to the ground as the other end of the gangplank dropped off the boat. They sloshed through the water, grabbed the side of the boat, and attempted to board.

Fink, weak from loss of blood, went to his wheelhouse and grabbed a lantern. The vengeance-driven survivors were falling over the side into the boat as Fink passed them heading aft. He pulled out his bayonet and drove it into a powder keg. He spread gunpowder on the deck of the boat and back to and over the top of about ten other powder kegs. He set the open keg on top. He raised the lantern and threatened to ignite the powder.

Two of the combatants jumped over the side and headed for the bank. The remaining pursuer scoffed at Fink and told him, "You don't have the guts."

Well, maybe he did or maybe he didn't, but he did drop the lantern, albeit from loss of strength or out of plain old cussedness. Fink headed toward the side of the boat on the river side, while his adversary followed his compatriots over the embank-

ment side. The kegs blew the boat to smithereens. Witnesses saw Fink up on the side of the boat just when it exploded. His body was thrown out into the river, flopping like a rag doll. The river was searched, but they never found his body. The old river rat was just where he belonged, rotting on the bottom of the Monongahela River.

• • •

On the way home, the kids fell asleep in the back of the wagon. I told Mary the war story about Mike Fink. She surprised me when she said Mike Fink got what he deserved. Shock must have registered on my face because she quickly explained, "Mike Fink hurt people and needed to be stopped. Pat Keegan was just a drunk who said something that offended you. You should have just walked away. People don't get the death penalty for being drunk and obnoxious."

She was right. I promised it would never happen again. I had overreacted and overreacting can be fatal.

• • •

Crazy John was elected president of the national bank by the board of trustees, but for a while it was in name only. When the national banks first opened, Joseph Biddle, the president of the main bank in Philadelphia, sent his brother Thomas to St. Louis to run the bank here. This really stuck in Crazy John's craw.

As the fates would have it, Biddle got into an argument with Spencer Pettis, a tough hombre who was running for state representative. Biddle waited and attacked Pettis while he was asleep in his hotel room. Pettis didn't file charges. He waited until the election results were in and then challenged Biddle to a duel. They stood only five feet apart because Biddle was near-sighted. They shot each other and died.

My brother George died from an infection on his brain. The doctor said it was caused by a bad tooth. By the time we got the letter from his wife Nancy, George had been in the ground for a couple of weeks. I couldn't believe it. George was such a good man. What a strange fate!

While President, Andy Jackson's government completely paid off the national debt but had to sink the national bank system to do it. T.H. Benton helped him, picking up the nickname "Old Bullion" while doing it.

Crazy John told me, "The government should be the last organization in the country to run a bank. To make money, you need money."

If the national banks made any substantial gains, the government withdrew at least 90% of the profit. Finally, President Jackson vetoed the National Bank Rechartering Bill, forcing the national banks to close. Crazy John handled the liquidation of the St. Louis branch. Unlike the rest of the banks in the country, whose final settlements left them in the six-figure zone of actual cash lost, the final settlement of the St. Louis branch was a loss of only $125.00.

Not bad for a crazy man!

Prosperity

*I*n 1830, my son George was born. He was a big baby and once again, Mary had a difficult time. Charlene Sullivan, her midwife, told me the next child could kill her, that is, if she recovered from this ordeal. When Mary was feeling better, I told her six children in the house were enough. She laughed and teased me about not paying attention. Lolo and Sophie were both 18 and not little girls anymore. On the baby issue, Mary couldn't agree more.

Mary had been waiting for the right moment to talk to me about Sophie. Sophie was sweet on Calvin, one of Uncle Daniel's slaves. They wanted to get married, but Calvin was a slave and Sophie was a free person. If she married him, she would be the wife of a slave and, thus, a slave again. Mary was afraid they would run away. I told her to talk to Uncle Dan.

Mary went to Uncle Dan's the next day and took Sophie with her. She sent Sophie to the slave quarters to wait.

Uncle Dan answered the door, "Mary! What a pleasant surprise! Come in, please. Deborah's napping. I'll get her."

"That won't be necessary, Uncle Dan. I came to see you."

"Me? Is there something wrong?" He pointed to a chair, "Please sit."

"No, Uncle Dan, there's nothing wrong. Not yet, anyway." She quickly explained about Calvin and Sophie. To her surprise, he knew all about the situation. He said, "I may be old but I'm not blind."

Uncle Dan sent for Calvin. Mary didn't know what was going to happen. Calvin arrived. He shot anxious glances at Mary.

"Mary here tells me you've been seeing Sophie."

"Yes, Master Bissell, but I . . ."

"No buts. Either you're seeing her or you're not."

"Yes, Master Bissell, but I . . ."

"Want to get married. Is that true?"

"Yes, but I can't . . ."

"Turn that girl back into a slave. I know."

"Yes, but . . ."

"You're a good man, Calvin, and a good worker." Uncle Dan paused. Calvin fidgeted. Uncle Dan finally broke the long silence.

"Well, I've been thinking it over and here's my offer. If you agree to stay and work for me, I'll grant you your freedom."

They heard a scream outside. Through the window they could see Sophie dancing for joy. They all burst into laughter. Mary hugged Uncle Dan who added, "Consider it an early Christmas present for all concerned."

Sophie and Calvin wed and Calvin became Uncle Dan's chauffeur.

• • •

1830 was a prosperous year for me. Settlers and drovers arrived every day, the mail stage now came twice a week, and my cut from the ferryboat business became substantial. Our bread and board business also did quite well.

Stumpy Fredericks and Sam Wiggins were glad when my keelboat was in dock. I ran one of the ferries for Sam. Larry ran the bed and breakfast for Stumpy, giving him a chance to take some time off and spend a few days in Alton. We hit him with some good-natured ribbing about his love life when he returned.

While Sam was away, Nahaboo and Larry tended his trading post on the west bank of the Mississippi. Sam's wife and two sons took care of the east side post. Thanks to his

father, Larry knew how to read, write, and count. Nahaboo
taught Larry how to barter and soon Larry was a savvy trader.

Nahaboo also taught Larry to swim. He took him to the
pool created by the beaver dam, and they were saddened to see
that trappers had captured or scared off the beaver population.
The unattended dam was just about washed away. It never
occurred to me that Larry didn't know how to swim. It
certainly explained his reluctance to get off the boat and slosh
through the water to get to shore. The poor kid must have been
scared to death.

Nahaboo also taught Larry about the night sky, naming the
different constellations and teaching him how to navigate by
them. Sometimes Larry spent the whole night stargazing, while
Nahaboo told tall tales. His favorite was the tale of the eternal
wrestling match between The Morning Star and The Evening
Star.

The foundry in the settlement of Carondelet made mighty
fine boilers. When the Memphis foundry was shut down by a
court suit, we got a lucrative contract to haul boilers to boat
yards in Memphis where they used the boilers to make steam
engines. This enterprise was arranged by Crazy John's uncle,
William Clark. He was a friend of my Uncle Dan, a former
governor of the Missouri territory, and a well-known explorer.

Uncle Dan invited Mr. Clark over for Sunday dinner.
Uncle Dan told war stories about William's brother, George
Rogers Clark, the Revolutionary War hero. Since he died about
the same time the 1st Bank of St. Louis was under siege, Uncle
Dan missed his funeral in 1818. William told us war stories
about his journey with Meriwether Lewis to explore the
northwest. Meriwether drove him crazy with his incessant
snoring.

Mr. Clark was in charge of the Bureau of Indian Affairs
and under a federal mandate to find jobs for the "civilized"
Indians. He placed many with the territorial Marshal's office.
Mostly he found them jobs that no one else wanted, like
loading heavy boilers onto boats. He knew I employed
Nahaboo. He convinced the owner of the foundry to use my
services. I was grateful.

I made the trip only three times, but the pay was exceptional. The Carondelet foundry wanted me to haul more boilers, but I didn't like being away from Mary and the kids for such long periods of time. Coming back up an unfamiliar section of river, all the way from Memphis, was tough and dangerous work. I decided I would just haul locally or not at all. Crazy John understood, but he also thought I was throwing away good money. I threw one of his favorite sayings right back at him, "It ain't always about the money."

Dorf came by at Christmas and entertained us with some "sleight of hand." The kids loved his act. He occasionally performed at the Old Salt Theater in St. Louis, a professional theater house. It had one tier of "box seats," which were benches placed advantageously. The theater boasted the classics, especially Shakespeare. Mary loved to go and I enjoyed it as well. We went to see *She Stoops to Conquer* and we ran into Junior and his wife, Emilie. Other than two bodyguards, he kept the less civilized members of his repertoire busy elsewhere.

Junior was always a gentleman when Mary was around. Finally, I realized why. He was sweet on her. Glory be!

Afterwards, Mary would comment that she didn't understand my dislike for him. I joked that even the devil would fall victim to her charm. She scolded me for saying such a thing, but I knew she liked it.

Marshall Dodge

1831. I helped Henry Wiggins haul a group of Mormons across the Mississippi. They camped on my grounds for a few nights but didn't take advantage of the bed and breakfast. Stumpy Fredericks was relieved. He thought Mormons had some strange ways. According to Stumpy, "One wife was one too many."

I heard the term "zealot" used before, but their leader, Joseph Smith, was the first person I ever met who filled that bill. There was a hungry fire in his eyes. He gathered his people around him and preached at sunrise and at sunset. His followers hung on his every word. Between feeding my animals and other chores, I caught bits and pieces of his sermons. I heard him use terms like "chosen one" and "the chosen." His supporters referred to him as "The Prophet."

He's not the first person in this neck of the woods to have that moniker hung on him. Nahaboo told us Tecumseh's brother, Terskwatawa, the Shawnee shaman, was also called "The Prophet" and had that same look in his eye. Terskwatawa claimed he received his messages from the "Master of Life." My Uncle Dan said both "prophets" were charlatans who used superstition to sway people to do their bidding. I wasn't so sure. Truly, Joe Smith was a mesmerizing speaker, and I got the feeling he really believed in what he was preaching.

The arrival of the Mormons caused such a stir Marshall Dodge came by. He asked me, "What do you think of 'em?"

It's not my habit to denigrate anyone or their beliefs, so I chose my words carefully, "I didn't get the full message Smith was preaching, only snippets, but his congregation appears to believe him. Maybe they have no choice. He has little or no tolerance for slackers."

"Well, I got reports that some of his followers want to leave but he won't let them. I'm gonna tell 'em all to move on."

Later, I read in the *Missouri Gazette,* a newspaper that would become the *Missouri Republican,* then the *Globe Democrat,* that the Mormons moved into Franklin County.

Crazy John's bank had a subscription to the paper. After reading the papers, he gave them to me, often dropping them off on his way home. I don't think that's what Joseph Charless, who founded the newspaper in 1808, had in mind when he said the paper needed a wider circulation. Charless and his wife also opened The Missouri Tavern, an inn that served just about anything but whiskey. It was a popular place at election time. T.H. spent every election night there. Later, it was called The Missouri Hotel.

Before Larry, Sophie, and Lolo came to live with us, one of the few people they trusted besides Father Saulnier was Henry Dodge. To help Larry overcome his reluctance to come stay with us, Marshall Dodge promised he would drop in as often as possible to check on their well-being. Now, to give you an idea how seriously Marshall Dodge takes his promises, let me tell you a little war story.

In 1814, during the War of 1812, Dodge was in charge of the Missouri Militia. General Henry Dodge and 350 Rangers and 40 Shawnee went to the Boone's Lick area to subdue hostile Miamis. They met up with Captain Ben Cooper and the local militia at Cooper's Fort. They picked up the trail near Arrow Rock and tracked the Indians to some nearby woods.

After a brief exchange of gunfire, very one-sided, the outnumbered Indians waved the white flag. They would surrender if Henry Dodge gave his solemn word he would spare their lives. He promised. When one of the volunteer militiamen from Boone's Lick found a rifle belonging to a Boone's Lick man, Cooper and his men demanded vengeance. They wanted the Indian who committed the murder executed as an example to the rest of the tribe.

True to his word, Henry Dodge refused to exact revenge for them. The locals became so enraged they raised their weapons and threatened to shoot all the Indians. Dodge pulled his sword so swiftly that witnesses later said the cutting edge appeared like magic against Ben Cooper's throat. Now, the cutting edge of a military sword is unbelievably sharp. Just placing it against Cooper's neck caused a thin trickle of blood to flow.

Dodge threatened to lop off Cooper's head if the dissidents didn't stand down. In the meantime, Dodge's 350 Rangers and 40 Shawnee had drawn their weapons and had the small band of militia in their deadly sights. Nathan Boone of Salt Lick, Daniel Boone's son, announced that he was standing by Dodge and his pledge. Soon, everyone cooled down and a disaster was averted.

Henry Dodge was a man who kept his promises.

• • •

One Sunday afternoon, while Uncle Dan was visiting, Marshall Dodge dropped by. Uncle Dan wanted to show off his new buggy. Calvin came along since he was Uncle Dan's chauffeur. Sophie came, too, but not before those rascals gave her a hard time. Sophie was such fun to tease

Sophie was late for everything and today was no exception. Uncle Dan and Calvin plotted their revenge while they waited in the carriage.

At last, Sophie rushed to the carriage all spruced up and ready to go. She was carrying a little handbag.

Calvin said, "Sorry, Sophie, my little sugargirl. We can't take you with us. Not this time."

"What? Why not?"

He and Uncle Dan made a big show of looking around to see if anyone was listening. Calvin said, "We got to do us some man talking!"

"Man talking?"

Uncle Dan chimed in, "That's right, Sophie. Man talking!"

"Man talking? What's man talking?"

Calvin whispered, "I can't tell you."

"Why not?"

"It's a secret only men can hear."

Uncle Dan added, "If we told you and you told someone else, then it wouldn't be man talking anymore."

Sophie didn't know what to say. She looked from one to the other.

With as straight a face as he could muster, Calvin said, "Nope, then it would be woman talking and we hears enough of that already."

Uncle Dan and Calvin burst into laughter. Sophie bopped Calvin with her handbag while Uncle Dan took cover.

At dinner, I asked Calvin, "How does the new buggy handle at full gallop? It looks fast."

Calvin answered, "Ask Master Bissell. He only lets me take the reins at the places where you can't drive fast."

Larry, Lolo, and Sophie were always glad to see Henry Dodge, since he was one of the few people, besides us, who cared what happened to them. It was mighty difficult for decent folk not to respect old Henry. He had an aura about him, an air of honesty impossible to miss. Nahaboo called him a "great spirit." Me, I'm just glad to call him friend.

Marshall Dodge, Uncle Dan, and I moved to the porch for an after dinner smoke. We sat on the big bench, with Marshall Dodge in the middle, a deliberate act so he could referee for me and Uncle Dan. Dodge lit up one of those runt cigars that smell like burnt vanilla, a New Orleans specialty. Uncle Dan packed his favorite Virginia blend into his pipe and set a match to it. I sucked on an unlit cigar left over from when George was born.

Uncle Dan and Henry kidded me about my reluctance to actually smoke. I told them, "Grandpa Bissell warned me people who smoke are getting ready to meet the devil."

Marshall Dodge slapped Uncle Dan on the back and said, "That makes us the devil's right hand men."

I snickered, "Two right hand men? The devil only has one right hand."

Uncle Dan looked at me, "How come you know so much about the devil?"

After a moment's silence, he and Dodge started heehawing like a couple of homesick mules. Mary stuck her head out the door and asked, "What's so funny?"

I told her, "Uncle Dan and Henry just struck a bargain with the devil."

We hunkered down for some serious conversation, more war stories. Marshall Dodge said Joe Smith and his Mormons weren't making many friends in Franklin County. Clyde Fellows, the mayor of Union, sent word to the Rangers' office that he'd appreciate some help in sending them on their way. The Marshall told us old Clyde, who was given to exaggeration, described the Mormons arrival as akin to the descent of a plague of locusts. The Mormons set up camp on the edge of the city limits and Clyde wanted them to move on. Dodge and a troop of Rangers sent them packing. They settled in Jackson County.

Marshall Dodge asked, "Have you seen today's *Missouri Gazette?*"

We hadn't, so he filled us in on a situation that could have repercussions for us all. Nat Turner, a slave in Virginia, led a rebellion. Several escaped, but it ended badly for most of the slaves. Federal authorities announced that anyone traveling with slaves or any freemen could be stopped and their papers checked. This didn't mean that the local authorities were required by law to return fugitive slaves, at least not yet, although there was a faction pushing for such a law.

Henry held his hand up to silence us before Uncle Dan and I started debating the issue. Marshall Dodge said, "I'm sworn to uphold the law and that's just what I'm gonna do, but I'm not gonna stick my nose into the business of every stranger who passes through."

He warned me, "Take extra special care of those freemen papers. There's a lot of 'finders' on the prowl."

He added, "Tom Keegan had a falling out with Junior

Chouteau. I found Keegan beaten to a pulp in the alleyway behind Stein's Pub. Junior's goons worked him over. Word on the street is he was skimming protection money. Course, Keegan won't talk or press charges. Now he's riding with Gil 'Patch' Kane, a finder."

"Thank's Marshall. I'll keep my eyes open."

As I did for Larry and Lolo, Uncle Dan kept Sophie and Calvin's papers at home in a safe place. Of course, if Sophie and Calvin ever decided to leave his estate, Uncle Dan would give them their papers, as I would Larry and Lolo. I kept their papers in a metal strong box I got from John Riley, an old Army buddy who drove the mail wagon from Springfield, Illinois, to St. Louis and back. I ferried him across the river hundreds of times.

I told Uncle Dan and Marshall Dodge, "John Riley told me they're building a post office in downtown St. Louis. Rumor is, Rufus Easton will be the new Postmaster."

After a few jokes about Rufus' sense of direction, the Marshall and Uncle Dan decided to call it a day. Calvin cracked the whip, and that unlikely threesome took off for home. I walked with the Marshall over to the hitching post. "Marshall, thanks again for the heads up on Keegan. I really appreciate your checking in on my family's safety while I'm away."

With a sly grin, he said, "My pleasure, Bissell. I'd come by to see that pretty little wife of yours any time."

He rode off, laughing like a loon. When I repeated what Marshall Dodge said, Mary got red as a beet. I laughed.

Marshall Dodge wasn't the only one to come by to check on Mary and the kids. Until April of this year, Lieutenant Jeff Davis routinely stopped by while on patrol. In April, he and Lieutenant Albert Johnson led elements of the 6th U.S. Infantry on an expedition to Wisconsin to participate in the Black Hawk War. They left by steamboat. His replacement was Lieutenant Meriwether Lewis Clark, William Clark's son and Crazy John's cousin. We watched Meriwether grow up. Now, he was watching over us. Time marches on.

Safety

$\mathcal{M}$ary was an excellent tutor. She was well versed in the Romance Languages and Mathematics. This was odd for a woman of her era, since math was considered a man's field. Her uncle, an engineer, taught her well.

She had several pupils, so there was a lot of traffic to my house, especially during the summer months when school was out. Mary tutored college girls who failed Greek, Latin, or French, and needed to make up courses. She taught math to the boys, over the objections of some of the more gender conscious among us. Some students came to prep themselves for college because they wanted to make a good first impression or, in most cases, it's what the parents wanted.

Mary had some adult students, people who wanted to improve their lot in life and hoped that education might open some doors for them.

Mary Easton Sibley, Rufus Easton's daughter, the wife of Major George Sibley and the founder of Lindenwood College in St. Charles in 1827, thought highly of Mary's teaching abilities. She offered her a full-time job teaching at the college. Mary was flattered, but moving to St. Charles in the immediate future was not an option. We had three small children to raise and my business was here at Bissell Point.

Mary didn't lack for students. Madam Rigauche, who ran a charm school for young ladies in St. Louis, sent girls to Mary for tutoring. Boys seeking to get into the Jesuit-run St. Louis Academy came to Mary to study for the entrance examination required at that school. Needless to say, people were coming and going at my place. I didn't worry about Mary and the kids as much as I would have otherwise. This didn't mean they were never exposed to danger. It just meant that the odds were reduced, and we had our safety plan.

• • •

We lived on a bluff. To the east, it was wide open all the way to the Mississippi. To the west was a series of hills. We cleared a lot of trees in that direction to get wood to build things like the bread and board, Sam Wiggin's trading posts, and my barn. The point is, you can see people coming. Mary could handle all the weapons we owned. If she saw trouble coming, be it nasty weather or nasty people, she and the children could take shelter in the hiding place.

I had a wine cellar in my basement. It had a brick floor and stone block walls. The east wall was a facade. We put the blocks up to make people think there was dirt on the other side of that wall. I built my house over a natural hole in the ground, the entryway to a subterranean cavern, a virtual labyrinth. I didn't know the full extent of this cave system, but I did know how to get to the river. I marked a path, using a series of markings as a code.

If you didn't know the code, you could very easily follow a false trail. When the river was high, it would back up into the cavern, making egress impossible. There were narrow spots on the trail that you had to squeeze through. It was often a tight fit for me, but I could do it.

We built a concealed trap door in the east wall near the top. It matched the block pattern and was only a quarter inch thick but it looked as solid as the rest. We put a series of O-rings into the wall and hung items from them, tools and what not. You could use the O-ring and the pry bar hanging on the center ring to open the trapdoor. We stacked barrels in front of this wall so Mary and the kids could reach the trapdoor, and to make people think we stayed out of that corner.

On the other side of the trapdoor was a wide ledge, a couple of phosphorescent rocks, a large basket on a long coiled rope, and a tall ladder. It was a long way down.

At the bottom of the wall, under the ladder, was a large alcove that was out of sight from prying eyes from above. The alcove was large and stocked with food, water, furnishings for comfort, a couple of lanterns, and a pair of shotguns.

In case of trouble, we had a safety drill. The goal was simple. Get everyone down to the floor of the cavern and into the alcove safely. Push the ladder to the opposite wall so no one could follow.

We practiced this safety drill, making it a game for the kids. We rewarded whichever child kept quiet the longest while the lights were out. At first, they were frightened by the semi-darkness, but soon they were at ease with the radiance from the shining stones. The shimmering rocks gave me solace, too. They reminded me of a near-extinct campfire, where the hot coals give off an energy that reaches into the heart as well as warms the flesh. I just hoped Mary and the kids would never have to play this game for real.

• • •

Oh, yes, in August, Doc Bernie and his wife welcomed little Bernard Farrar into this world. Doc was busting his buttons. It was my turn to tease new fathers.

The Captain's War Story

1832 began sadly for me. On February 9, my mother passed away. I made the long, sad journey to Windsor to see her laid to rest. She left the house to my sister Eunice and her husband, Joseph Winter.

An old friend from Fort Bellefontaine, (Col.) John Miller was elected governor of Missouri. He signed into action a bill that made Jefferson City the permanent site of the state capitol.

John was once the head of Indian Affairs for the U.S. Army. In early 1809, he arranged a meeting with leaders of many Indian nations in an attempt to convince them that Tecumseh and The Prophet, with help from the British, would lead them to their doom. Omaha, Shawnee, Sioux, and Delaware attended the meeting and agreed to stay neutral. Fox and Sauk, Iowas, Kickapoos, and Winnebagos didn't attend and cast their lot with Tecumseh's Federation of Indian Nations.

Also in 1832, St. Louis University was chartered as a college and Carondelet was officially incorporated as a city by the St. Louis County Court, which was located in the City of St. Louis. Carondelet was governed by a board of trustees. It's first board chairman was John Leitensdorfer. Dorf never ceased to surprise me.

I helped Sam Wiggins ferry a circus across the river. They were to be part of the Independence Day celebration on the riverfront. On the ferry ride, one of the performers told me they had a fighter who was unbeaten, a mean and nasty man. The circus hands hated him, but he was tolerated because he made them a lot of money.

He was called "The Mongolian Mauler" and billed as a wild man from the frozen steppes of Asia. Those New York circus folk must have figured us for rubes. I was looking forward to seeing this wild man.

At noon, they would bring this madman out in chains and place him in a huge cage. Challengers could put up $50 to win $500 by entering the cage and beating The Mauler in a no-holds-barred wrestling match.

So that's why Nahaboo asked me for $50 of his money. He didn't trust banks, so I kept his cash in my strong box. He planned to challenge The Mauler. He was risking an awful lot of money and I tried to talk him out of it. Nahaboo laughed and said, "Nahaboo win. $500. Easy way."

The 4th of July arrived. Mary was eight months pregnant and feeling well. The whole family went to the St. Louis riverfront to enjoy the holiday fair. Machingo and Nahaboo joined us. Food vendors, craftsmen hawking their wares, pony rides for the wee ones, horseshoes, plate shooting, dunking booths, and other contests of skill were the order of the day.

The traveling circus was an added attraction and was housed under a multicolored tent. For a small admission fee, we would see clowns, acrobats, trick shooters, and animal tamers. This was the premiere performance for this circus west of the Mississippi and people came from miles away to attend. We had to stand in a long line to get tickets.

I ponied up for tickets for Mary, Larry, Lolo, and the little kids. Nahaboo shook his coin pouch as he paid admission for him and Machingo. Crazy John and Dorf saved us seats in the first row of temporary bleachers, a row of benches on angle rails, constructed especially for spectators. We sat smack dab in the middle of the arena. I sat on one end with Mary. Machingo, Nahaboo, John, and Dorf sat on the other end. The children sat in between.

A fanfare of trumpets and a drum roll opened the show.

The ringmaster was a pipsqueak with a basso voice that belied his size. The children giggled at the deep voice emerging from such a little man. He looked like a picture of a fox I saw in my son James' book of *Grimm's Fairy Tales.*

He touted himself as The Great Gambini, the world's greatest circus master. The barker previewed each act, exaggerating flamboyantly; what a bag of puffery and bilge. The acrobats were skilled, the animal tamers brave, and the clowns funny, but as noon approached, the audience became restless. They began to chant, "Mauler, Mauler."

At noon, the trumpets blared again, this time accompanied by a peal of bells from the old Basilica of St. Louis The King. It was an odd combination.

(The new church was under construction and would be finished in 1834).

Amid the blare of trumpets and the beating of a drum, the tent flaps opened and four men entered the arena, pulling a heavy chain. Struggling at the end of the chain was a gigantic strong man.

His arms straining against the pull of his captors, the wild man was hauled through the entryway into the circus arena. He threw back his shaggy head and dug his heels into the ground, resisting with all his strength. In the end, it was to no avail. They dragged him to the middle of the arena.

The savage beat his chest, the clanking of man-made metal a sharp contrast to his feral cries of belligerence. Chains wrapped his arms and were connected to shackles on his biceps and wrists. Other chains continued from each wrist and were attached to a long chain used to lead him about.

He was huge, as tall as I was, with slightly wider shoulders. He was horribly disfigured. A thin layer of pine tar covered thick scar tissue left from the healing of his horribly burned face. In places, it looked as though it had been burned to the bone.

He was wearing a bearskin cut like overalls. Around his waist was a thick belt with a skull-shaped buckle. The bare portions of his chest and shoulders were covered with scars and tattoos. On the top of his left arm near the shoulder was a tattoo of an anchor with a snake wrapped around it. I knew that tattoo! When The Mauler turned toward me, I was sure of it. The Mauler was Mike Fink!

Fink knew I recognized him and he smiled, a ghastly grin splitting his damaged face. He began to circle the arena, his chains just long enough to keep him from reaching the first row of spectators. When he neared, small children screamed and ducked away; some clambered into the next row of seats.

When his handlers pulled him back, the kids chuckled, denying that they were ever frightened. Mary told our kids not to be scared; that it was all make believe.

Four men with spears joined the other handlers and, holding Fink at bay, they forced him into the cage. The huge cage was made from bamboo and hemp. A sign over the door said, "Enter at your own risk."

I heard a familiar voice behind me. I turned and spotted Junior Chouteau sitting two rows up, his ever-present contingent of bodyguards surrounding him. The crowd roared. I turned back and saw that Fink was manhandling one of the spearmen. He lifted the man above his head and tossed him halfway across the ring. He reared like a bear and howled, his body glistening with sweat and obviously coated with oil.

The animal trainer walked into the cage and cracked his whip several times until The Mauler quieted and stood still. The attendants removed the chains and ran out of the cage. As the crowd applauded, the trainer strolled from the cage. When the cage door slammed shut, Fink ran about the cage, grunting and screaming and beating his chest.

People in the stands mimicked Fink, beating their chests like apes. Fink stood still and glared at the crowd. In his thunderous voice, Gambini launched into his act, beginning the tale of The Mongolian Mauler.

• • •

In Russia, parents tell their children the legend about a monster so hideous that, if one looks into its eyes, death follows. The monster comes into your village at the darkest hour, when his powers are at their peak. He pulls out the heart of every villager, even the kulak, and enjoys a midnight feast. *(A little snickering and nervous laughter.)*

His prey do not die. His victims awaken the next day. All memory of the frightful event is stripped from their minds, but they are left with a feeling of doom. That moment of terror before the monster struck flits around in their skulls, but it never settles down long enough for them to grasp it. For the remainder of their days, gloom resides where once was a heart, and they never feel sunshine in their souls again.

(When Mary told the story of this day, she would call Gambini the Master of Hyperbole.)

 Nahaboo announced in a loud voice, "Rat Man most wondrous teller of tall tales."

People shushed him. I glanced down the bench. Mary held little Mary in her lap and had a protective arm around James. Bravely sucking his thumb, little George sat between Larry and Lolo, whose eyes were as large as saucers. I suppressed a laugh.

The Great Gambini continued. The mightiest warriors of the Mongol tribes cannot stand against this creature, so they join forces with their brothers to the south, the Cossacks. A mighty horde forces this abomination all the way across the Siberian wasteland. Many horsemen and horses fall victim to the icy cold fingers of winter.

The tatters of the vast assemblage stop at the fringe of the Arctic Circle and turn back. The vile Mauler continues headlong to the North Pole. He survives by eating polar bear and uses walrus tusks for toothpicks *(snickers from the crowd)*. The Mauler reduces glaciers to powder with a single blow and slaps his hands together to create deadly blizzards *(more snickers and guffawing)*.

The creature treks across Canada, clearing forests and leveling settlements along the way *(cheers)*. The Canadian government sends its best troops to apprehend the brute, which they call Sasquatch. Before they can capture him, the behemoth crosses the border. He ducks under Niagra Falls, washing off months of accumulated grime, and enters the United States. The monster is hungry and eager to feast on American hearts *(a chorus of boos and catcalls)*.

Then Gambini boomed, "Without further ado, ladies and gentleman, I give you The Mongolian Mauler!"

• • •

The Mauler bowed, his muscles rippling. The crowd cheered, clapped, and booed, producing a cacophony of noise that was sustained for several moments. It was sheer bedlam.

After another fanfare, Gambini signaled for silence. Gambini barked the challenge. In the full light of day, the creature was at its weakest. If he was ever to be defeated, the time was now. Anyone brave enough to enter the cage to defeat The Mauler in a no-holds-barred wrestling match could win $500. All they had to do was put up $50 of their own money.

Gambini spelled out the rules. Enter at your own risk. Anything goes. Pin your opponent's shoulders to the ground while the referee counts to three. The referee would strike the ground with the flat of his hand, accompanied by the drummer, who would echo the count. The animal trainer would stand by to stop the beast from going for his vanquished opponent's heart!

Contest entrants were skeptical. They shouted, "Who's the referee?" and "Are we gonna get a fair shake?"

The pipsqueak shouted, "The Mongolian Mauler doesn't need help from any man!" *(Loud jeering and booing)*

Gambini waved for quiet. Then he introduced the referee, one of St. Louis' favorite sons, Senator Thomas Hart Benton. The crowd went wild, cheering and clapping, and stomping its feet. T.H. passed us as he strode to center ring. He yelled, "I haven't seen a group of people this wild and out of control since the last session of Congress."

T.H. wore a bowler hat, his lucky poker shirt, and a pair of bright red suspenders. He had his sleeves rolled up to his elbows and an ace under a garter on each bicep. Ever the showman, he pulled his suspenders way out and let them slap him, just like the clowns. There were more cheers.

Oh, brother. The circus really was in town.

Gambini asked, "Who will be the first man brave enough to pit his courage and wrestling prowess against The Mauler?"

There was silence. Gambini looked in my direction. Fink just stared at me. A voice to my right rang out, accepting the challenge, then another. Eight men piled out of the stands and headed toward the cage, Nahaboo among them. Those fools must have thought The Mauler to be a sham. I knew otherwise. Fink was dangerous.

A hand clamped my shoulder. I looked up and was surprised to see Uncle Dan, since earlier this week he was feeling poorly. He squeezed in next to me. Indicating Fink, he asked, "Is that who I think it is?"

"If you're thinking Mike Fink, you're right."

Uncle Dan swore, adding, "And I thought cats had nine lives, not rats. Do you plan to fight?"

Mary piped up, "He's going to sit and watch is what he's going to do."

Before Uncle Dan could retort, the crowd started yelling. The first contestant had entered the ring. T.H. stood next to the cage entrance. Fink was still motionless. The first challenger was one of Henry Dodge's Rangers. He had taken off his long coat but wore the rest of his uniform. It's lucky for him Henry wasn't around. The Marshall wouldn't like this.

The Ranger, who was smaller, had to rely on speed and agility. He feinted right, then went to Fink's left. Bam! Fink's right arm tracked him and he landed a haymaker right on the chin. The Ranger went down—so much for speed and agility.

Fink reared back and roared. He ran to the nearby cage wall and threw his back against it. The bamboo and hemp gave just enough to catapult him through the air. Fink landed heavily on top of the Ranger. T.H. scurried in, slapped the ground three times, then hustled back out. Fink kicked the poor fellow in the ribs for good measure and then stepped back and folded his arms. As the handlers helped the injured Ranger out of the cage, an unhappy Gambini went over and whispered something to Fink.

I glanced around the circus tent and saw children everywhere. I thought that maybe kids shouldn't be watching this freak show. I hoped the other parents followed Mary's example and told their children that it was "just pretend."

Well, it wasn't "just pretend" for Mike Fink. He was out to hurt people. I hoped Gambini told Fink to control himself. If he kept smashing people after they were down, no one would want to fight. No matches. No money!

The Mauler smashed his next three opponents. The crowd groaned when Fink hit one fellow so hard he knocked his jaw off the hinge. He dislocated Horst Weiser's shoulder and kept twisting his arm as he screamed in agony. Fink continued to deliver vicious blows after each match was over. The crowd got surly. A scuffle broke out between two fellows in the stands.

After each match, Fink stood motionless, staring at me, daring me to take the challenge. Well, I wouldn't play his game. I told Mary, "We should leave."

She said, "Nahaboo's next. Let's leave after his match."

Nahaboo was the first man of equal stature to fight The Mauler. He locked up with Fink, trying to use his center of balance to knock Fink off his legs. Fink gave him a headbutt and Nahaboo stepped back, blood on his forehead.

Fink rushed him, going for a tackle. Nahaboo deftly stepped to one side, hooked his right arm under Fink's left arm and across his back, slipped his right hip under Fink, and gave him a terrific hip toss. Fink landed on his back and Nahaboo fell on him, going for the pin. The crowd went crazy.

Before T.H. got close enough to slap the ground, Fink threw his left arm over Nahaboo's head and turned over, getting out of the pin predicament. Nahaboo was on the madman's back. Grunting ferociously, Fink stood up. Nahaboo kicked his legs out from under him and pulled him sideways. They went down in a heap.

Nahaboo was high on Fink's back and the slick-downed Fink ducked out from under Nahaboo's grip. Now, Nahaboo was on his haunches with Fink behind him. Fink hit him with a vicious forearm at the base of his neck. Nahaboo flattened for a second and then tried to rise. Fink grabbed him by his hair and jerked his head back. He gave Nahaboo a horrific chop right across his throat. Only Nahaboo's great neck muscles kept it from being a fatal blow.

Holding his throat, Nahaboo fell forward. Shocked, I heard people in the stands yelling, "Finish off that stinking Injun."

Fink started stomping on Nahaboo, who rolled away from him and somehow managed to get back on his feet. He was wobbly on his legs and Fink saw it. Smelling blood, Fink rushed in and got Nahaboo in a fireman's carry. He lifted Nahaboo above his head and held him there, no mean feat. I expected a body slam and a pin. Instead, Fink brought him down over his knee. We could hear the snapping sound as Nahaboo's back broke.

Nahaboo cried out once and lay still. Machingo howled with rage as Fink began to kick Nahaboo. My stomach rose in my throat.

Machingo, Dorf, Crazy John, Larry, and I jumped to our feet and raced toward the cage. The Mauler's handlers got there first. They jumped Fink and brought him to the ground. He was back up in an instant, tossing his attackers around like rag dolls.

As we entered the cage, Fink started back toward Nahaboo. Crazy John, just ahead of me, tackled Fink. They rolled on the ground with Fink ending up on top. He reached back with his right arm to smash Crazy John. I grabbed Fink's wrist, halting the downward swing. He looked up at my huge paw and then at me.

Through clenched teeth he said, "Bissell."

I said, "Fink," and did something I couldn't help. I smashed his ugly face with my right elbow. Fink snapped back and landed flat on his back. Crazy John jumped up and out of the way. Fink scrambled to his feet and stumbled, blood rushing from his flattened nose.

Fink snarled, and I braced for the onslaught, but his handlers intervened. Fink caught the arm of the first man trying to subdue him and flipped him through the air. He didn't let go of the arm until he heard it snap. The other attendants pulled out saps, leather sacks filled with something metal and heavy. They started smacking Fink, the blows thudding off his beefy body. Ignoring the pain, he grabbed one of them by the throat and squeezed the man until his eyes bulged.

A gunshot rang out.

The Great Gambini stood at the entrance to the cage, a huge pistol in hand. The little man shouted, "Back off, all of you!" He pointed the pistol at Fink, "That goes for you too, Mauler."

Like an animal reacts to the report of a gunshot, Fink swiftly backed up to the far wall of the cage. As Gambini held Fink at bay, we tended Nahaboo.

A couple of clowns arrived with the stretcher they used in their comedy routine, Doc Bernie one step behind them. He knelt to examine Nahaboo, Machingo on the opposite side. A few minutes later, Doc Bernie rose slowly and said, "He has no feeling in his legs."

I asked, "Is the damage permanent?"

Doc said, "We'll just have to wait and see."

Larry was beside me. I put my arm across his shoulders to comfort him. I heard someone in the crowd shout, "Nigger lover."

I hugged Larry even tighter, then went to help Machingo, T.H., and Crazy John get Nahaboo onto the stretcher. The clowns picked up the stretcher and followed Doc Bernie out of the cage. Machingo went with them.

I looked into the stands. Mary and the kids were gone. I grabbed Gambini by his coat collar and, as we followed Machingo, I said, "You're gonna pay for this."

I heard the crowd roar. The next thing I knew I was face down in the dirt. I rolled over just in time to avoid a kick to the head. I scrambled to my feet and faced Fink.

I made a quick perusal, noting every spot where Fink might have a hidden weapon. With a swiftness that surprised him, I slapped him hard across the face. It was a beautiful slap and it sounded like a crack of lightning. Fink growled and rushed me.

I did a simple side step and trip. He fell forward on all fours. Before he could rise, I kicked him right in his huge rump. The crowd roared with laughter as Fink splayed out on the ground.

He put his hands under him for leverage and spun his legs

toward me. I neatly jumped over them before they could trip me. But Fink was quick. He reversed the direction of his leg sweep and caught the back of my legs as soon as I touched down. I collapsed on my back.

When my shoulders hit the ground, he was on top of me. He clobbered me with a terrific right. I saw stars. Then a nasty left snapped my head the other way. He started raining blows on my head. I couldn't take much more of this.

I tried rolling from side to side, putting my arms up for protection, throwing elbows on the returns. He punched me under my arms, which hurt like hell. I attempted to roll completely over but he kept his weight high on me to prevent that. I tried to wrap up his arms so he couldn't pummel me, but he was slicker than a snake oil salesman. He kept swiveling and ducking under and through my arms and then started punching me again.

We continued this dance for a while. I heard the crowd going crazy, but it was a far off sound, like someone yelling through a tunnel.

In desperation, I reached down and grabbed his belt with both my hands, freeing him to punch away. He was still high on me, up toward my shoulders. With a mighty heave, I pulled him up toward my head, using my knees to help push him up and over me. It was a temporary respite.

I rolled onto all fours just in time to receive a kick to the side of my head. I went out for an instant. My ribs were aching, possibly broken. His next kick awakened me. I rolled away from him but he followed, kicking away. He drove me up against the cage wall.

All I could do was grab his right foot with both hands and try to twist it 360 degrees. He toppled and landed on all fours. I was directly behind him. He did a mule kick with his free foot and caught me right in the groin. An empathic groan escaped from the males in the crowd. I dropped his foot and doubled up in agony. I tried to straighten up but a wave of nausea overwhelmed me and I heaved.

Fink laughed and pushed my face down into the puke, which made me retch even more. He stepped back and played to the crowd. Half of them were cheering and half were booing. He made a throat-cutting gesture.

I managed to get to all fours, but my whole body was trembling. Fink stepped behind me and grabbed the top of my head. He put one knee in the middle of my back. He intended to snap my neck. He said, "You're done, Bissell."

In desperation, I twisted to one side, knocking his leg from my back as I jerked my head loose from his grip. I was still under him so I threw one arm between his legs and put the other in the middle of his chest, grabbing the bearskin. I raised him above my head. With a strength that surprised even me, I got my feet under me and stood, holding Fink above my head. With a sudden motion, I drove Fink headfirst into the ground. The crowd went crazy again, some booing and some cheering.

Fink managed to twist his head to the side and his right shoulder absorbed the impact. It was a severe blow. I staggered back a few steps.

Fink rolled slowly to his feet. His right arm thrashed about, his shoulder obviously dislocated. His arm snapped back into place, his one shoulder now lower than the other. He circled warily, then rushed forward to tackle me.

I brought my knee up and it met his nose head on. I could hear the gristle and bone rearranging as his head snapped back, and he went down. It was music to my ears. Fink slowly rolled to his feet again. Blood was running from the hole where his nose used to be. He wiped the blood from his nose with the back of his hand.

Fink was livid. While he was looking at the blood on his hand, I took advantage of the opening to clap my hands as hard as I could over both of his ears. I was sure I burst his eardrums because blood began to trickle from both ears. He was tottering, his center of balance gone.

I drove the heel of my big right hoof into his left instep. A loud crunch accompanied the blow and a collective moan went up from the crowd. Fink bellowed in pain and hobbled around on one foot, trying to turn away from me. I kicked Fink as hard as I could in the hamstring of his left leg.

(Anyone trained in the art of frontier hand-to-hand combat

knows that sticking a knife in the back of someone's leg is as effective as sticking them in the heart. If you hit a man there, you could kill him.)

Fink's left leg shot forward and he went down in a heap, landing on his back. Like a broken bow, his left leg drew up and he clutched the back of it. I leapt as high as I could, raising my elbow above my head and came down, all 18 stone *(252 lbs.)* of me, driving my elbow into his solar plexus. There was a great whooshing sound as the air was driven out of him. I stopped my attack and watched him roll around on the ground, gasping for breath.

The crowd yelled, "Finish him! Finish him!"

I waited. As he thrashed about, the dirt and straw on the floor removed much of the oil from him. Good. My hands were already way too dirty.

Fink got his breath back. He coughed up blood, then sat, his back against the cage wall. He raised his arms in a gesture of surrender. Keeping a wary eye on Fink, I bent and put my hands on my knees, taking a couple of deep breaths myself. Once again the crowd chanted, "Finish him. Finish him!"

Machingo, Uncle Dan, T.H., Dorf, Crazy John, and Larry headed across the arena to congratulate me. Suddenly, Machingo pulled his knife and threw it straight at me, narrowly missing my left ear. The crowd erupted and the din was even louder then before. I looked behind me and saw Fink standing a few feet from me, a dagger in his hand. Machingo's knife was sticking through his throat. Fink dropped his dagger and fell to his knees, toppling forward in a heap.

I didn't need a doctor to tell me he was dead.

As Gambini passed me, I pointed to the "Enter at your own risk" sign above the door to the cage. I told him, "The Mauler should have read the fine print."

Then my friends were congratulating me, pounding me on the back. I ached all over. I yelled, "Hey! Take it easy! I've taken enough of a beating for one day."

Crazy John did more than congratulate me. He handed me a fistful of money. That crazy Irishman was making bets while I was fighting for my life. A large portion of the money we won was Junior's. I didn't know whether to thank John or to punch him.

I had to get home. I broke my promise to Mary and, with her abrupt departure, I didn't know what was waiting for me there.

• • •

As it turned out, Mary was probably more exhausted than I. She gave birth to our new daughter, Anna.

That's right. Mary and I had another child. It was Mary's easiest delivery. My friends usually never stick their noses in my business or so they say. They wouldn't let me slide on this issue. They knew Doc Bernie advised us not to have another baby. Uncle Dan, Crazy John, Dorf, Sam Wiggins, Stumpy Fredericks, Henry Dodge, and even some of the parents of Mary's students got in line to slap me down—verbally that is. I couldn't take anymore physical punishment, not in my battered condition.

My battle with Mike Fink was Anna's favorite war story, since it happened on the day of her birth.

Death in the Family

1833 got off to a terrible start. Uncle Dan finally succumbed to the fever. I thought the old man was indestructible, so his death knocked me off my pins. People from all over the country sent condolences. Many of the city's blue bloods attended his funeral, probably to get their names in the paper. He left Franklinville Farm *(The Bissell House)* to his wife.

The City of St. Louis proposed building a statue in Uncle Dan's honor, but the project was shot down. Judge J.B. Lucas called in all his markers and made sure the city bigwigs voted against it. Too bad! Uncle Dan would have loved it. Oh well, the pigeons can find some other target.

With the money won at the circus, I purchased a steam engine for my keelboat. I also bought steam engines for Sam Wiggins' ferryboats in exchange for a bigger percentage of the earnings. A Carondelet foundry built the boiler engines and the Carondelet shipyard installed them. I had them add a paddle wheel to the keelboat. The first time I took it out I was astonished. I was now the proud owner of a river racer.

Crazy John thought I'd be better off buying a whole new boat, but the *Pole Cat* and I had been through too much together. With the extra money from the ferryboat business, I didn't need to spend as much time hauling river cargo, but I did anyway.

With Nahaboo down with his back and since Larry was finished with his home schooling, I used Larry as a pole man. He wasn't tall, but he was broad and strong in the shoulders. Just because we had a steam engine, it didn't mean we used it

121

all the time. Fools who did that usually ended up at the bottom of the river.

It was about five months before I fully recovered from my fight with Fink. My cracked ribs healed quickly enough and Doc Bernie helped me get my dislocated jaw back in place. The broken bone in my right hand took longer to mend, since I started using it before it completely healed.

The worst damage was done by that mule kick to my privates. With my gonads in serious need of repair, my sex drive went south. At least it kept Mary from getting pregnant. Doc Bernie advised me to be patient, that there was an excellent chance my condition would improve as my body healed. He was right.

As Doc Bernie predicted, Nahaboo's broken back mended. Some of the bone fused, so bending was almost impossible for him. Fortunately, he got well about the same time Henri Picot quit working for me. Henri's uncle died and left him a hefty sum of money and some land in Kentucky. He was a good worker and a decent man. I wished him well.

Nahaboo came back aboard as my helmsman. Standing for long periods of time caused his back muscles to cramp. Nahaboo never complained about the pain, but we knew he was hurting. So I installed a seat with a high back in front of the helm. He was stubborn about not sitting down while the rest of us were working, but he gradually came to see that his physical comfort was an important asset to the running of the *Pole Cat.*

Henry Dodge and two regiments of dragoons went upriver to Wisconsin to help General Henry Atkinson and the U.S. Army in their pursuit of the Fox and Sauk leader, Black Hawk. Henry's son, Augustus, went with him. The Fox and Sauk were enemies of the Sioux and Omahas. About 100,000 Indians, 35,000 of them braves, were involved in the conflict. Black Hawk was finally captured. He was 66 years old.

A new leader rose among the Indians, a Keokuk named Joe Smith. He chose this name because Joe Smith, the Mormon leader, called himself The Prophet, a name used by Tecumseh's brother, Terskwatawa. Turnabout is fair play.

In Carondelet, Dorf was part of a committee that passed an ordinance against the discharging of weapons inside the city limits. Of course, there were all kinds of exceptions. The militia was exempt, and you could fire at game in the air or in trees.

The town hired a constable to enforce the ordinance and levied a $2.00 fine on violators. Dorf told me they passed the ordinance to abolish dueling within the city limits. He said people dying in the streets was bad for business and population growth. I can't argue with that.

They also passed an ordinance regulating the cutting of firewood in Carondelet. Carondelet citizens supplied the City of St. Louis with most of their firewood.

One of the more important ordinances they passed affects us to this day. It was called a Blue Law. They made it illegal to make an apprentice, a servant, or a slave work seven days in a row. Employers and owners were required to give help a day off. It was the custom to give half of the fine levied against offenders to the informant. Needless to say, there were people who tried to take advantage of the system.

Also in 1833, the British abolished slavery in the British Isles. They had outlawed slave trading in 1808, a move that made black-market slave trading even more lucrative. The English imposed stiff penalties for violating this edict. Slave ships would dump their cargo if interception by British ships was pending. Tragically, hundreds of slaves ended up at the bottom of the sea.

 Joe Smith and his Mormons were driven out of Franklin County. In a close race, Dan Dunklin was elected governor of Missouri.

Best Laid Plans

1834 looked to be the best year of my life. I had fully recovered from my injuries. Lolo got herself a boyfriend, the carriage driver who brought students from Madam Rigauche's charm school to our house for tutoring. The ferryboats were running nonstop. I had more delivery orders than I could fill. My bank account was growing. The kids were healthy and happy. My friend, Henry Dodge, returned from his mission in Wisconsin and was hailed as a hero. Crazy John was making money hand over fist. Dorf was held in high esteem by the citizens of Carondelet. Life was good.

Then I got greedy.

It was early August, just a few days before my wedding anniversary, and the weather was weird. It was chilly. Dark clouds and high winds, accompanied by cold drizzle, were constant. If autumn was coming this early, it was going to be a nasty winter.

(In 1810, it snowed in July and August was cool. It got hot in September and then the rest of the year was as cold as I could ever recall. Spring came late in 1811.)

Machingo came to visit. He and Nahaboo called the winter of 1810-1811 the harshest of their lives, one that saw the deaths of many members of their tribe. They called it The Winter of Sorrow.

The Indian brothers felt this unseasonable cold portended dark times ahead, maybe even The Day All Return. I don't dismiss other people's beliefs. However, I didn't see this unusual cold snap as a sign that Ragnarok, the Norse version of the end of time, was around the corner. It was just what we Easterners called an Alberta Clipper. They come early some years.

I was thinking about pulling the *Pole Cat* off the river for a few days when the Army offered to pay me a tidy sum to run some much-needed supplies to the troops at Fort De Chartres. I thought, fine, with my new steam engine, I'd make decent time and be back for our anniversary.

This fort was slightly upriver from Ste. Genevieve, except it was on the Illinois side of the Mississippi River, so the Army couldn't just haul the supplies from JB down to the fort overland. Originally built in 1720, the fort was named after the Duke De Chartres, the son of the French Regent. It was rebuilt three times before it was turned over to the British in 1789.

The fort fell into disrepair when the British abandoned it after the War of 1812. It would be rebuilt and fall into disrepair many times. The U.S. Army was refurbishing it again. It had the reputation as being one of the strongest forts in the United States. I had seen it from the river. I wanted to get a closer look.

Mary didn't want me to go. She thought I should stay near home and help Sam Wiggins. We were doing well financially and she thought it didn't make sense to take chances on the river with the weather so unpredictable. I told her she was worrying for nothing. We were familiar with that part of the river and we would be back in a couple of days, in plenty of time to celebrate our anniversary and long before a serious cold snap could freeze the river. Despite her objections, I took Larry and Nahaboo and left, much to my everlasting regret.

The river was high for this time of year but manageable. The trip down was uneventful and the Army supplied me with manpower for loading and unloading. However, the temperature dropped and a couple days of freezing rain kept us from leaving Fort De Chartres. We took off on the day of my anniversary, hoping to make the 50 miles back upriver in time for dinner. Ten miles upriver, we hit a snag.

It took us several hours to disengage from the tangle of trees that held us. The freezing water hampered us. We could work on cutting away the snag for only so long before we had to get out of the water and warm ourselves. Both Larry and I were miserable. We finally ran some rope to shore and, with the help of the soldiers accompanying us, we pulled the *Pole Cat* free. We were lucky we weren't using the steam engine when we snagged. It might have sunk us and, at the very least, we wouldn't be free now. We started back upriver, more slowly this time.

Mary's Last Stand

*M*ary's war story took place on our anniversary. Mary gave blankets to Lolo and James and asked them to sit on the widow's walk to scan the river for the return of the *Pole Cat*. They used one of the government-issue spyglasses I brought with me from Fort Bellefontaine.

Stumpy went to Alton to check on a sick friend. Mary suspected Stumpy had a girlfriend. I didn't say anything, but ever since Sam Wiggins took Stumpy up to an Alton bordello a couple of years ago, Stumpy went up there every chance he got. Can't say I blame him. A woman is more likely to dance with a man who has both legs.

It was Sunday. Sam Wiggins and Gustav Hesse worked one of the ferryboats from 6:00 a.m. to 9:00 a.m., since several church groups relied on the ferryboat to bring portions of their congregations across the river. Sam and Gustav went home for dinner but returned by 6:00 p.m. to haul people back.

Lolo and James came down from the widow's walk occasionally to warm up and drink hot cider in front of the fireplace. Then it was back to the roof to lookout duty. They concentrated their vigil east on the river, so they didn't see trouble blowing in from the west.

Mary heard gunfire but dismissed it. Every Sunday, some group held a turkey shoot. Shooting contests came with the territory. After checking on Anna, Mary went to fill the birdfeeder hanging from the back porch. It was a high porch, the doorway to it on the landing halfway upstairs.

I didn't want my back door to be on ground level, so I built the porch high. It afforded us a slightly better view to the west and gave us the advantage of higher ground in an attack. The short rolling hills offered cover to people approaching from that direction. The high porch helped negate that a little. The widow's walk was our real crow's nest.

Mary opened the door and was surprised to see a small black man leaning on the porch rail, gasping for breath. How odd! He was dressed like a Ranger and his clothes were soaked. He looked vaguely familiar.

Mary figured he was a runaway slave. She asked, "Who are you?"

He tried to talk but all he could do was rasp and cough. He had to move his whole body to turn his head. She was shocked to see rope burns on his throat. Somebody tried to hang this man!

Her Christian nature bested her cautious nature and she led him inside. When she tried to get him to sit, he got excited and tried to talk, choking and pointing toward the back windows. Mary looked out and saw movement, way off in the distance. She yelled, "Mary, fetch Lolo and James from the widow's walk."

She grabbed my other spyglass from the mantel and went back for another look. She spotted two riders crowning the hill to the west just up from Rocky Bottom Creek. They weren't far off. One of the riders got off his horse and knelt on the ground. It was obvious he was looking for tracks. He said something to the fellow still on horseback and pointed in the direction of our house. Mary's heart skipped a beat. The tracker mounted and the pair wheeled about and headed toward Bissell Point.

Mary looked at her dining room table, nicely set for a special anniversary dinner. She quickly went about the house and closed the drapes. She went back to the kitchen window and took up the spyglass in time to see the two riders top

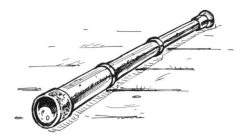

another hill. Her heart skipped another beat when she recognized one of the riders. The eye-patch was a dead giveaway. It was Gil Kane. The other rider was undoubtedly her husband's ex-buddy, Pat Keegan.

Figuring they were about six to eight minutes away, Mary sprang into action. She was relieved to see Lolo, James, and little Mary in the hallway. Hastily explaining about the run-away slave, she gave Lolo the keys to the wine cellar. "Take the children and the slave to the basement, open the trapdoor, and get everyone on the ledge. Send the man down the ladder immediately, Lolo."

Mary barred both doors and ran to our bedroom to fetch Anna from the crib. As she picked Anna up, an odd thought struck her, considering she was in the middle of a crisis, "Anna's getting too big for the crib."

Anna wasn't happy at the rude awakening and began to cry. Mary shushed her as she hustled to the basement.

Lolo was waiting on top of the barrels in front of the trap door. Mary handed Anna to her and Lolo set Anna on the ledge, putting her finger to her lips, shushing her again. When she told Anna to remember the "be quiet" game, Anna complied. Lolo gave Mary a hand up and they entered the adit to the cavern.

Mary pulled the trapdoor shut. The phosphorescent rocks lit the interior. Lolo started to speak but Mary hushed her, indicating she should go down the ladder. The slave was holding the base of the ladder. Lolo went down the ladder just ahead of James. When James was safely down, Lolo climbed halfway back up.

Mary heard glass breaking. The finders were forcing their way into her house! Mary lowered George, and then Anna, in the basket. Lolo stayed under the basket as it lowered. Mary was about halfway down the ladder and sweating profusely when light poured in from above. Someone had opened the trapdoor!

Mary moved faster as Lolo herded everyone into the alcove. As Mary neared the bottom of the ladder, her right foot missed a rung and she couldn't hold on. She fell. Her left foot caught between two rungs and she twisted upside down. She was just close enough to the ground to hit her head on the stone floor, hard.

She temporarily lost consciousness, but the sharp pain in her ankle brought her back to awareness. Someone was tugging at her left foot, removing it from the ladder. Her ankle throbbed with pain. Lolo pushed the ladder to the opposite wall as Mary got to her knees and then helped Mary to her feet and into the alcove.

Mary lay down on one of the cots in the alcove. She was bleeding from the back of her head and fighting against the pain in her ankle. An anxious Lolo went to the emergency kit we kept stored in the alcove and grabbed a big ball of cotton. She pressed it against Mary's head wound to stop the bleeding. Mary put her hand up to hold it in place. Lolo put James in charge of keeping George quiet. She set Anna next to Mary. A shout from above silenced everyone.

Tom Keegan yelled, "We're not here to hurt anyone. We're just here for the nigger. Send him up and we'll leave."

Mary put her fingers to her lips, indicating silence. She handed Anna to Lolo and pulled a shotgun from under the cot and cradled it in her arms.

Lolo whispered to Mary, "That old man's no runaway slave. He's no slave at all. He's Odysseus Williams, Larry's father."

A second voice threatened. It was Gil Kane. "Send that nigger up now or you'll all pay."

He fired his pistol. The report echoed through the cavern, startling everyone. Lolo hugged Anna close, her hand over

Anna's mouth. She whispered over and over that everything was all right.

Odysseus, who had been sitting on some sacks of flour, stood up and headed out of the alcove. Mary, realizing Odysseus was surrendering to save them, got up and blocked his way, bad ankle and all.

"Odysseus, there's no reason to give yourself up. Keegan and Kane can't get to us, and Sam Wiggins or my husband will show up soon. Strange horses and a broken window will alert them to the danger. All we have to do is wait."

Then her ankle gave out and she dropped to one knee, using the shotgun to break her fall. Luckily, the gun didn't go off. Odysseus helped her back to the cot. He tried to take the shotgun from her but she refused to give it up. They could hear talk from above. A second later, the light from above disappeared.

After what seemed an interminable length of time, someone opened the trapdoor again, the light flooding the upper cavern. Once again, Mary signaled for quiet. After a few seconds, a rope dangled from above. They could hear someone grunting as they climbed down the rope. The roof of the alcove was about nine feet high. As soon as Pat Keegan lowered himself enough to realize there was an alcove, it was too late. Mary had him dead in her sights.

She was almost close enough to touch him. She told him, "Climb back up that rope or meet your Maker."

He looked up and then back at Mary. His feet weren't far from the ground. He let go of the rope, drawing his weapon as he fell. I guess he wanted to meet his Maker. Before he could get off a single round, Mary cut him in two.

The shotgun's recoil knocked Mary off her pins. She landed on her backside, striking her head on stone a second time. She was out cold.

Gil Kane cursed loudly, then yelled, "This ain't over yet. I got dynamite. Send the nigger up or die."

He waited on the ledge. "You got ten minutes!"

Lolo was tending to Mary. Blood pooled beneath Mary's head.

Odysseus stood up to help and immediately sat back down. He had reached the end of his strength. His heart was fluttering and a ringing filled his ears. Odysseus slumped over onto a sack of flour.

Lolo said, "You better stay down, Mister Williams. You don't look so good."

Odysseus looked at Mary and Lolo and croaked, "How is she?"

Lolo said, "She's hurt bad."

Odysseus sat up, "Looks real bad. I think she's dyin'. Cuz of me! I gotta go afore I get somebody else killed."

Lolo pointed to Keegan's body, "He's gonna kill us anyway. Stay here. I'm gonna go for help."

She turned to go and stumbled over George. James, Little Mary, and Anna stood next to him. Little Mary said, "Is mommy all right?"

Lolo wanted to cry. "I don't know, baby. I'm gonna get help."

She picked up Anna and set her next to Odysseus, "You think you can hold onto her?"

She didn't wait for an answer. She picked up the shotgun and reloaded it.

"I'm going with you."

"No, you're not, James" Lolo handed him the shotgun. "You're gonna stay here and guard these kids."

Like his mother, James was small and he had her dark hair, but at this moment he looked like his father. One look at the glint in his steel gray eyes was all Lolo needed. She knew James would fight to the last before he let anyone harm the family.

"I'm going." She leapt out of the alcove. She was across the cave in a flash. As she entered the maze, a gun thundered and splinters from a piece of rock hit the back of her neck.

Lolo had been through the maze a hundred times before. She raced Sophie and Larry to the river and she always won. But that was all in fun, just a game. This time she raced against death.

Phosphorescent paint marked the trail and she knew the code. She ran quickly. The stone floor was wet and slippery and she fell several times. At the end of the maze, she skidded to a halt. The river was high and the cave was filled with water. Her heart sank.

Lolo was a poor swimmer and was afraid of the river. She knew the dark water was freezing cold. Panic set in.

She just couldn't do it! She turned to retrace her steps and put a hand to the back of her neck. She touched something wet and sticky. She quickly pulled her hand back. Her fingers were covered with blood. She was bleeding.

She looked at the blood on her fingers and thought of Mary lying in a pool of blood. Then Little Mary's voiced filled her head, "Is mommy all right?" Lolo sobbed.

● ● ●

Kane realized that the people in the alcove couldn't see the entryway Lolo took into the maze. So what if he missed! He laughed and said, "Looks like there's one less nigger to shoot when I get down there."

Silence.

"Seven minutes." He looked at his watch. It wasn't running. He started humming to himself.

Back in the alcove, the kids were plotting.

James said, "He got Lolo. We got to do something. He's gonna blow us up."

George, "Or bury us alive."

Mary, "How's he gonna get his dynamite down here?"

George, "He's gonna throw it down. Girls are so stupid."

"Are not!"

"Are too!"

"Quiet! Both of you! I'm trying to think."

George, "That's a first."

James ignored him and looked around the alcove for anything that could help. What was he gonna do?

"Six minutes!" Kane's voice echoed in the cavern. He must have liked the sound of it. He repeated, "Six minutes."

• • •

Lolo looked at the mark just above the water line. It was the last one in the maze. The exit to the river was about sixty yards away. Could she swim sixty yards? That was how many feet? A voice in her head commanded, "Stop! Stop it! Stop thinking and just do it!"

Taking a deep breath, she plunged into the freezing cold water. Every muscle in her body contracted and an icy hand squeezed her heart. She panicked. Time stopped.

Lolo began to swim and she could feel the grip on her heart lessen. After a time, she came up for air and bumped her head against the roof of the cave. She kept going. Her lungs were burning and her body was freezing. She came up again and bumped her head again. Only this time there was a small gap between the cave roof and the water. She gasped for air.

• • •

"Three minutes. Make it easy on yourself and give up. Ain't no nigger worth dyin' for."

Lolo struck out again. Her limbs were getting heavy and she couldn't think clearly. She struck for the surface.

"Two minutes."

Lolo broke the surface and took a big gulp of air. She was between the *Antelope* and the *Pole Cat,* only ten feet from shore. It may as well have been a hundred. She fought for consciousness and started to sink.

"One minute."

• • •

Ex-Ranger Gustav Hesse was sitting on the bench in front of the trading post waiting for Sam Wiggins. Gustav heard a splash and went to investigate.

• • •

"Times up! Send the nigger up or I'm goin' for the dynamite."

Silence.

• • •

Lolo felt strong hands pull her from the water. A voice she didn't recognize said, "Are you crazy, girl? What are you doing in that freezing water?"

Lolo's teeth chattered. She couldn't talk. Gustav wrapped her in his long coat, saying, "Easy girl. Easy. We need to get you inside."

• • •

"Have it your way. I'll be back." Kane went through the trap door and waited. When he closed the trapdoor, the light from above was gone.

James said, "He's goin' for the dynamite." He ordered his brother and sisters, "Get to the maze. Get far back so the explosion can't hurt you. Mary, take Anna. George, help Mister Williams."

George said, "Aint you comin'?"

"And leave mom? Never. Now get!"

They went. James got as close as he could to the wall opposite the alcove and hunched down. A few minutes later, light shone down from above.

• • •

Gustav was trying to break the lock on the trading post door when Sam Wiggins showed up. He looked at Hesse and then Lolo all wrapped up in the Ranger's coat and said, "What in blazes is going on?"

Gustav said, "I wish I knew. We need to get this girl near a fire."

• • •

This was his final bluff. Kane yelled down, "You wanna die? I got the dynamite."

A boy's voice answered, "I don't believe you! Let me see it."

Kane was bewildered. He'd been sitting up here all this time afraid to stick his neck out 'cause of some kid? He went to the ledge and peered over.

James let him have both barrels at once. Most of the pellets struck just below the ledge but some hit Kane right in the face. Kane scrambled back from the edge and reconsidered.

• • •

The pot belly stove in the trading post gave off welcomed heat. Lolo was finally able to tell Sam and Gustav what happened. They grabbed their weapons and headed for the house.

Rescue

*W*iping the blood from his face, Kane decided the nigger wasn't worth it. He'd go, but he'd leave them something to remember him by. He found a can of kerosene and went upstairs. He dashed it over the floors and slopped it on the walls.

He was dousing the hallway when Sam stepped through the broken window, Gustav right behind him. Before Kane could strike a match, Sam had the barrel of his .75-caliber Brown Bess rifle between Kane's shoulder blades. As Wiggins made Kane raise his arms, Gustav slipped Kane's pistol from his holster. He jammed it into his waistband and raised his shotgun. Wiggin's clouted Kane with the butt of his rifle, putting him down and out.

They shouted for Mary. When she didn't answer, Sam went to the cavern access and yelled again. Everyone in the cavern was relieved to hear his voice.

• • •

Larry, Nahaboo, and I arrived about two hours later. I was surprised to see Doc Bernie's carriage and Marshall Dodge's horse in front of the house. The doors and windows to my house were all open. What was going on? Did one of the kids get hurt?

Marshall Dodge met me on the front porch. Through the open door, I could see Gustav and Sam sweeping up sawdust that looked oily and grimy. What happened?

The Marshall looked grim. He quickly told me what happened and grabbed me before I could rush into the house. He told me, "Doc Bernie says it looks bad for Mary."

I tore loose and rushed into the house past Sam and Gustav. Doc Bernie met me at the top of the stairs. The look on his face spoke volumes. "I've done all I could but it's in someone else's hands now," he said. "Mary's asking for you. Try to keep her awake."

Mary lay in the middle of our huge bed, looking even smaller than usual. Her eyes were closed when I entered. I sat next to her on the bed and pushed a curl away from her cheek. She opened her eyes and smiled. "Don't be afraid."

I was trembling. I tried to respond but choked on my words. She told me, "Take care of the kids."

Then she stopped breathing.

Her eyes were open. I just sat there, not knowing what to do. Finally, I reached over and pulled her eyelids down.

I gazed at her for a long while, then rose to go tell the children and my friends Mary was gone. I nearly jumped out of my skin when I heard Mary start breathing again, the first breath an audible intake of air. She opened her eyes and said, "Anna's too big for her crib now."

Then she closed her eyes and stopped breathing, this time for good.

I heard Anna bawling in the other room. The next thing I knew, I, too, was crying like a baby.

● ● ●

We buried Mary not far from the house, under the elm where I had buried my father.

(In 1854, we moved both graves to the family plot in Bellefontaine Cemetery. That elm tree died a short time later.)

My heart was eased when I saw the large turnout for her funeral. Ten years of tutoring brought her many friends.

Larry, Lolo, and Sophie were inconsolable, for Mary was mother to them. Crazy John was as heartbroken as I. Crusty old Marshall Dodge and battle-weathered John Leitensdorfer were equally stricken.

Machingo and Nahaboo assured me that Mary was in the bosom of her ancestors and would be beside me in spirit for the rest of my journey in life—good words from warm hearts.

Junior Chouteau attended the burial and offered his condolences. His sorrow seemed genuine. Ah, Mary. You even touched the heart of the devil.

I became a hermit that winter. I knew in my mind I had to keep going, but my heart was broken and my spirit diminished. Thankfully, I had the children. I discovered I needed them as much as they needed me.

James and I suffered from the same malady—survivor's guilt. I told him, "You did all you could and I'm real proud of you."

I reassured him that her death wasn't his fault. It helped ease my feelings of guilt as well. I told him, "Your mother, wherever she is, is glad we're alive. She would want us to be happy."

Little Mary needed constant reassurance that I wasn't going away as well. Her mother used to tell her bedtime stories. Now it was up to me. If she awoke in the middle of the night, I was the one to comfort her. Her needs filled me with a sense of purpose.

George was enigmatic. He spoke well when he did speak. He just didn't speak much. When he did, he sometimes shocked me with his child's insights.

And Anna. Blessed Anna. She was just the medicine I needed. She was the spitting image of her mother. With her baby magic, she slowly unraveled the knots in my heart and helped me to live with sorrow.

Travail

*O*dysseus Williams' war story was one of bad luck. His wife died giving birth to Larry. He was a slave for another eight years. After 30 years of servitude, Odysseus and his son were given freeman papers by their owner. He joined a caravan of ex-slaves in search of a better life and left Kentucky.

The caravan headed west, crossing the Mississippi at St. Louis. Just outside of Herculaneum, the caravan halted for an extended rest.

Odysseus was attending to "private business" in the woods when the raiders attacked. A stray round grazed his head, knocking him loopy. He toppled backwards off a cliff and hit the ground hard, severely spraining his neck.

When he awoke, the first thing he thought about was Larry. He immediately set about trying to find his way back up the cliff. His neck hurt so badly he couldn't bear to look up. He had to lie down to see the top of the bluff. He was afraid to shout for fear he'd bring more gunfire.

He tried skirting the cliff to find easier access back up to the wagons. He walked for a long time, occasionally lying down to look up, before he heard voices ahead. He withdrew into the brush and furtively inched his way forward. He got close enough to recognize that the voices weren't speaking English or French. Indians!

He crawled away but didn't get far before the Indians caught him. Ironically, he was captured by the same Fox and Sauk Indians that would soon kill the outlaws who slaughtered his caravan. Later, the Indians crossed paths with a couple of Frenchmen who traded them rifle ammunition for the "esclave." The Indians wanted more, but relented when the Frenchies claimed the slave was damaged goods.

Whenever Odysseus tried to tell them he was a freeman and that his son and friends were in danger, they struck him and laughed. The Frenchmen took him southwest to the Winter plantation where they gladly sold the troublemaker and left.

When Odysseus tried to explain to his new master, Old Man Winter, that he was a freeman and had the papers to prove it, he was beaten and told to shut up. His only recourse was to escape. Larry needed him!

When Odysseus attempted his first escape, he was caught. Old Man Winter's sons, Lester and Herschel, introduced him to a little game they called "Hang the Nigger."

They put a rope around Odysseus' neck. They threw the rope over a stout limb on their favorite tree and tied the end of the rope to a saddle horn on Lester's horse. They led the horse away until Odysseus' feet were just far enough off the ground to strangle him.

Odysseus would claw at the rope and his arms would flail wildly until he passed out from lack of air. The old man's sons would lower him down until he regained consciousness. They repeated this little game over and over, all the while drinking and laughing. When they tired of it, they lowered Odysseus to the ground. Then they kicked the stuffings out of him before taking him back to the slave pen. Odysseus' poor neck was never right again.

Odysseus soon discovered he wasn't the only freeman on the plantation who was forced back into slavery. Other Negro wagon trains going west were plundered by outlaws who took all the belongings and sold the blacks back into slavery.

About six months after Odysseus arrived, Marshall Dodge and a large posse visited the plantation. Odysseus and the other illegal slaves were herded into a large cellar so they wouldn't be discovered.

Old Man Winter suspected the Marshall knew he obtained some of his slaves unlawfully. Newcomb, the black straw boss, overheard the Marshall's conversation with the plantation owner. It seemed cordial enough.

The Marshall said, "We're on the lookout for renegade Indians who killed some settlers near Jeff City. Figured it might be the same bunch that killed some fellows up near St. Louis earlier this year."

"Who'd they kill?"

"A bunch of cutthroats. They attacked a caravan of black settlers up on the Big River. Killed most of 'em."

"Most of 'em?"

"Yep. Everyone 'cept a couple of teenage girls and a young boy. One of the adults may have survived. Don't know fer sure."

"What'd you do with them nigger kids, Marshall?"

Dodge ignored the racial slur. He said, "Took 'em to a Catholic priest in Carondelet. He found 'em a home with a ferryboat operator in St. Louis."

During this conversation, Marshall Dodge kept looking about, making Old Man Winter nervous. Winter said, "Well, Marshall, as you can see there ain't no renegade Injuns here. So, if you'll excuse me, I got me a plantation to run."

"Well, keep your eyes open."

"I'll do that."

Dodge and his posse rode off.

When told this story, Odysseus' hopes soared. Larry was alive. He had to be. He was the only young boy in the caravan. It sounded like the Marshall was on to Old Man Winter as well. Odysseus vowed he would escape and be reunited with his son. This promise kept him going during the dark years of his imprisonment.

Newcomb asked Odysseus, "Why'd them outlaws shoot up all them folks you was travelin' with? A nigger ain't worth nothing to 'em dead."

Odysseus had asked himself the same question. He thought he knew the answer, "It was Old Cal."

"Old Cal?"

"Calvin Jackson, our wagon master. Swore he'd die before he'd let anybody put shackles on him again. Musta shot someone with that rusty old pistol of his and got everyone killed."

"Damn!"

"I figured that old pistol would of blowed up in his hand if he ever tried to use it. Reckon the old fool must have got that gun to work, at least once. Old Cal got all those people killed."

Newcomb, the nasty rope burns on his throat a memento of his own sufferings, pointed to Lester and Herschel's favorite tree and said, "I wish I was Old Cal."

• • •

One night, during a session of "Hang the Nigger," Lester and Herschel got so drunk Lester passed out after Herschel staggered off to bed. Fortunately, he lowered Odysseus to the ground before succumbing to the spirits.

Odysseus awoke with the rope still around his neck so he kept his eyes shut, waiting for the eventual beating. When he heard Lester's snores, Odysseus sneaked a peek and saw him sprawled on the grass. Herschel was nowhere in sight.

His throat aching inside and out, suppressing a cough, he slipped the noose from his neck, climbed up on Lester's horse, and lit out. No one discovered he was missing until daybreak.

Lester and Herschel, after a tongue-lashing from their father, wanted to pursue Odysseus, but their daddy said, "No. I'll hire me Pat Keegan and Patch Kane out of Farmington. Those boys'll get my horse and that nigger back. I'll hang that horse thief myself."

Odysseus knew he had done nothing to deserve the punishment of these cruel farmers, but taking the horse would be construed as horse stealing. If they caught him, they would hang him. No Lester and Herschel game this time. Near dawn, he approached Farmington. He led the horse behind the post office and into their corral.

Because Odysseus could write and count, Lester shirked his duties and used him to do his inventory work. Odysseus had a pencil and paper in his overalls. He wrote a note addressed to the post office manager, briefly telling his story. He would leave the horse here and hoped they would make sure it got back to Lester. He wrote that he was no horse thief. He thanked them. He stuck the note halfway into the saddle-bag, securing it so it wouldn't blow away but visible enough to be seen.

His ruined throat tickled and he fought a constant urge to cough. He climbed into the back of the wagon carrying the mail that was marked for St. Louis. He found a comfortable spot underneath the canvas and lay still.

His mind raced. What if they needed to load more mail on the wagon? What if they saw the horse before the mail wagon left? Would they start looking around? What if no one saw the note? Lordie, he hoped another horse wouldn't get curious and munch on it. Would this tarp muffle the sound of a coughing fit?

He heard someone climb into the buckboard on the passenger side of the wagon and, a few minutes later, the driver climbed aboard. Lordie! He forgot that someone always rode shotgun on the mail wagon. Now he'd have to sneak past two people. Then the wagon lurched forward. He was on his way!

The mail wagon stopped in Herculaneum, and Odysseus heard the driver tell someone named Jesse they had a couple of crates for him. The mail carriers came to the rear of the wagon and started to roll back the tarp. Fortunately, the Jesse fellow stopped them and insisted they come on up to the house and eat before lunch got cold. They'd get the crates later. The mail carriers happily accepted the invitation.

Fearing discovery, Odysseus climbed out of the wagon and was immediately stung by the cold. The temperature had dropped so much he could see his breath. He made his way to the river and headed north along the bank. Following the Mississippi would lead him to St. Louis. The wind was fero-cious. His raw throat burned with every breath he took.

About noon, the Farmington postmaster discovered the extra horse in the corral and the note. He took the note to the constable's office. Old Man Winter was there. The angry old man had come to the constabulary to press charges against Odysseus and to offer a reward of $50. He had already rousted Keegan and Kane from a drunken stupor and had sent the finders off in pursuit of Odysseus.

After reading the note left by Odysseus, the newly appointed constable drew up a wanted poster for a runaway slave but not for a horse thief. Old Man Winter didn't like it but figured he could wait. The nigger would get what was coming to him when Kane and Keegan brought him back to the Winter plantation. He'd make an example of him in front of the rest of his slaves.

Old Man Winter went home. He would see to it that Lester and Herschel would spend their days working—boiling pitch in anticipation of Odysseus' return.

Two of Marshall Dodge's Shawnee scouts spotted Odysseus just before sunset. He was huddled behind a rock, blowing on his hands and rubbing his bare feet, obviously a victim of exposure. They approached him so silently they nearly gave him a heart attack when he looked up and saw two Indians in Ranger uniforms. He tried to get up to run but his stiff limbs just wouldn't cooperate. Thunderation! Indians dressed like white men. Now what?

Odysseus was relieved they spoke English. The Shawnee said they were Rangers and asked, "Are you a runaway slave?"

He rasped, "I am a freeman."

"A freeman has papers. You have papers?"

"No. No, I don't. I lost 'em." He looked from one to the other. "Please. I can explain."

To his surprise, they let him tell his story unimpeded. Meanwhile, one of the Shawnee made a most welcome fire. When they told him the story about tracking the bandits who attacked his wagon train, he almost fell over. How about that? Those killers got butchered themselves.

Larry! Maybe they knew about Larry! With diminishing vocal capacity, he asked, "There was a young boy, my son, Larry. Do you know what happened to him?"

The short Ranger said, "Son alive. Live with Captain Bissell on Bissell Point."

He pointed upriver.

When he heard Larry was alive, he broke down and wept. Tearfully, he begged them, "Take me to my boy."

Sadly, the Ranger said, "Cannot do. Orders strict. Find runaways. No papers. Take to Ranger Headquarters."

The Rangers fell silent. Odysseus continued to weep. An unspoken message passed between the two Shawnee. The taller of the two said, "Believe story. Take to son in morning."

Weeping unashamedly and coughing uncontrollably, Odysseus thanked them. One Ranger gave him a blanket and an old Ranger jacket. Then he cobbled some moccasins from hide for him while the other fixed some food. It was the best meal of Odysseus' life.

They set out after breakfast, following the river, the cold north wind in their faces. The taller of the two Shawnee said, "Rangers call me Smiley. Call partner Bad Shot." He laughed. "Bad Shot good with bow and arrow. Bad with rifle."

Smiley rubbed a nasty smelling ointment on Odysseus' throat. Odysseus climbed up behind Smiley on his horse and Bad Shot gave him a blanket. From the distance, people might figure he was an Indian squaw. At least the trio hoped so. Besides, Odysseus needed to stay warm. He was suffering from exposure. After coughing all night, his throat was so sore he could barely speak. As the day wore on, his voice disappeared completely.

Outside Carondelet, they debated whether to skirt the town or stick to the riverbank. They decided to stay close to the river. It was Sunday. Businesses were closed and most people were staying home. It was very quiet and they made their way through Carondelet without incident. Traveling as silently as they could on the cobblestone streets of the riverfront, they reached the boundary of St. Louis and continued toward Bissell Point.

The stillness was broken. Two drunken teenage boys yelled wisecracks from the rooftop of a warehouse about how ugly Smiley's squaw was. They rode away as the boys' drunken laughter filled the air. Five minutes later, these same boys saw Pat Keegan and Gil Kane pass by. Even drunk, they knew better than to yell anything at those two. They weren't surprised to hear gunshots shortly thereafter.

The Rangers and Odysseus rode a fair distance due west to ford Rocky Branch Creek. With the Mississippi unseasonably high, the creek had risen and was over its banks in spots. As Smiley pointed out the Bissell Mansion in the distance, a gunshot cracked and a metal bee buzzed past Odysseus' ear.

Smiley jerked forward as the bullet ripped through his head. Odysseus' hands around his waist kept Smiley from tumbling to the earth. A second shot and the horse pitched forward, throwing Odysseus and Smiley to the ground. Odysseus landed on top of Smiley's body, the wind knocked from his lungs. As he lay there, gasping for breath, Odysseus heard more gunshots. Luckily, the horse was between him and the shooters.

Shortly, Bad Shot crawled behind Smiley's fallen horse. His horse was also shot dead. He reached up and pulled Smiley's rifle from its scabbard. Bad Shot said, "I shoot. You run. Bring help."

Odysseus knew that even with two rifles Bad Shot couldn't hold off those buzzards for long. He scrambled over the hill and ran. He was almost to the Bissell home when the shooting stopped.

Minutes later, Odysseus was on the porch when he heard the report of a different weapon, a single shot from what, in all likelihood, was a pistol. He knew what that meant. Then the door opened and Mary saw him on the porch. You know the rest.

• • •

It was a bittersweet night for Larry. He regained a father, but lost a mother. Odysseus blamed himself for Mary's death. I didn't. Like most soldiers, I was a fatalist. When it's your time, it's your time. I'd seen too many people step into death's snare by trying to avoid it. Actually, I admired the man's courage and tenacity. Odysseus had a huge heart, just like his son.

Odysseus had no worldly possessions and nowhere to go, so I asked him to stay. He rasped his thanks. Stumpy's good leg was acting up, and he could use some help with the bunkhouse. I wasn't so sure I did Odysseus a favor. With his voice so weak and damaged, Stumpy had a new victim whose ear he could bend all day.

Poor Odysseus' reunion with Larry was short-lived. Over the winter, Odysseus developed a hoarse cough. His throat swelled and he had difficulty breathing. The doctor called his nagging cough the croup. He could hardly speak, but he thanked me repeatedly for being so good to his son. I told him Larry was a joy to us all. Odysseus died before spring.

I thought about how Odysseus cried when I returned his freemen papers. He had thought they were lost forever. I mourned the fact that he needed the papers at all.

Tom Keegan and, eventually, Gil Kane got what was coming to them. At his lawyer's insistence Gil Kane received a change of venue. Kane was still found guilty of murder and hanged.

Small consolation. Mary, Smiley, Bad Shot, and Odysseus didn't have to die.

I am haunted by their deaths.

MJ

1835. Good friends expand a family. Crazy John, Dorf, and even Marshall Dodge stopped by to check on my well-being.

Lolo accepted a proposal of marriage from Madam Rigauche's carriage driver and would move out soon.

Crazy John suggested, "You're a good-hearted fellow and a good father, but you could use some help."

"You may be right. I need to get back to work and the children need a tutor."

One of Crazy John's clients had a daughter who was a fine tutor but couldn't find work. She was raised by her father, an ex-soldier and a bartender for The Missouri Hotel. He saw to it that she got a good education. However, after spending most of her youth hanging around army posts and then the hotel bar, she was a little rough around the edges. Many people were uncomfortable around her.

Crazy John said, "She's a good woman. Just needs a chance."

Since I certainly could use the help, I asked, "What's her name?"

"Mary Jane Douglass."

"Whoa! I can't have another woman named Mary in my home."

"Nobody calls her Mary. Just MJ."

I finally capitulated.

Just before spring, Mary Jane Douglass became the caretaker and tutor of my children. She was excellent with languages but not nearly as up to snuff on math as my Mary. Her best subject was drama.

She was a tall, strong woman, with broad shoulders. Far from pretty, she had a large nose and a square jaw. Every morning she came to the mansion on horseback, the horse a gift from her father. She wore pants when she was riding, which was considered extremely unladylike, but I didn't care. The children liked her and she was an excellent instructor. God knows I needed the help.

MJ would change into a dress after arrival, only because Crazy John convinced some people to send their kids for tutoring and she didn't want to upset their parents' sensibilities. She stayed in the guestroom and tended to the children on the occasions I was gone.

She had a thorough knowledge of weaponry. Her father, wise in the ways of the frontier, knew that every gun counted and taught her how to use them. That knowledge comforted me.

I admit we didn't treat MJ kindly. When she wasn't around, the children called her Horse Face. We teased her mercilessly. Her voice was deep and gravelly, and sometimes we'd mimic her. She'd just give us a dirty look and go about her business while we had a good laugh. One day, I heard her guffawing with Stumpy. My mule started heehawing, which I thought was appropriate. I figured even a jackass likes company.

Stumpy told me later that MJ was the funniest woman he ever met. She knew more salty jokes than a sailor. Too bad she was so strong-willed and opinionated. Not a day went by we didn't argue over some trivial thing. I had a second battle-axe in the house.

Near summer's end, Old Man Winter, Lester, Herschel, and five of Winter's hands rode up to my front porch. MJ met them, shotgun in hand.

Larry and I were down at the trading post jawing with Sam

Wiggins and Tom Miller, since MJ got real testy if we were underfoot while she was tutoring.

Sam loved telling Larry funny stories. Larry's laugh was infectious. After every joke, Larry would say, "That's a good one, Sam. That's a good one."

Sam repeatedly told Larry he was a "good audience."

When we saw the riders and then MJ on the front porch with that scattergun, we high-tailed it up there. I was wearing my sidearm. Tom Miller handed Larry one of his shotguns and a pistol to stuff in his belt.

As we approached, Old Man Winter and his boys turned to face us. I identified myself and asked, "What do you want?"

Winter demanded reparations, "I want my money for that darkie you stole from me."

That really irked me. Larry, too. I had to put my hand on Larry's shotgun to keep him from raising it. Larry started to protest but stopped when I told him, "Hush up."

Lester said, "Let's take the uppity little nigger, Pa."

That did it! I said, "I'm only going to tell you once. Get off my property."

Old Man Winter laughed as his boys lined up alongside him. He said, "You're in no position to be giving orders."

Admittedly, he and his men had the advantage of numbers and the higher ground, but we had more mobility, being on foot. The odds still appeared to be in their favor. However, they made a near fatal mistake. They forgot about MJ. I heard her cock the twin hammers on that double barrel she was toting. We all looked her way.

She had the shotgun leveled at Old Man Winter. A chill went up my spine when she spoke. That husky voice of hers carried a ton of malice. She hissed, "You got it all backwards. You're the one in no position to give orders."

She spat and said, "Numbers or no numbers, no matter what happens in the next few minutes, one thing is certain. I'll blow your fat ass to kingdom come!"

When he started to back his horse away, she barked, "Stop."

Winter froze. In a command voice that would give an old

first sergeant a run for his money, she ordered, "The rest of you maggots, drop your weapons."

Old Man Winter stared long and hard at her. She stared right back, a wicked smile on her ugly mug. Wisely, he ordered his men, "Okay, boys, do as she says."

As we gathered the weapons, MJ snarled, "Now get the hell out of here."

I added, "You can pick up your weapons at Marshall Dodge's office."

We never made fun of MJ again.

• • •

Old Man Winter and his boys went to Marshall Dodge to register an official complaint. Henry told him, "You don't have a legal leg to stand on, Winter. Now take your ugly mutts and get out of town."

Old Man Winter bellyached, "I'm gonna take this up with the governor."

Dodge replied, "While you're at it, give Governor Dunklin my regards. Tell him thanks for the invite to his daughter's wedding."

Old Man Winter groused a bit, but even a bigot like him knew when to quit. He wasn't about to tangle with Henry Dodge and his crew. Besides, he needed to get back to his plantation before those idiot Benson brothers burned it down.

On the way back, he promised himself there was no way he would let that river rat Bissell and his homely girlfriend get the better of him. He'd sit tight for a while and then hire someone to do his dirty work for him. No one would be the wiser. Thus he arrived home in a nasty mood. He told his boys, "Get me a nigger."

Old Man Winter's slaves learned quickly that resistance was futile. So the slaves walked meekly to the hanging tree and took their lumps. Newcomb was no exception, until today.

He waited until they were almost under the tree where Old Man Winter stood, rope in hand. He walked between the two brothers, their shoulders almost touching. Newcomb was left-handed and easily pulled Lester's pistol from his holster.

He put the first bullet right between Old Man Winter's eyes. Then he shot Lester in the side. When he turned to face Herschel, a bullet struck Newcomb in the chest and knocked him on his back. Screaming obscenities, Herschel emptied his pistol into him.

He jumped on Newcomb and punched him repeatedly until he was too tired to swing any more. He got up to tend to his father and brother. They were dead.

Newcomb was dying. Herschel would go to his grave wondering what Newcomb meant when he said with his dying breath, "Old Cal was right."

Actors and Irishmen

1836. James was 10 years old and small for his age. He hated school and groused about it all the time.

George was 6 and just the opposite of James. He was big, very bright, and eager to learn.

Anna, 4, was a bundle of energy who got into everything. I called her Queenie.

Mary, 8, told me she wanted to be an actress. She had never been in a theater. Where did she get that notion? When I asked her why she wanted to be an actress, she said, "I want to be just like MJ."

When I asked her, MJ seemed insulted by my ignorance. She said, "I've been a thespian for years."

• • •

In 1819, William Turner and his family were the first troupe of professional actors to perform in St. Louis. Up to that time, amateur productions were held in a blacksmith shop, which was also the site of many elections.

That same year, N.M. Ludlow, the famous actor and director, came to St. Louis and, like the Turners, he lived at The Missouri Hotel. He and Turner's troupe competed for the St. Louis audience. In 1820, Samuel Drake's company began performing in the City Hall ballroom. All three troupes opened with a double bill, as was the custom. They opened with the same lead play, *The Honeymoon,* at all three theaters. This was also the lead play at The Old Salt Theater the night it first opened. It was a very popular play.

• • •

MJ told me, "I'm in rehearsal for a show right now. It'll be performed at Berger's House."

Berger's House was a brick home on Church Street that had been converted into a theater. I heard it was strictly amateur.

I asked her, "How long have you been acting?"

She replied, "Since I was ten."

I let out a long whistle, "That's young."

She launched into the story about how she caught the acting bug while working backstage. Mr. Turner used her mainly to keep an eye on his sister Charlotte, the prop lady, who was known to fall down on the job due to a drinking problem. MJ was supposed to tell Mr. Turner if she saw Charlotte taking a nip or if she just smelled liquor on her breath. MJ never did. Occasionally, Charlotte let MJ have a sip of mint julep from her flask. Between the two of them, they got the job done.

I was aggravated to hear that. I said, "What kind of adult would encourage a child to drink liquor, especially a little girl?"

MJ laughed and mimicked me, "Especially a little girl." That stung. "You men think you own the world, don't you?"

Well, I didn't take that bait. After a couple of rounds with my dearly departed wife, that was an argument I learned to avoid. Instead, I changed the subject. "What part are you playing in your show?" I asked, stupidly adding, "It's hard for me to imagine you on stage."

She stiffened and said, "I suppose so. You'd have to have an imagination to do that."

I wisely departed. What an irritating woman!

• • •

With just 5 months left in his term, Governor Dan Dunklin resigned to take the post of Surveyor-General for Missouri and Illinois. Lilburn Boggs, Missouri's new governor, opened a new state penitentiary in Jefferson City. Then he hosted an official going away party for Henry Dodge in

downtown St. Louis. Henry's contributions in the Black Hawk
War made him so popular in Wisconsin he was appointed
Territorial Governor. T.H. Benton, Judge Lucas, and other local
bigwigs regaled us with long-winded speeches. I'm sure old
Henry Dodge would have been happy to skip the formalities.

Later, we had an unofficial party at my house. No
speeches, just words from the heart. Lolo, Sophie, Larry, and I
thanked the Marshall for his help. Dodge took great delight in
ribbing Lolo and Sophie. They were both pregnant.

Crazy John presented Dodge with a going away gift, "Here
you go, Henry, an official 1st National Now Defunct Bank pen.
Now you have no excuse for not writing."

Dorf performed his magic act. I was surprised when he
told me, "I get paid to do my magic show now. I got tired of
doing it for free for amateur troupes."

"Ever see MJ act?"

"Yes, she's pretty good, don't you think?"

"I wouldn't know. I've never seen her perform."

"Why not?"

"You don't want to know."

• • •

Crazy John's uncle, William Clark, and John Miller, his
assistant at the Bureau of Indian Affairs, paid us a visit. Mr.
Clark told us he added a wing to his house for his new
Museum of Indian Relics and Natural History Objects. He
bragged it was the only museum of its kind west of Cincinnati.
John Miller said it was a fabulous collection.

As I said earlier, John Miller was a colonel in the U.S
Army back in 1809. I'm still grateful to him for convincing the
Omaha, Shawnee, Delaware, and Sioux to not join Tecumseh's
federation of Indian tribes. If all those tribes had joined
together, I might not have lived long enough to tell this part of
the tale.

Challenges

1837 brought us a new President, Martin Van Buren. He was Andy Jackson's Secretary of State in his first term and his Vice-President in the second term. The Army sent a young engineer to St. Louis to redesign the St. Louis waterfront and to figure a way to divert the swifter current on the Illinois side to the Missouri side of the river. The channel was 75 feet deep on the Illinois side.

The Army hired my boat and crew to take this young 1st Lieutenant, Robert E. Lee, on a tour of the Mississippi River. He was an engaging fellow, much like his father, Light Horse Harry Lee. I told him how Uncle Dan and my pa served under his father during the Revolutionary War and how I met his father at Fort Pitt when I was a small boy.

He gave me a funny look and said, "So, you're that Bissell, the boy who whipped Mike Fink."

He revealed that it was one of his father's favorite stories, a David and Goliath tale. We had a good laugh when he said, "How a colossus like you could be cast as David is beyond me."

Lee engineered the reshaping of the St. Louis waterfront. The Army blasted out the stone ledges and created a gentle slope to the river. The city covered the new water egress with cobblestones. They used stone from the ledges to build a retaining wall just north of downtown to redirect floodwater away from the warehouse district.

Lee and I spent considerable time together that summer as I hauled materials for him. His crew constructed a gigantic pier from Bloody Island to the Illinois side of the river. The pier succeeded in diverting the current to the Missouri side.

I was impressed with Robert E. Lee. Diversion of the river was no small feat. The Mississippi River is a powerful force of nature.

• • •

Junior Chouteau challenged the ownership of my land. In 1815, when Congress passed the settler's rights legislation that allowed people to replace the land they lost in New Madrid due to the earthquakes, they stipulated that the owner needed to live on and work the land. I was in the U.S. Army at the time. How could I be in two places at once? Obviously, I left and came back, a violation of ownership terms.

In 1818, the newly formed St. Louis Land Office set a minimum price of $1.25 acre for new settlers in Missouri. Judge J.B. Lucas was appointed by the state to rule on land claims. In the following years, he ruled on over 5,000 land cases and decided in favor of the plaintiff on about 1,250 of them. He even rejected a claim made by Daniel Boone. Judge Lucas was not a popular fellow. Naturally, my Uncle Dan's land claim never came into question back then.

Now, in 1837, Junior put in a claim for my land, perfectly willing to pay the least amount for it. Jed Parsons, one of a slew of lawyers who worked for Junior represented him. T.H. Benton defended me. With Judge J.B. Lucas presiding, Junior didn't have a chance. Once again, Judge Lucas didn't want to risk exposure. He knew I was aware how he and his sons got their land. So, of course, he ruled in my favor. Junior was hopping mad. He tore into his lawyer, embarrassing the man in open court. It was almost worth all the trouble.

• • •

Missouri troops took part in the Seminole War in Florida. The old Missouri state capitol building burned to the ground. How convenient! The government founded the U.S. Arsenal at Liberty, Missouri. The State Bank of Missouri was established with Crazy John as President of its Board of Directors, just in

time for a big money scare. The Sisters of St. Joseph established the St. Joseph's Institute for the Deaf. With just five
months left in his term, Governor Dan Dunklin resigned to
take the post of Surveyor-General for Missouri and Illinois. In
1843, he would adjust the boundary line between Arkansas and
Missouri.

Lolo had her baby, a boy she named Henry.

Of all the significant events that occurred in 1837, the
most memorable was the start of another war story for me.

MJ and I got married.

It didn't matter that she was 30 years younger than I. The
kids were happy for me for the most part. It took James a
while to warm up to the fact that MJ was his stepmother. I
think he still carried some guilt over his mother's death.

I made a very interesting discovery on our wedding night.
MJ wore a thigh holster, which held a derringer. She said she
had worn it since she was 16. She didn't answer when I asked
her why.

Potpourri

1838. Business was steady and I was making good money. I planned to send my boys to college. James turned 12 and was still on the waiting list to get into the St. Louis Academy. He wasn't happy. Mary, George, and Queenie *(Anna)* still received tutoring from their new stepmother, MJ. I received a few lessons from her myself. Oh, and MJ was pregnant.

Sophie died in childbirth. The baby, a girl Calvin named Mary, lived for three days and she died as well. I didn't realize how much joy Sophie brought to us all until she was gone. We all missed her.

William Clark, our old friend, died under mysterious circumstances in an inn in Tennessee.

There was a general uprising against the Mormons in Missouri. God-fearing Protestants and Catholics demanded their heads. Judge Samuel D. Lucas called out the state militia and issued orders that Joe Smith be shot. Since cold-blooded execution was not in the province of the state militia's duties, they turned Joe Smith over for trial. Story has it that, en route to Columbia, Smith paid his guards $1,000 to allow him and his companions to go free. He eventually showed up in Quincy, Illinois. Sam Wiggins wondered if he unwittingly hauled The Prophet across the river.

• • •

1839. Dan Dunklin was beset with a boundary dispute with Iowa. Crazy John contended with what was called The Money Panic of 1839. There was a run on banks all across the country. Thanks to confidence instilled by Crazy John, his bank was the only bank west of the Mississippi River that didn't suspend operations. Money that was drawn from the bank, however, was deposited in insurance companies and The St. Louis Gas Light Company. The gas light company was chartered to provide lights for the city but acted mostly as a bank until 1842.

MJ and I had a daughter, Cornelia. Charlene Sullivan, the midwife, said the delivery went without a hitch, adding that MJ was built for having babies. I wasn't sure how I should respond to that bit of information, so I kept my mouth shut.

• • •

1840. Emil Mallinckrodt, a fruit tree grower, bought the land east of me. He was devoted to his trees. When a ship sailing to America containing 600 seeds sank, he saw to it those seeds were rescued. Emil and his orchard were a welcome addition to the area. Many times, the wind carried the sweet scent of fruit blossoms our way. I swapped him peaches for apples. Eventually, he had wonderful peach trees of his own.

In Independence, Governor Boggs was shot in the head and survived. The Mormons were suspected. I put George's name on the waiting list for the St. Louis Academy. MJ was pregnant again.

• • •

1841. Our new President was William Henry Harrison, and his Vice-President was John Tyler. William Henry's father was Benjamin Harrison, one of the signers of the *Declaration of Independence.* William Henry was a General in 1811. He and Tyler led the troops that defeated Tecumseh and the British in a battle on the Tippecanoe River in central Indiana that broke the back of Tecumseh's Indian Confederation. Harrison earned the nickname, Tippecanoe.

Later, the Army killed Tecumseh and captured his brother, The Prophet, at Thames. At the end of the War of 1812, the government released The Prophet, who lived in England on a pension until 1826.

The dynamic duo's campaign slogan, "Tippecanoe and Tyler, too," worked. Harrison died a month into his term and Tyler became the President. Among other things, Tyler established the U.S. Weather Bureau and annexed Texas, an action that eventually led to a war with Mexico in 1846. Some Texans named a city after him.

From 1841 to 1845, Henry Dodge represented the new Territory of Wisconsin in Congress as a Democrat. I chuckled every time I read in the paper that Henry Dodge got into some kind of scuffle with some politician. I'll bet he and T.H. Benton terrorized Congress.

Also in 1841, the state established the University of Missouri, a state college in Columbia, Missouri. That sure made the Protestants happy. Up to this time, most of the universities in or near Missouri were Catholic or run by a Catholic faculty.

• • •

MJ gave birth to another daughter, Sophie. My family was getting bigger and my house was getting smaller. At least, it seemed that way. We have four bedrooms upstairs. Lolo was gone and Larry shared Nahaboo's tepee. MJ, the baby, and I were in one bedroom. The other five children—two boys and three girls—shared two bedrooms.

We also had a guest bedroom. James and George shared a room, but I knew that couldn't last much longer. They fought about every ten minutes. The three girls shared a room, but when Mary turned 13, she asked for a room of her own.

We wanted to keep the guestroom, so I asked James, "How would you like to move to the bunkhouse? You'd have to share the worker's quarters with Stumpy."

James happily agreed. He was "sick of being around little kids all the time." Stumpy's back was acting up and he could use James' help.

George moved to the attic.

I gave Mary the boys' old room, with the stipulation that if our family got any larger, she would have to share again. She pouted for about a minute, then started moving her things to her room.

• • •

1842. The Army hired me to haul supplies to Fort De Chartres, under the supervision of 2nd Lieutenant James Longstreet, a friendly fellow with an eye for the ladies. He found St. Louis a most hospitable place. I invited Longstreet to see one of MJ's plays and he accepted. He was the life of the cast party.

Later, MJ told me, "It was sinful the way some of those actresses threw themselves at that man." Smiling wickedly, she said, "I can see why!"

• • •

I read in the paper that the Supreme Court ruled in *Prigg v Pennsylvania* that states need not return fugitive slaves. This ruling created hordes of finders who, up to this time, had been few. The only finders I had encountered were Tom Keegan and Gil Kane. I could see trouble brewing.

Doc Bernie sold the last of the 1,000 acres he acquired in 1815 and bought 255 acres not far from Bissell Point. His estate would one day become the site of Hyde Park.

• • •

1843. What is it with MJ? She gave birth to another daughter, Lucy. I guess she just didn't know when to quit! Sophie couldn't pronounce Lucy's name so she called the baby Ludy. Soon we all called her Ludy and the nickname stuck. Few people know that her real name is Lucy.

Mary's two-year reign as queen of her room ended. Ironically, we moved the real Queenie *(Anna)* in with her. Mary pouted at first, then accepted her. Queenie was much better at schooling, so Mary took the opportunity to copy her workbook assignments.

Larry read in a periodical about cabs in New York City. People made money by hauling people around in carriages. It sure sounded easier than working the river. These cabbies charged for the distance traveled, which was figured by amount of time traveled. Huh?

Larry earned good wages for his work on my boat and he saved almost every penny he earned. This money was drawing interest in a savings account in Crazy John's bank. During the Money Panic of 1839, Larry got nervous and wanted to withdraw his money, but Crazy John talked him out of it.

Larry told me he was planning to buy a carriage and start a cab business in St. Louis. He was excited about the venture and he expected me to be excited for him as well. I wanted to be, but I just couldn't manage it.

I told him, "Larry, it just won't work. If it was such an easy way to make money, everyone would be doing it and you'd get routed by the competition. St. Louis isn't New York City. Where are you going to find customers?"

Larry disagreed, "People need a way to get to work, Cap'n, and a way to get to church, and children need to go to school."

I knew he had to face the truth, so I lowered the boom, "Larry, you're black. White people just won't use your service. I'm sorry but that's the way it is."

I continued, "You'll pay hell getting a license from the city, if you get one at all. On the river, you have the support of the crew. In the city, you'll be on your own. Some customer or competitor could rob and kill you, and every finder who comes through town will give you grief. The more unscrupulous ones just might help you lose your papers."

Larry started to speak and then stopped. He realized I was right but didn't want to admit it. We didn't talk the rest of the day.

The next morning, I walked down to the ferry landing. Larry and Nahaboo were already manning the trading post.

When Sam mentioned Larry looked a little down in the mouth, I told him about Larry's business scheme.

Sam screwed up his face, which was a snap for him, and said, "I think you oughtta let that boy buy his carriage, Lewis. Some days we get a whole passel of passengers on foot. You know how testy they can get when they find out they're still five miles from town."

He was right. I'd heard the complaints myself. Sam continued, "They may as well pay Larry to take them into town." He snickered and added, "In case you're too old to recall, buggies are fun to drive."

Sam added he was sick of hearing me complain about hauling James to the St. Louis Academy on cold winter days. He reminded me that, on the days I could work the river, I had to get up earlier to hitch up the work wagon and haul the boy to school.

Since his well-to-do classmates arrived in style, James was embarrassed to be seen with me and made me drop him down the street from the school. I wouldn't let him walk to school, knowing that led to truancy.

The Academy boys also had to contend with the growing criminal element in the streets of the city. Gangs of boys, either orphaned or abandoned by their parents, roamed the streets looking for easy prey. There was a stigma attached to being a student at the Academy. The students were seen as "goody two-shoes." In fact, one semester James Fitzpatrick was beaten and robbed. The ruffians stole his shoes.

If Larry had a carriage, he could get up early and take them to school. Maybe he could provide the same service for other families. It turned out to be a good plan.

Aunt Deborah died and left Franklinville Farm *(The Bissell House)* and surrounding property to her only surviving son, James. The property now included approximately 2,300 acres, 25 buildings, and over 30 slaves.

Although James inherited the family home in 1843, he didn't take permanent residence until 1849 after he married Anna Haight Christophers.

• • •

1844. Larry bought his carriage and proved me wrong. He turned a profit from his new enterprise, hauling people to the city limits and children to school.

George, James, Larry, and I were fishing one Sunday morning off the riverbank. Larry pointed upriver and said, " I'm going up by that rock. Stumpy says that's where the fish are biting."

James said, "That's the same thing you told us last Sunday."

George added, "When you came back empty-handed."

I chimed in, "Again."

As Larry walked upriver, he yelled back, "You'll see."

We all laughed. I asked the boys how Larry was doing with his taxi service.

James told me, "Fine, but I don't see how. Larry never stops talking."

"So, what's new?" I pulled my line out of the water. My bait was gone again.

"He tells the same old war stories over and over again."

"They don't like 'em?"

James got a nibble. His cork bobbed up and down for a second then stopped. "No, his passengers lap it up, especially all that Viking stuff."

George, now in his first year at the St. Louis Academy and a daily passenger of Larry's, said, "What else are they going to do, James. Jump out of the carriage?"

James countered, "I've thought about it!"

"Larry makes those tales more exciting every time he tells them."

"That doesn't surprise me. All that time he spends hanging out with Stumpy and Sam isn't wasted. He's learning from the masters." I tossed my line back into the water.

Larry loved that carriage. When Crazy John visited, he and Larry would race. Larry still worked on my boat, joining me after he made his drops. If we didn't get back in time for Larry to make his pickups, Mary would do it for him, for a nominal fee, of course. I think she did it because most of Larry's customers were boys. That's how she met her future husband, William Morrison.

I didn't think much of the idea of Mary driving a carriage, but MJ supported the idea. It was a done deal.

Academics

$\mathcal{J}$ ames was in his last year at the St. Louis Academy. He was trim and athletic. He took after my brother George, small in stature, big in heart. He excelled at the game of lacrosse. I knew that playing that game was the main reason James attended school. I thought it was a real stroke of luck that lacrosse was played at the St. Louis Academy. I was wrong.

(In 1636, a Jesuit missionary observed a tribe of Hurons playing a game with a hide-covered ball that was hurled from a curved stick with a pouch at the top. The Hurons called the game bagataway. The curved stick resembled a bishop's croiser and the Jesuit priest renamed the game lacrosse, a French word that means 'the crook'.)

George was also an excellent athlete. For his size he could run well, not as fast as James, mind you, but pretty darn fast. George was a little over six feet tall and weighed 14 stone *(196 lbs.)*. When I was his age, I was a little under six feet tall and weighed 11 stone *(154 lbs.)*.

George was going to be a monster.

The Academy placed the students into four classrooms, dividing them not by age but according to their academic skills. "A" was the top class and "D" was the bottom feeder. James was in "C" class all four years.

The Catholic Church maintained the Academy, but its main financial support came from its alumni. The majority of the students were scions of the rich and powerful. Needless to say, some students were treated better than others.

James fell victim to this caste system. Jack Parsons, a senior, was a bully and a teachers' pet. He was a big kid but he was slow and not very athletic. His mother died when he was young and he was raised by his father, Jed Parsons, a lawyer who provided legal assistance to the school. Jack Parsons and James were bitter rivals.

As I learned from my experiences with Mike Fink, bullies like to stick together. Unlike Fink, though, most bullies are cowards and run in packs. Jack Parsons was no exception. He was the head of his own little gang.

Jack was in "A" class, not because he deserved it, but because he was Jed Parsons' son. After scoring extremely high on his entrance exam, George was placed in the "A" class.

The classrooms competed against each other in athletic contests. The most notable competition was for the trophy awarded to the champions of the annual lacrosse tournament.

To raise funds, the school held a fair every fall. They played the championship game of the lacrosse tournament on the same day. They invited the families of students and encouraged them to bring friends. The lacrosse tournament was very popular and rare. Lacrosse wasn't being played at any other school in America at that time.

James was quick as lightning and the best player in school. Scouts from the new professional lacrosse league in Canada came to watch him play. For three years running, James and "C" class won the tournament. Jack Parson's class was a distant second. None of the games were even close.

James' final tournament was a week away. During a pickup game at recess James bloodied Parson's nose with the end of his lacrosse stick. It was an accident but Parsons screamed bloody murder.

With his gang behind him, Parsons said, "You've just made a big mistake, Bissell. We're gonna mess you up!"

"And how are you gonna do that?" James asked just before he took off running. The bullies gave chase but they couldn't catch him. George came out of the school and James ran up to him and stopped. So did the bullies chasing James. They were out of breath and breathing hard. James wasn't even winded.

George said, "Is there a problem here?"

"No problem. Just helpin' these fellows get in shape."

• • •

James got called on the carpet for bloodying Parsons' nose. MJ went to school to talk to the principal, Father Ducat. She took care of the school business. After all, she was the tutor in our family.

Parsons' father was present. He demanded, "That hooligan should be expelled or at the very least suspended. That's what the Academy would have done in my day."

MJ argued, "It was an accident. James doesn't have a mean bone in his body and doesn't need to cheat to win."

Father Ducat knew MJ was right. He was in a difficult position. To appease Jed Parsons he suspended James, but for only three days. That way James could play in the lacrosse tournament. Seeing James Bissell play lacrosse was a big drawing card and good for the school's coffers.

Jed Parsons was upset over this development and, as usual, he took his anger out on Jack. As they left the school, he said, "When I was at the Academy, they would have tossed that peon out."

"I know, father."

For the 100th time he told Jack, "My class won that trophy four years running. I'm just asking you to win it once! Is that too much to ask?"

"No, father."

"Listen to me, you jackass! My class reunion's this year and I don't want to spend the whole evening listening to Harry Haig gloat!"

"I know, father! I know. But you never had to play against a player like James Bissell. He's the best lacrosse player in Missouri. He's being scouted by the pros."

"He's just one player, Jack. He's not a whole team. How about your team, son? Surely you have some players worth a damn?"

"Bissell's brother George is on my team. He's just a freshman but he's almost as good as his brother."

"Well there you go. You can win."

"But..."

"But, but, but! Excuses! That's all I ever get from you." He smacked Jack on the back of his head. "I don't want to hear any more excuses!"

"Dad, please!"

"Shut up!" Jed placed his face as close to Jack's as he could get. His breath reeked of alcohol and tobacco. Jack wanted to turn away but knew better than to do it. His father's voice quivered with anger as he warned, "Listen to me, boy. I don't care how you do it! Just win that damn game! You got that!"

"Yes, father!"

"I didn't hear you!" He cuffed Jack across his face.

Jack shouted, "Yes, father!"

Jack was desperate to please his father and had to devise a plan to win the game. He could come up with only one solution. He used George's presence on the team as a smoke screen to cover his scheme.

He bragged that with George on the team they couldn't lose. Parsons told James, "I can't wait to get you on that field, Bissell. This year you're gonna lose and your brother's gonna help me."

A week later, Jack Parsons made his move. He knew Larry dropped James and George off at school early every morning before going to work on the *Pole Cat*. James and George usually went to their respective homerooms.

Larry dropped the boys off at school. George went to the library on the second floor to do research for a paper. James went to his homeroom to nap.

James sat in a desk in the back and laid his head on his desk to sleep. He awoke with a start as strong hands clamped on his shoulders and the back of his neck and head. He tried to push up but to no avail. Two sets of burly arms held his arms. A third person had him by the back of the neck and head. He couldn't see his attackers.

Someone with tremendous strength grabbed his right leg and pulled it sideways. James screamed as his groin muscles tore. The attacker stretched his leg and set his foot on the seat of the desk opposite him. He tried to pull his leg back. He heard someone say, "Hold him one more second."

It was Parsons. He was sure of it. A second later something struck him on the right knee. His leg bent in a direction it wasn't meant to go. His knee had been torn to shreds, a crippling injury that would plague James for the rest of his life. James let out a loud wail.

Someone rabbit-punched him on the back of his neck and he saw stars, but he didn't lose consciousness. The pain in his leg wouldn't let him pass out. The attackers fled before James could get a look at them, but he knew who they were.

Brother Tucker was George's homeroom teacher. He was alone in the principal's office when he heard James scream. He went to investigate. He stepped into the hallway and heard someone hit a door hard behind him. He turned and saw several boys going out through the back door of the school. He only saw the back of his head but he was sure the last one out was Jack Parsons.

He turned and headed the opposite way. George Bissell had just descended to the first floor and was heading toward him. Brother Tucker heard someone moaning and followed the sound to homeroom "C". James was writhing on the floor. Brother Tucker rushed to him and said, "What happened? What's wrong?"

Through clenched teeth, James answered, "My leg! They've broken my leg."

"James!" George was in the doorway.

"He needs a doctor. Hurry."

George took off. He was out of the school in an instant and onto the hard pavement. He turned in the direction of Doc Bernie's house and took off. He prayed that Doc Bernie would be in.

It was about two miles to Doc Bernie's and George wasn't built for long distance running. He tried to set a pace he could handle. After a mile, he was gasping for breath. He thought, "I can't go on. I've got to stop."

He slowed down. A vision came unbidden into his mind. It

was of James, an eight-year-old boy holding a shotgun and saying, "And leave mom? Never."

At the memory of his brother's bravery, tears came to George's eyes and waves of emotion rippled through him, energizing him. With renewed determination, he picked up his pace. His breath came in short gasps and his lungs burned. He screamed at himself, "Keep going you tub of lard. You can do it." Then a miracle took place. He got his second wind.

Doc Bernie had just climbed into his carriage when he heard a shout. He turned and saw George running toward him. He turned his buggy in that direction and rode to George who was bent over, gasping for breath. Before he could ask, George climbed up into the buckboard and panted, "It's James, Doc. He's hurt real bad. You gotta come. You gotta."

They arrived at the Academy. Doc Bernie immediately gave James laudanum for the pain and examined his knee. He said, "Good Lord, this boy's knee is mangled!"

He asked Brother Tucker, "What the hell happened to this boy?"

Before Brother Tucker could answer, someone said, "That's what we intend to find out." It was Father Ducat, the school principal.

"Brother Tucker, come with me."

George and several students helped carry James to Doc's buggy. Doc told George, "You better come with me. At least, until we find out what happened here."

Brother Tucker told father Ducat what he saw and heard. Father Ducat asked, "These boys you saw leaving the school. You didn't see their faces, did you?"

"No."

"Then how can you be sure one of them was Jack Parsons?"

"I just know."

"No! You don't know anything! Understand me?"

"Yes, Father."

"We can't scandalize the son of a school patron on such flimsy evidence."

"James Bissell told me one of them was Jack Parsons. He recognized his voice."

"He didn't actually see him?"

"No, Father."

"Then he has no proof. We can't take the word of the son of some ferryboat operator over that of the son of the school barrister."

"But, Father . . ."

"But nothing! Keep your mouth shut! Understand?"

"Yes, Father."

Father Ducat softened, "Brother Tucker, I can see how you could be confused. This all happened so quickly. This is obviously the work of those street toughs who make it their habit to harass our students. They're getting bolder. Remember what happened to the Fitzpatrick boy?"

"Yes, Father."

"Good. Now you'll speak of this matter no more. To anyone! Understand?"

"Yes, Father."

• • •

Larry, Nahaboo, and I were heading down to the landi- when Nahaboo pointed to the southwest and said, "Doctor come." Larry and I turned and saw Doc Bernie's buggy in the distance.

Larry said, "That's George with him!"

It sure was. I said, "Something's wrong here."

Nahaboo and I carried James to the guestroom. I was sick at heart when I saw James' leg. His dream of playing professional lacrosse was over. From the looks of his injury, I thought he'd be lucky to walk again. Doc Bernie reassured me that the leg would heal.

James told me what happened. I had to resist the urge to go hurt some people. Larry was as distraught and angry as I was.

I told him, "Easy, Larry. We can't go off half-cocked."

"But, Cap'n, I gotta do somethin'. I can't just sit here."

"Then find Crazy John and tell him what happened."

Crazy John came and he brought T.H. Benton with him. "I figured you might need some legal advice before you did something stupid . . . or after you did."

I told them what James told me.

Crazy John said, "Those sons a' *(censored)!* Unbelievable!"

T.H. said, "And criminal if you ask me. But schools have their own set of rules and their own justice system. Too bad."

"Why so?"

"If this were a criminal case, you might be able to convince a jury that the Parsons kid did it. Juries are swayed by emotion. School faculties are influenced by the size of their patron's purse strings."

"But a religious order runs this school. Surely they don't sell justice to the highest bidder."

"No, but like yours truly, there are times when a person has to do what they think is best for the majority. A scandal like this would stain the reputation of the school. They could lose funding and enrollment. They sidestep the truth to protect themselves. Denial is their sword."

"What can we do?"

"Nothin' legally, not unless James is willing to lie and say he saw his assailants."

"James doesn't lie."

"We know," T.H. and Crazy John said simultaneously.

"I've got to do something."

T.H. said, "Let's find out what kind of poker players these people are."

T.H. explained his strategy. It was a good plan. I thanked them for their support and went to talk to George.

I told George, "You can't go back to school until I've talked to your teachers. These thugs may be out to get you as well."

"Let 'em come. I'm not afraid of 'em."

"I know you're not, George. But maybe you should be. Just a little, anyway."

"But . . ."

"This isn't an argument, George. This is an order. Stay put!"

"Yes, sir!"

I softened, "I just don't want to see you hurt, son. That's why I need to talk to these people."

"They're not gonna listen to you."

"Why not?"

"You're not a lawyer or a doctor. To them, you're nothing."

"We'll see. Now I want you to do something for me."

• • •

Crazy John delivered my request for an audience with the senior faculty members to Father Ducat. The priest was unnerved by the celebrity of the messenger.

He said, "Mr. O'Fallon, are we talking about the same Lewis Bissell here?"

"I hope so. One is enough."

Father Ducat dismissed the joke. "Lewis Bissell . . .the ferryboat operator."

"The one and the same."

Ducat accepted my request, although he thought it odd that I insisted on holding the meeting early in the morning on a school day.

• • •

Crazy John told me, "Father Ducat said to advise you that Jed Parsons would be in attendance as their counselor."

"That shyster." I remembered the day Junior dressed him down in court.

"He suggested," John cleared his throat and mimicked Father Ducat, "that if Mr. Bissell can afford it, he should bring legal representation as well, so he doesn't get in over his head."

"Too late."

"Father Ducat's never met you, has he?"

"I've never talked to the man, but I'm sure he's seen me. I've been to every one of James' lacrosse matches."

"With Sam Wiggins, right."

"And MJ and the kids."

"Well, I get the impression he thinks you're Sam Wiggins."

"Sam Wiggins?"

"Don't worry. I won't tell Sam. I know how riled he can get when he's been insulted."

I now understood why the Greeks killed the messenger.

• • •

I decided to dress for the occasion. I took my uniform out of the cedar chest and put it on. It was a little snug.

MJ asked, "Are you really going to wear that?"

"Yes."

"Why?"

"Credibility. Being a captain in the U.S. Army gives me more credibility."

"But you're no longer in the Army."

"Once commissioned, always commissioned. I could retake my commission tomorrow. I'd be at the bottom of the list seniority-wise, but I'd still be a captain in the Army."

"That's scary."

"Oop's. Almost forgot."

I took the saber General Sinclair gave my father back in 1791 off the wall and strapped it on. Uncle Dan thought dad deserved a medal for valor after that battle outside of Fort Wayne where dad got his skull creased. Sinclair gave him the saber instead. It was another of dad's prized possessions.

"What's with the sword?"

"T.H. said 'Denial is their sword,' or something to that effect. I want to be able to defend myself."

"It's not a good idea."

"It's my birthday today. Humor me. Now grab your wrap. We don't want to keep T.H. waiting."

MJ, and I met T.H. outside the school and entered. Students were still arriving. School would start shortly. Several students recognized MJ. She'd tutored them. They guessed why she was here. Everyone in school believed Jack Parsons crippled James.

Father Ducat and Jed Parsons were waiting in Ducat's office. Parsons heard the talk around school but was still in denial about his son's part in the incident.

T.H. entered first and Ducat sprang to his feet.

"Senator Benton, what a pleasant . . ." His voice trailed off when he spotted MJ.

"Father Ducat, Mr. Parsons, I believe you know my clients, Captain Lewis Bissell and his wife, Mary Jane Bissell."

"You're Lewis Bissell?" Father Ducat looked confused. There were three chairs in front of Ducat's desk. We didn't wait for an invite. We sat.

Parsons said, "That he is. Hello, Bissell."

Parsons sat with his arms folded. He had gained considerable weight since last I saw him. With his heavy jowls, he resembled a bulldog.

"Parsons."

"We're here about this ugly matter concerning James Bissell." T.H.'s voice had a steel edge to it.

The words were barely out of Benton's mouth when Parsons blurted, "One mention of my son's name and I'll sue you for slander."

The gloves were already off.

I didn't hesitate, "Well, I guess we'll see you in court then."

"Where you'll lose."

T.H. took a piece of paper out of his pocket and set it on the desk in front of Ducat. It contained a list of names.

"We have a witness."

"A witness!" Parsons' face was red. "You can't have a witness. My son could never hurt anyone like that."

He looked at Father Ducat who had turned white.

"Take a look at that list of names," I challenged. "I think you'll recognize them."

I got the list of names from George. It contained the names of Jack Parson's gang members.

Parsons studied the list, then threw it back down on the desk, "This means nothing. You don't have a witness. You're bluffing."

T.H. countered, "Well, then, I suggest you call these boys in and question them—one at a time. They should be in class by now. Oh, and we'd like to add Brother Tucker's name to that list."

Father Ducat knew we had them. The boys wouldn't have time to get together and fabricate a story. None of them had the gumption to stand on their own. One of them was bound to confess.

Father Ducat wasn't sure what Brother Tucker would say. If legal action were taken, the scandal could deal a crushing blow to the school.

Ducat said, "What do you want from us, Mr. Bissell?"

Parsons bellowed, "Father Ducat!"

"Mr. Parsons. Please! Let's see if there's some way we can resolve this matter amicably."

T.H. said, "My clients wish to do the same thing. Tell them what you want, Lewis."

I said, "My son George is also a student here. He's in your "A" track. I don't want Jack Parsons in the same room with him. Understood?"

"Agreed."

"This is preposterous!"

"Sit down, Mr. Parsons."

"I want your personal guarantee that no harm will befall my son George during his stay here. No repercussions!"

"Agreed."

"Parsons, I want to hear your personal guarantee as well." I placed my hand on the hilt of the saber. "Well?"

It finally sank in that perhaps his son was guilty of this misdeed and, if so, he may have been the catalyst for his son's actions. He took a deep breath and said, "You have my word."

T.H. muttered, "For whatever that's worth."

"Now as for my son James, we . . ." My voice faltered. MJ rescued me.

"We want him to be able to graduate this year."

"This year? But how? If his injuries are as severe as you claim, he won't be able to attend class."

"We know that," MJ continued. "We want you to send his lessons home with George. I'll administer his tests. I won't go easy on him."

Father Ducat mulled it over. I cleared my throat. He responded.

"Agreed, but on one condition. He'll have to come here to take his final exams. Hopefully, he'll be well enough by then. It's the best I can offer."

"Fair enough." MJ picked the list of names off the desk and we left.

• • •

The Academy was aware that Jed Parsons had a drinking problem. Up until now, they had looked the other way. Father Ducat realized Jed Parsons was more of a liability than an asset. The school dismissed him as their legal representative.

Parsons lost face and social status. He was too embarrassed to show up at his class reunion. He took more and more to the bottle. The more he drank, the more he took his anger out on his son.

He railed against Jack, "How could you do something so stupid?"

"But father, you told me . . ."

"To win the damn game. Not maim someone."

The arguments were one-sided. If Jack argued back, his father beat him. Jack was afraid of his own father.

Jack's life was a living hell. He came home from school, sneaked into his house, and locked himself in his room. He wouldn't come out until he was sure his father was asleep or passed out. Angry and confused, he started carrying a derringer for protection. In his confused state of mind, he placed the blame for his father's lack of affection for him on James Bissell.

• • •

Doc Bernie drained James' knee several times a week and wrapped it tight. He gave James some crutches.

Doc told him, "James, you'll still need to have your knee drained regularly, but you can use it for short periods of time. Rest it and use it. Rest it and use it. Understand? That's the only way it'll improve."

James convalesced for six months. George brought him his homework and study lessons. At first James was depressed and uncooperative. He wouldn't eat and he wouldn't study.

MJ and I were at the end of our rope when Stumpy said, "Let me talk to him."

James was sleeping. Stumpy entered his room and sat on the chair by his bed. When James woke up and saw Stumpy, he sat up and asked, "What are you doin' here?"

"Visitin' an idiot."

"What?"

"You heard me." He loosened the strap holding his leg, "Asides, I want to show you somethin'."

He removed his wooden leg. The end of his stump was an ugly mass of scar tissue. It looked swollen.

"Not too pretty, is it?"

"No. Put your leg back on. Please! What's wrong with you, Stumpy?"

"Nothin's wrong with me, James. It's you what's got the problem." He put his leg back on. "They tell me you've been actin' like the end of my leg here, all nasty and ugly."

"I don't know what you mean. Now get out of here." James lay back on the bed and rolled away from Stumpy.

"I'll go all right, but not before I've had my say. I know your hurt boy. I've felt it myself. Now listen to me."

James lay still, his back to Stumpy.

"I was just like you, James. When I lost my leg, I thought it was the end of the world. I didn't have anyplace to go. I didn't know what to do. People offered me nothing but pity, which was the last thing I wanted. I became mean and nasty. People didn't want to be around me, which is just what I wanted. At least, that's what I thought."

Silence.

"Then your pa hooked me up with Will Root and I got me this leg." He rapped on it.

"When I had no place to go, he offered me this job I got here."

James stayed silent.

"People looked at me like I was a freak. It didn't bother me, though. Cuz of your ma."

That got his attention, "My ma?"

"Your pa, too, but mostly your ma. From time she met me until . . ." his voice trailed off.

James was sitting up and looking at him, "Go on. I'm listening."

"This is hard to explain, boy. Your ma, she never once looked at me like I wasn't a . . . man. Somehow, she made me feel whole. Ya understand?"

"I think so."

"Your ma's gone, rest her soul. But your pa's still here and your brothers and sisters, and MJ. They're all good people, James, and they're hurtin' right along with you. They deserve better than you been giving them."

James burst into tears. Stumpy went to him and hugged him. "Let it go, boy. Let it go."

Stumpy paid James regular visits and James' disposition improved.

• • •

The night before his return to the scene of his torment, James told George, "Jack Parsons and his buddies did this to me. I've laid in bed for the past six months thinking of ways to get even."

George said, "Me, too. But I promised dad I wouldn't do anything. But if you got something in mind, I'm not going to let you go it alone. What are you gonna do?"

"I'm not gonna do anything. Revenge is stupid. It just gets more people hurt." He paused. "Mom told me that."

"What are you gonna do?"

"Take the tests and graduate. I hope."

"What if Parsons wants to start something?"

"I'll just stay out of his way."

"If you can."

"Yeah." James was quiet a moment. "George?"

"What?"

"I'm afraid."

• • •

The next morning I helped Larry hitch Buck to his carriage and I told him, "Larry, wait for them. James' knee is pretty swollen this morning. I don't know if he can last the day."

"No problem, Cap'n."

So Larry dropped off the boys and waited outside the school in his carriage. He dozed off and was awakened by the sound of angry voices.

James and George were in front of the school. George was arguing with a large boy. James was behind George. Larry thought the boys were going to fight so he got out of his carriage.

He heard George say, "Leave my brother alone, Parsons. Haven't you done enough damage?"

Parsons said, "What's wrong, gimp? Need your little brother to protect you now?"

James turned his back to him. Parsons reached past George and pulled one of James' crutches from under him. James grabbed the fence railing to keep himself from falling. He yelped in pain.

Parsons threw down the crutch and turned to walk away.

George saw the red cube. He picked up the crutch and whacked Parsons on the head. Parsons fell to the ground. A second later, James was beside George.

He took back his crutch. He said, "You fool!"

Parsons rolled over on his back, holding his head. He brought his hand down and it was covered with blood. He was enraged. He got to his feet and pulled a derringer from his pocket. He said, "Bissell!"

George turned to face him. As Parsons squeezed the trigger, Larry crashed into him, causing the shot to go through a school window.

"Sorry, boy, but nobody hurts my brothers."

"Brothers?"

Father Ducat emerged from the school. Parsons dropped the derringer on the ground and said, "This crazy nigger tried to shoot me."

"That's a lie!" It was Brother Tucker. He was looking out

the shattered window. "I heard a ruckus and came to the window just in time to almost get shot."

He shot a defiant look at Father Ducat. "Mr. Parsons pulled the trigger."

Parsons wailed, "I was just protecting myself, Father. Look at this."

He showed Father Ducat the blood on his head. The priest saw it and demanded, "What's going on here?"

"Bissell hit me with a crutch, Father."

He looked at George and James. "Well, speak up. Which one of you is responsible?"

Before George could answer, James said, "I am."

James and Jack Parsons were expelled from school. George graduated from the St. Louis Academy in 1848 and went on to graduate from West Point.

Miscellany

*J*ames was sweet on a girl whose father was a typesetter. So James learned how to set type and soon we had a free subscription to the *Missouri Republican*. I guess I should have spent more time reading that paper. MJ was pregnant again.

• • •

Joseph Smith and several followers were arrested in Carthage, Illinois. They were charged with conspiracy to undermine the local government by targeting certain officials for termination. Some still believe he ordered the shooting of Governor Boggs of Missouri in 1840. An angry mob pulled Joseph Smith from the jail and shot and killed him.

• • •

1845. We had another daughter. We named her Anne, after MJ's mother. Since Anna was now called Queenie, we didn't think there would be any confusion. Hah!

Some fellow came up with an idea to hitch a team of horses to what looked like an oversized train dining car and haul people in it. They called this monstrosity an omnibus. It had wheels and didn't run on a track. It followed a route from 3rd and Market Street downtown to the ferry landing at Bissell Point. Junior Chouteau helped with the financing to put it into operation. I have to admit he was progressive. For years, he helped finance scientific expeditions to the West.

DAN PATTERSON '02

This transit service didn't last long. The weight of the car was so great, it required at least six horses to pull it, eight horses on a muddy day. Often, there would be more horses working than people riding the omnibus.

John Looney took a smaller dining car and converted it to a lunch diner on wheels. Much lighter, it took only two horses to pull. From a sliding window on the side of the car, he sold food to go. What a unique idea! Dock workers, foundry workers, millers, you name it, were glad to see the wagon with the word "LUNCH" emblazoned on the sides pull up at their places of business.

James K. Polk was President in 1845. He fought in the War of 1812. He was one of the few politicians to basically run his campaign on a single promise and then actually come through on it. He vowed to annex California and the Southwest, which he did. Wisconsin achieved statehood and our old buddy, Henry Dodge, became the first U.S. Senator from there. There was a German Communistic Colony established at Bethel.

• • •

1846. The Mexican War began. Colonel John C. Fremont, son-in-law of T.H. Benton, led a successful campaign in California. The new U.S. Arsenal south of St. Louis was brimming with ammunition and arms and provided jobs for 500 workers. The arsenal made a nice profit selling weapons and ammo to settlers heading west, as well as provisioning military expeditions.

Over the last decade, Machingo spent time each season with Cloud Bank, the tribal medicine man, learning the ways of the shaman. Cloud Bank deemed Machingo his successor and told him he must truly become Magic Hands.

Machingo was at Bissell Point visiting Nahaboo. While adding another figure to the tepee to mark his visit, he suddenly stopped and told Nahaboo they must return to their village. They left immediately. We learned later that Cloud Bank had died. How Machingo knew is a mystery to me.

A terrible cholera epidemic had swept through his tribe, killing over half of his people. Over 200 died, the highest casualties among the elderly and the young. Machingo could do nothing to hold the plague at bay. He watched helplessly as friends and loved ones suffered a horrific death. I knew how he felt.

It was an extremely wet spring. Rain fell night and day, but the cleansing rains arrived too late for Machingo's people. The survivors placed the bodies on biers and torched them. Later, Nahaboo told me the steady downpour forced them to relight the funeral pyres many times. Machingo told Nahaboo that The Morning Star and The Evening Star could not stop weeping because the hurtful smoke from the pyres of so many little ones stung their eyes.

Cloud Bank was one of the first victims of this epidemic and Machingo became the healer. The new shaman was presented with an impossible task, a test he could only fail. It didn't matter that no one could have stemmed the tide of this tragedy. Machingo's grief-stricken people found him lacking. He lost face and became an outcast.

He spent the rest of his days on the road, mostly in and around St. Louis. Many times he stayed with Nahaboo and

Larry here at Bissell Point. He returned to his tribe shortly
before his death.

• • •

Due to the tireless efforts of John Clemens and others
during a meeting in his law office in Hannibal, Missouri, the
Hannibal & St. Joseph Railroad, the first trans-state railroad,
was incorporated. This action got the attention of the movers
and shakers in the rest of the state, T.H. Benton among them.

Dred Scott was a slave who had been passed between the
Blow family and the Emerson family of St. Louis. Captain
Peter Blow was his original owner. When Captain Blow left
Jefferson Barracks for assignment elsewhere, he left Dred in
the hands of the widow Emerson. She rented Dred to people to
perform odd jobs and do menial labor. He lived up to his
reputation for being lazy. I know.

On occasion, Mrs. Emerson hired Dred out to work for a
cold storage company downtown. They sent him to the St.
Louis docks to unload cargo. On the few occasions he helped
us unload, he was no help at all. His favorite excuse was his
back was out. He'd shuffle about until the job was done. Then
he'd miraculously recover.

Peter Blow's sons, Taylor and Henry, felt somehow
responsible for Dred's behavior. Henry Blow was the husband
of Minerva Grimsley, whose father was Colonel Thorton
Grimsley, the inventor of the dragoon saddle.

In 1846, because he had spent some time in the free
territories of Illinois and Wisconsin, Dred sued Mrs. Emerson
for freedom for him and his family. He lost his case.

Mary turned nineteen and asked me if she could go to
work in the kitchen at Lindenwood College in St. Charles.
Mary Sibley, the lady who founded the college with her husband, was a friend of our family. She once asked Mary's
mother to teach at the college. Mary would board and work
there. I saw no reason to stand in her way. MJ told me later
that William Morrison, the fellow she was sweet on, was
attending classes there.

MJ was pregnant again.

• • •

1847. We had a son, Lewis, Jr, Since MJ named our last child after her mother, she felt it only right to name the new baby after someone from my side of the family.

The Hannibal & St. Joseph Railroad was officially established. The City of St. Louis was finally illuminated by gaslights. Telegraph lines ended on the Illinois side of the river. They tried to string telegraph lines across the Mississippi by putting huge masts on each side of the river and a third mast on Bloody Island and running lines across, but the river and river traffic wouldn't cooperate. Passing ships and roosting birds interrupted service. So telegrams had to be ferried across. Great day in the morning! What a lucky break for Sam Wiggins and me!

• • •

1848. Mary married William Morrison in Mound City, Illinois, where he and his father operated a wood mill. Soon I was hauling lumber for them in my boat.

The French and the Danes abolished slavery. August Dodge, Henry Dodge's son, became the first U.S. Senator from the new state of Iowa. He served from 1848-1854. They opened a Presbyterian church in Carondelet, the first non-Catholic church in this area. Many German immigrants to the United States settled in Carondelet.

Chaos Reigns

1849. Gold was found in California. A huge influx of people heading west caused the population of the City of St. Louis to grow until it was surpassed only by the population of New York City. We ferried people across the river practically non-stop. About half of the people traveling to California didn't have the funds or the means to go further, so they sought employment in St. Louis.

Overcrowding led to unsanitary conditions, followed by an outbreak of cholera, a disease generally caused by drinking water containing fecal matter. Cholera can also get into food-stuffs. It's an ugly death. One's body can no longer retain anything. Retching and diarrhea are followed by cramping and death.

An early cholera victim arrived by steamboat and was blamed for the epidemic. Cholera is not easily transmitted as an airborne illness, but at that time people believed it was. The epidemic was worse in the north side of the City of St. Louis and that area was quarantined.

Several prominent Northsiders, people like Henry Blow and Judge Wilson Primm, fled to South St. Louis and Carondelet. Distraught Carondelet civic leaders passed an ordinance that would fine people for bringing infected non-Carondelet citizens into their sector.

Anyone who serves in the military knows the conse- quences of drinking befouled water. The Army's Standard Operating Procedure is simple—boil your water. St. Louis newspapers warned people to boil their drinking water.

Illiterate and lazy people failed to perform this simple ritual and died as a result. Ignorance is bliss, until the cramps take hold.

Some people thought the disease was carried here by steamboat. Some fool torched the *White Cloud* and soon the whole St. Louis harbor was aflame. Twenty-three ships were swept up in the fire and dozens of local warehouses burned to the ground, close to $3,000,000 in damage.

Larry, Nahaboo, and I saw the flames and smoke and set out in the *Pole Cat* to help. Our mission turned into a war story.

Using our sump pump and hose, we sprayed river water on the burning ships. Nahaboo manned the wheel while I operated the sump pump and Larry handled the hose. We had to keep backing away from the flames. The heat was so intense, the water turned to steam. Hot vapor sprayed back toward us. Nahaboo moved us to and fro just out of reach of the flames. We were making progress, until a powder keg went off on one of the boats.

The *Pole Cat* was showered with debris, a heavy flaming spar landing midship. Larry picked it up by one end, burning his hands and shoulder in the process. Balancing the giant torch on his shoulder, he made his way to the side of the boat. A shot rang out from shore as some idiot shouted, "Look! There's the nigger who started it!"

As Larry was heaving the spar over the side, a bullet struck him in his stomach. From my position at the sump, I saw Larry stagger backward, clutching his belly. Then he fell to the deck.

As I rushed to where he lay, a couple more shots whizzed by. I ducked down and looked toward shore. I saw three figures standing on a warehouse dock, rifles in hand. As if trying to make up for a grievous mistake, fate took a hand. Something volatile was stored in that warehouse and it exploded, wiping out all three bushwhackers in one fell swoop.

We got Larry back to the house as quickly as possible. I sent James to fetch Doc Bernie, who was working in the quarantined section of the city. James was gone a long time and I became apprehensive. Finally, he returned with a doctor. Doc Bernie had taken ill with the cholera, so Dr. William Taussig came to tend to Larry.

Doc Taussig was working toward his medical degree from St. Louis University and was helping Doc Bernie with the cholera victims. He examined Larry and bandaged him up. He told us, "The bullet's lodged in a bad spot. I can't remove it. It'll have to stay where it is."

Larry carried that bullet in him the rest of his life.

• • •

Dr. Taussig was a hero to the citizens of St. Louis and Carondelet. For his efforts to thwart the dread cholera epidemic, he was made a member of the St. Louis County Council. By fall, the disease had run its course. An average of 86 people died per day, ten per cent of the local population, including Doc Bernie and my precious little son, Lewis, Jr.

I had never seen a coffin so small.

• • •

Another soldier, Zack Taylor, old "Rough and Ready," was now our President. Railroad talk was in the air. The National Railroad Convention was held to determine whether we should build a transcontinental railroad across the top, through the middle, or at the bottom of the nation. T.H. Benton made his famous "railroad speech." His impassioned words convinced those present to run the railroad through Missouri.

The Pacific Railroad Company was incorporated in Missouri. They were allowed seven years to build track and ten years to finish it. Incorporators included Crazy John, Ernest Angelrodt, James H. Lucas, Wayman LeDow, Thomas Allen, Henry Shaw, and Junior Chouteau.

Junior, a railroad baron, imagine that. Junior didn't spend much time in St. Louis anymore. He was busy in New York running his business empire.

The State of Missouri passed a bill commissioning the
Illinois-St. Louis Wire Suspension Bridge Corporation to build
a toll bridge across the Mississippi River. Tolls were not to
exceed one half-ferriage cost now received at Wiggins Ferry. It
turned out to be a lot of hot air. I was 77 years old before a
bridge was completed across the river. I turned 60 in 1849.

Harbingers of War

1850. Zack Taylor died in office and Vice-President Millard Fillmore, the Commander of the Army of the Rio Grande, became President. Another old soldier was President; I guess they like war stories in Washington. Congress passed *The Compromise of 1850,* a stern fugitive slave law. The Supreme Court decision, *Scott v Stanford,* appeared to give slavery new support and set the stage for the Civil War. The Town of Kansas, eventually Kansas City, was incorporated. The first telegraph lines were strung across Missouri.

The town of Bremen was incorporated in 1850 by the four principal property owners: George Buchanan, E.C. Angelrodt, N.N. Destrehan, and Emil Mallinckrodt. A city was growing up around me. I sold a fair-sized portion of my land to German settlers. I now had enough money that I could retire, but I refused to sit around and die on the vine. I kept working.

I found out the hard way that Doc Taussig received his medical degree from St. Louis University. Cholera struck southern Illinois. It was quickly contained before it reached epidemic proportions, but not quickly enough for my family. My daughter Mary, who lived in Mound City and was pregnant, was stricken with this vile disease.

Now, I shouldn't have done it, but I took the *Pole Cat* down the Mississippi to the Ohio River and then up the Ohio to Mound City to get Mary and bring her to St. Louis for treatment. We put in at the boat yard in Carondelet. Dorf was waiting to pick me up in his carriage and he took me to Doc Taussig.

I begged Taussig to come to the boat to treat her. He pointed at his new degree and told me he'd taken the Hippocratic oath to treat all sick people. Of course, he'd come.

Doc Taussig's efforts were for naught. Mary died and her baby was stillborn.

George was a recent graduate of West Point and an Ensign in the Army. We corresponded regularly by mail. Still mourning the loss of little Lewis, the news of his sister's death compounded his sorrow.

Queenie's latest beau was a struggling young lawyer, Henry Haight. I remember the day Queenie introduced him to me. She bragged, "Daddy, Henry is a graduate of Yale."

It was too easy. In my most serious voice, I said, "Well, nobody's perfect."

Henry and his father had a law office in St. Louis. Henry followed the "Gold Rush" wave of prospectors to California. Tales of claim jumping and arguments over land assessment led him to believe his legal skills would be in demand there. Queenie fell into a state of depression after Henry left. 1850 was as hard on us as 1849.

Dred Scott won his case in a retrial in 1850 on the argument that a slave taken to a place where slavery was prohibited, by law, must become a freeman. Mrs. Emerson appealed to the Missouri Supreme Court and in 1852 the decision was reversed. By then, Mrs. Emerson had moved to New York and handed ownership of Scott and his family to Taylor Blow. Now he was Taylor's problem.

• • •

In 1851, Nahaboo passed away in his sleep. Somehow Machingo knew his brother had died and showed up at midday. It took him the rest of the day and part of the evening to build a funeral pyre of wood. It stood about six feet off the ground and Machingo carved totems on the four corner posts where the support posts were affixed to the funeral bier.

Larry and I helped Machingo lay his brother on the bier. Machingo said, "Evening Star is bright, but we must wait for Morning Star."

While Machingo retired to Nahaboo's tepee and dressed in his most colorful raiment, we made a fire. Machingo painted his face and wore a headdress of feathers, the colors vivid even by the light of The Evening Star. We listened as Machingo sang and performed the "bird dance" around the fire, a traditional dance performed by many Native American tribes.

(William Clark told me he believed the name Pawnee came from the Native American word, pani, which means "red bird.")

Machingo motioned for us to join him, so we did. To my surprise, the longer we danced and chanted the more refreshed I felt. We danced the night away. When the sun's rays peeked over the horizon, MJ and the kids joined us.

Machingo lit a torch and carried it to the pyre. He dropped the torch and said, "Fly, little brother."

We stood in silence while Nahaboo's body was reduced to ash and carried away on the wind.

MJ murmured, "What an odd way to honor the dead."

I replied, "My ancestors would disagree with you. They did the same thing."

Larry agreed, "Ceptin' they placed the body on a boat. Right, Cap'n?"

"That's right, Larry, and the ceremony took place at sunset, not dawn. I want to go the same way."

Larry said, "Me, too."

MJ and the kids laughed and headed for the house.

I said, "Larry, we'll just have to do it for each other. I'll let you go first. It's the gentlemanly thing to do."

It took him a second, then he broke into a broad grin, "All right, Cap'n, all right!"

Machingo took Nahaboo's pony and sled. He told Larry that Nahaboo wanted him to have the tepee. This upset some of my new neighbors who thought the tepee was an eyesore and should be torn down. To hell with them!

• • •

Queenie received monthly letters from Henry Haight, which temporarily cheered her. If a month passed without a letter, she was a bear to live with.

Some good things happened in 1851. MJ gave birth to another son, Taylor. He was the spitting image of Lewis, Jr.

Christian College was established in Columbia. Construction was begun on the first Missouri passenger train, *The Pacific.*

• • •

In 1852, the passenger train was completed. The citizens of Missouri were proud. Steamboat travel was always risky business. Only a few days after the train's completion, the steamboat *Saluda* exploded at Lexington, Missouri. Someday, a railroad company would run tracks through the Rocky Mountains to the West Coast. Travel by rail would be the quickest and least troublesome way to go.

It's a hard thing recovering from the loss of a child, be they grown or a baby. I was so busy helping my seven children with their day to day affairs, I forgot to feel sorry for myself. They affirmed that old saying, "life goes on for the living."

Queenie still railed at the postal service if she didn't get her monthly letter from Henry Haight. MJ and I figured if "you can't lick them, join them."

We arranged for Queenie to get a job at the post office, thanks to Crazy John's prodding of our old postmaster, Rufus Easton. Queenie was fascinated by the wanted posters that hung on the post office walls and soon her room was filled with them. My daughter was strange!

James was sick of setting type for the *Missouri Democrat,* literally. The fumes from the ink made him dizzy and gave him headaches.

James was familiar with the river and the workings of the boat. As boys, he and George spent many hours with my crew and me on the Mississippi. With Nahaboo gone, I needed a new helmsman. James could sit at the helm and keep the weight off his bad knee. As MJ liked to say, James "fit the bill."

The newspaper didn't want to let him go, but they wished him well. There went my free subscription.

• • •

1853. Franklin Pierce was now President. He appointed Jefferson Davis his Secretary of War. Pierce led an effort to buy Cuba from Spain, and he also created the U.S. Court of Credit.

Eliot Seminary *(eventually Washington University)* and Westminister College were chartered. Central High School, the state's first public high school, opened.

Doc Taussig was elected mayor of Carondelet. Primus Emerson bought the Carondelet boat yard. He retained the workers and named his new business, the Carondelet Marine Railway and Dock Company.

In an attempt to compel the Supreme Court to make a ruling on the *Missouri Compromise,* Roswell Field took up Dred Scott's cause. In 1853, he entered a new suit in the Federal circuit court knowing full well they'd rule against him. However, it gave Field the opportunity to appeal to the U.S. Supreme Court.

It was several years before the matter was settled. Dred's reputation as a slacker grew, but he had gained a bit of notoriety and it became the "in thing" to be able to say that Dred Scott "once" worked for you. After once, they never hired his services from Taylor Blow again.

• • •

1854. George stopped to visit us on his way to an assignment at the Presidio in San Francisco. The old Spanish fort became the property of the U.S. government when California became a state in 1850. George and a troop of soldiers from Jefferson Barracks were going to lead a wagon train of settlers to the West.

James and Larry took George out on the *Pole Cat.* It's the first time the three of them had been together in years.

George asked James, "How do you like working on the boat?"

"Best job I ever had, if you want to call it a job. Working with Larry makes it a real adventure."

Larry playfully punched James on the arm, "What you talkin' about? Cap'n says I'm the best snag man on the river. Did I ever tell about that time we wuz workin our way back from Hannibal . . ."

"Yes . . ."

" . . . 'bout 100 times."

"Oh."

George asked, "How's the leg, James?"

"Okay. I have my good days and my bad days."

"Ever think about Jack Parsons?"

"Only on my bad days."

They all laughed.

"What happened to him?"

Larry said, "His daddy died from a heart attack 'bout a year after you left for West Pint."

"West Point."

"Oh, sorry." Larry looked at James. "I thought you told me that was a drinkin' school."

They all laughed again.

"Jack Parsons inherited his daddy's estate. He gave it all to charity."

Larry added, "Took a vow of poverty."

"Joined the Jesuits."

"Are you pulling my leg?"

"No way. Couldn't get my hands around it anyway."

"It gets better. Tell him, James."

"Now he teaches physical education at the Academy."

George said, "Well, I guess he knows all there is to know about that."

They fell silent for a moment.

Finally James said, "Father Tucker says he's a changed man and he's trying to do some good. He said Jack was as much a victim I was."

"You believe that?"

"Not rightly sure. Maybe."

"How about you, Larry? What do you think?"

"Don't know. Ain't as smart as you fellas."

"That's not saying much."

They laughed again.

Larry's tone turned serious. "I know one thing for sure. You're some of the luckiest people I know. Hell, I'm one of the luckiest people I know."

"How so?"

"I was raised by your ma and pa."

• • •

During a party we hosted for George, MJ and I pulled him aside and had a long talk with him about Queenie. She still pined for her boyfriend, Henry Haight. We thought a change of scenery might be just what the doctor ordered.

Queenie got excited when we told her our plan. She didn't mention Henry. She said she was ready for some adventure. So she headed west with George. It was a bittersweet parting.

• • •

The New York Stock Exchange had been in business since 1792. With Crazy John's advice, I had invested some money in the stock market, so I was well off financially.

MJ was tossing around the "retire" word. I hate to admit it, but I was 65 and beginning to feel my age. Oh, I was as strong as ever, but my muscles and joints complained a lot longer and louder after strenuous physical activity. We reached a compromise.

I stopped hauling cargo up and down the river. Instead, I concentrated on helping Sam Wiggins. With the steady stream of people heading to the West, there wasn't any dearth of people to ferry across the Mississippi. The *Pole Cat* was a welcome addition to Sam's fleet.

I didn't need the money, but it did provide a nice source of income for James and Larry. Besides, I liked going out on the river in the *Pole Cat.* The transition from life on the Mississippi to life as a landlubber would be hard for me. I was grounded sooner than I thought.

I read in the paper that the little fort I helped build in

Nebraska while on the Yellowstone Expedition was now the
site of the city of Omaha. Our youth comes back to haunt us.

Henry Blow was elected a state senator in 1854 despite the
Dred Scott fiasco. He openly opposed the extension of slavery.

It was rumored that St. Louis was going to annex Bremen.
Ann Farrar, Doc Bernie's widow, sold her estate to the City of
St. Louis. I heard she got well over $30,000 for her property.

• • •

1855. Queenie was in California for less than a month
when she became engaged to Henry Haight. After receiving
her letter, MJ insisted we go to California for Queenie's
wedding.

I remember well her argument for going. I never uttered
one word about not going but she "sensed" my reluctance.

"Queenie wants Cornelia to be her maid of honor but she's
too young to travel that far alone."

"I suppose."

"We can't leave the smaller children at home alone, so
Sophie, Ludy, Anne, and Taylor will have to come with us."

"Lolo could watch them."

"You don't have to worry about the bunkhouse. Stumpy
will take care of it."

"I'm not worried about the bunkhouse."

"James and Larry can keep an eye the *Pole Cat* and the
house."

"I'm sure they'll be all right."

"No, wait. Larry can keep an eye on things here. James
should come with us and attend his sister's wedding."

"If he wants to. He's a grown man, you know."

"Most importantly, Queenie wants her father to give her
away."

"I know that."

"Well, we're going. I don't care what you say."

"I know."

She was right. I didn't want to go. The thought of traveling
2,000 miles overland with five kids and a wife while perched

on the buckboard of a rickety old wagon just didn't appeal to me. How could I get out of this without actually saying "no" to MJ? Could I let my daughter down?

I thought long and hard about my argument for not going. I imagined how it would go.

"MJ, I'm too old."

"You're too old to travel but not too old to work."

"It's too risky."

"More risky than risking your life out on that river every day?"

"It's too expensive."

"Tightwad!"

The argument was going badly. Luckily, I didn't have to finish my train of thought. Shortly after the arrival of Queenie's first letter, a second letter arrived stating that she and Henry were leaving immediately for St. Louis to be married here. Hallelujah! Saved again!

I let MJ plan the most elaborate wedding we ever had at Bissell Point. It was a lot of work and nerves got stretched a bit, but compared to traveling across country it was a breeze. Everything went off without a hitch, figuratively speaking.

• • •

The Gasconade R.R. Bridge disaster left 34 dead and 100 injured. Investigators believed it was a combination of factors that led to the derailing of the passenger train. The train was going too fast and several loose spikes suggested the track was poorly maintained. Gasconade Railroad executives claimed they were the victims of foul play but couldn't prove it. No one wanted to be the fall guy for this catastrophe.

• • •

By the dock at our ferryboat, several people, including Crazy John, Emil Mallinckrodt, and a little old black lady, Mary Meachum, kept johnboats—square-backed rowboats used for fishing. It was one of the best places to put into the river and we were willing to share.

*(In the future, the railroad built a train trestle, the
Merchants Bridge, near this site.)*

When the river was calm, Crazy John and I would go out
early in the morning when everything was quiet. Sometimes
Larry joined us. We'd see Emil and usually one of his sons out
on the river as well. We'd drop anchor, then our lines. We
seldom caught anything, but as Crazy John would say, "It ain't
always about catching fish."

Mary Meachum would be out some mornings with a
boatload of people. Larry loved Mary's fishing hat. She had
more lures and fishing gadgets on it than the limit allowed.
Some days, she'd go all the way over to the Illinois side to
fish. The current on that side was much swifter.

One morning, I wondered aloud, "Why does she do that?
You can't catch fish in that fast water."

Larry and Crazy John laughed. Crazy John said, "That's
what I like about you, Bissell. You catch on to things so
quickly."

Larry said, "Yours isn't the only ferry in town."

It took a bit, but I finally got their drift. Mary Meachum
was a brave soul, as her war story will attest.

We had an early spring. April was beautiful. The winter
thaw sent a lot of water our way and the river was up. Crazy
John and I fished off the side of the *Pole Cat,* but it wasn't
quite the same as being out on the river.

By late May, the river had dropped some. Near dawn,
Crazy John and I were carrying our poles and fishing tackle
down to the dock when we heard gunfire.

Across the way, people were chasing runaway slaves. They
called themselves Illinois authorities, but I'm sure it was
Missouri law enforcement agents working outside their
jurisdiction. The real Illinois authorities just looked the other
way. St. Louis police were waiting by the dock on this side of
the river.

An article in the paper reported the incident. Eight or nine slaves were ferried across the river to a spot where a black abolitionist, who called himself Freeman, was waiting to assist them. Three of the slaves belonged to Henry Shaw. Mary Meachum was arrested and her johnboat was confiscated. She was charged with harboring and assisting slaves to escape.

The paper said Mary was the widow of John Meachum, the founder of the First African Baptist Church in St. Louis. Some fellow named Isaac helped with the rowing. He was arrested and released. I never did find out what happened to Mary. The paper never mentioned her name again. I hope she got away.

• • •

About a month later, MJ told me that Larry and James were taking the *Pole Cat* out late at night. They wouldn't be gone long. One guess as to what they were up to. This slavery issue was so confusing. There's the law and then there's the right thing to do. MJ and I let on like we didn't know what the boys were doing.

• • •

1856. MJ felt cheated that she didn't get to take that trip to California. So I took MJ and the family on a cruise in the *Pole Cat* to New Orleans. I regaled them with war stories about my exploits in the War of 1812. They listened politely, but the telling of ancient deeds by old war-horses usually falls on indifferent ears. I wasn't deterred. I told my tales anyway.

The citizens of Bremen voted in favor of being annexed by the City of St. Louis. Bernie Farrar's old estate was turned into a city park, Hyde Park, named after an area in London.

People rented sections of the park for gardens where they grew vegetables and herbs. The park was fenced off to keep the gardens from being crushed underfoot by cattle when cowhands drove their herds to the ferry landing to take them to the stockyards across the river.

On nice days, MJ and I would take the children for an evening stroll. Occasionally, we'd walk to Hyde Park. Quite often we saw young Edward Mallinckrodt in the park, asking people questions about the different plants, especially the medicinal herbs.

Some of the gardeners told me Edward had some kind of laboratory in his father's barn. They whispered things like, "Lord knows what goes on in there!" and "He's up to no good."

T.H. Benton's political career came to an end and so did his life. His doctor said he died from something called cancer; his death was a torturous experience. There's something to be said for a bullet to the head.

• • •

Stumpy Fredericks also died, just before Christmas. Before coming to work for us, the Army was the only family he ever had. Stumpy's parents were killed in Ohio by robbers when Stumpy was a small boy. Having that in common may be the reason he and Larry hit it off so well. I don't know.

Anyway, we were surprised when a woman showed up at Stumpy's funeral. She said she was working in an Alton bordello when she met Stumpy. Her husband had died from cholera. She had no skills and two small children. Stumpy helped her get out of the bordello and begin a new life. He gave her money until she got steady work as a charwoman and was able to support herself.

I always wondered what Stumpy did with his money. Bless that old rascal's heart! We offered her any of Stumpy's belongings that she wanted. We were surprised when she asked us for Stumpy's leg. Then again, that leg was Stumpy's pride and joy. Of course, we let her take it.

James took Stumpy's death harder than any of us.

The bed and breakfast business died with Stumpy. I no longer needed the income and it had become a pain to deal with city authorities and all their rules and regulations. What happened to the free in free enterprise?

We tore down the bunkhouses and threw the lumber and bunk beds in my barn. I used the lumber from the bunkhouse for firewood.

The beds took up a lot of space, so I placed an ad in the paper. I was surprised by the quick response. I practically gave the bunk beds away, all except Stumpy's.

Stumpy had carved the names and birth dates of all my kids on his bunk bed, girls on the headboard and boys on the footboard. He used to tease me that he had to do it in order to keep track. MJ said, "Well, I think we should keep at least one. In case we have extra visitors."

"Very practical," I said.

"Let's keep Stumpy's. Nobody's gonna want that old thing, anyway. It's all carved up."

"Right," I said. "Sentimental fool." I threw a canvas over the bunk bed and forgot about it.

Slow Going

1857. There was a financial panic that caused farm prices to drop and a late frost insured the loss of many crops. Several south county farmers, Ulysses S. Grant among them, sought other means of income. Grant turned to cutting and delivering firewood to area families. It was hard work and the competition from the coal industry cut severely into his profits. Grant started supplying shoring timber to local mines and the work served him well.

(There are numerous caves under St. Louis. Since 1820, bituminous [soft] coal was mined in an area now bounded by Grand Avenue, Arsenal Street, Gravois, and Kingshighway Boulevard. Missouri has one of the largest coal reserves in the Western Hemisphere, and under the St. Francois Mountains sits the largest identifiable lead ore reserve in the world.)

I met Grant while visiting Dorf. He was a genial fellow, not given to boasting like some West Point graduates I've known. St. Louis County needed a superintendent of roads. Grant studied engineering at West Point, so he applied for the job.

Doc Taussig, who was the superintendent of the county council and an abolitionist, didn't trust Grant. Grant's wife, Julia, came from a family that owned slaves and this cast suspicion on him. He didn't get the job.

James Buchanan was elected President. He was in command of the troops that defeated Santa Anna at Buena Vista in the Mexican War. He made an attempt to stem abolition but failed.

208

Jefferson Davis resigned as Secretary of War and regained his position as U.S. Senator from the state of Mississippi.

In 1857, the Supreme Court ruled on Dred Scott's case. Their decision helped the cause of slave owners and infuriated abolitionists. While denying Dred Scott and his family freedom, they declared the *Missouri Compromise* to be unconstitutional, insuring slavery in all states and territories. This was a decision that helped propel the nation toward civil war.

After the verdict, Taylor Blow set Dred and his family free. Dred's taste of freedom was short-lived. He died about a year later.

It took a month for mail to get to California. Congress authorized the Postmaster General to spend whatever it took to improve this service. John Butterfield, a popular Southerner, was awarded a franchise. The Postal Service would send the mail by wagon to St. Louis and Memphis, where the mail would be ferried across the Mississippi River to be picked up by The Butterfield Overland Mail Service.

Butterfield's main purpose was to deliver mail. However, the mail service was allowed to make additional money by hauling passengers as well. The Federal government subsidized this franchise to the tune of $600,000.

Butterfield purchased 1,000 horses, 500 mules, and 100 Concord Coaches. They established way stations every 10 miles. They hired 750 men to operate these stations, drive the gaudy red and green coaches, or to ride shotgun.

It cost three cents to send a letter "By the Overland Mail"; it was necessary to mark these words on your letter. It cost passengers $200 to travel to San Francisco, $100 to return to St. Louis.

During the "gold rush" of 1849, one of the quickest ways to get to California was to take the steamboat to Venezuela, the train across country, and another steamboat up to California. Cornelius Vanderbilt and some New York investors built the railroad in Venezuela.

In 1855, the train line in Panama was completed and the trip by train was much shorter than the one across Venezuela.

This trip took about 35 days. The mail coach left every
Monday and Wednesday and the trip took about 25 days. The
St. Louis route and the Memphis route merged at Fayetteville,
Arkansas, and headed west.

• • •

Taylor loved fantasy stories, from fairy tales to Norse
mythology to stories of knights and dragons. On his birthday,
our family celebrated by taking a cruise on the *Pole Cat*. I
wanted Taylor to see a new St. Louis landmark, Picot's Castle.

Louis Picot built his castle and parapets from stone hauled
from his own quarry to the tall hill next to St. Joseph's
Convent. Even with supplying most of the material, the project
cost him close to $40,000. The four-story high tower was
magnificent and could be seen for miles. Riverboat pilots went
out of their way to see it. Taylor was delighted with the castle,
and so were we.

Vacation

1858. We received a letter sent "By the Overland Mail" from the Reyburn family of San Francisco. They invited MJ, the children, and me to attend the wedding of their daughter, Virginia, to our son, George. What? George wrote regularly and never mentioned that he was seeing anyone!

The Reyburns offered to pay our passage to San Francisco and back, a whopping $2,100. Also, they would put us up. MJ was ecstatic. Odin's Beard! There was no way I was getting out of this trip.

MJ, Taylor, Cornelia, Sophie, Ludy, Anna, and I went. James and Larry stayed behind to "take care of business." James hated missing George's wedding but his knee was acting up again. I envied them. Traveling two thousand miles across country with five women and a seven-year-old boy is probably a form of punishment in hell.

The women complained about everything. "This coach is too small." "It's too hot!" "It's too cold." "Does he have to hit every bump in the road?" "Are we there yet?"

The coach was designed to carry six passengers on the inside and one to ten passengers on top. I took up a lot of space and it was crowded. Taylor and I spent a great deal of time riding on the top of the coach.

The stagecoach stopped at way stations every ten miles. We picked up the occasional passenger, but none of them were going as far as we were. I was grateful for the company of another man, no matter how brief. The coach changed horses frequently, drivers less frequently. One of the saving graces of

the journey was the affability of the drivers. They were
friendly and courteous and, in many cases, downright
entertaining.

Some way stations were clean; others were appallingly
filthy. At our driver's advice, we didn't go into several places.
We endured extreme heat and cold. It was a hard, hard journey.

We traveled west to Warsaw, then south to Springfield,
then further south to Fayetteville. Down south again to Fort
Smith, then southwest the rest of the way to Fort Belknap, Fort
Chadbourne, El Paso, Fort Yuma, and Los Angeles.

The last 100 miles or so to Los Angeles was all desert. It
was abominably hot. As we approached the city, I thought,
"This is madness. What kind of fools would build a city on this
infernal wasteland?"

As we headed north to San Francisco, the air got cooler
and the ground cover greener. There were fields of wild
flowers on the east side of the coastal road and stark cliffs and
the Pacific Ocean on the west. We marveled at the incredible
beauty. My first sight of San Francisco Bay was one of the
highlights of the trip.

The cities I named were main mail pickup sites, but people
also left mail at way stations and sometimes flagged us down
on the road. On some stretches of the trip, the driver wouldn't
stop for anybody, claiming it was too dangerous, too many
brigands.

Sometimes people raced up to the coach and chucked mail
through the window. Not knowing their purpose kept me on
my toes. I was wearing my pistol and had my rifle tied down
on my luggage. When I rode up top, I untied my weapon and
held it across my lap. The driver and guard welcomed extra
artillery.

When we arrived in San Francisco, our conditions
improved greatly. The Reyburns were well-to-do and treated us
like royalty. George's father-in-law, Eugene, was an engaging
fellow, born and raised in Tennessee. He arrived in San
Francisco in '49 and saw the folly of trying to compete in the
already overcrowded gold fields.

Realizing the miners would need something on which to

spend their gold, he sank his fortune into several dance halls. They were hugely successful, and he used the capital gained from this endeavor to go into the import/export business. He made a fortune, invested wisely, and then married the daughter of a newspaper owner.

They lived on Nob Hill. I got the impression his wife, Cora, thought her daughter was too good for my son. George's only saving grace was the fact that he was a graduate of West Point.

Cora didn't know what to think of us, especially MJ. I hit it off with George's future father-in-law. When all was said and done, we were birds of a feather. I called him Reyburn and he called me Bissell.

Reyburn, Taylor, and I went to the Presidio for George's bachelor party. He told me that meeting George was the best thing that ever happened to his strong-willed daughter. She thought women were treated as second-class citizens and needed to do something about their position in life. Reyburn said he wondered if Virginia hated men. George certainly disproved that theory.

My son-in-law, Henry Haight, was the Reyburn's lawyer. That's how Virginia met George. Queenie convinced Henry to play matchmaker. That was my Queenie, all right, always sticking her nose in other people's affairs.

(They say behind every successful man there's a good woman. Years later, Henry Haight would become the Governor of California.)

Mrs. Van Snoot, as George and I privately called her, arranged Virginia's bachelorette party, a trip to the theater to see Shakespeare's *Macbeth*. MJ and the girls dressed in their best clothes and were delighted to go. They loved the theater.

The women were in the theater lobby waiting for Queenie. Thinking MJ and the girls might not understand the play, Cora thought it necessary to explain *Macbeth*.

She began, "Shakespeare is difficult to understand, even for the well-educated. *Macbeth* is such an intricate play. So many names. Mac this and Mac that. Perhaps I can make it easier for you to follow the story. Let's, see. Where shall I begin?"

MJ said, "Girls, where should she begin?"

Cornelia suggested, "You could start where Macbeth and Banquo meet the three witches."

Sophie followed, "And they tell Macbeth he will be King of Scotland and that Banquo's descendants will be King as well."

Ludy said, "And they warn him about MacDuff."

MJ cackled, *"No man born of woman can harm him."*

The girls applauded MJ's performance.

Anna said, "I like the part where Macbeth decides to murder King Duncan but gets cold feet. Lady Macbeth convinces him to do the foul deed. Do the voice, Sophie."

Sophie deepened her voice and played MacBeth,
"Come thick night,
And pall thee in dunnest smoke of hell,
That my keen knife see not the wound it makes
Nor heaven peep through the blanket of the dark
To cry, 'Hold! Hold!"

The girls applauded Sophie, who curtsied. A small crowd joined in the applause.

Ludy continued, "Macbeth murders Duncan. Lady Macbeth covers up the murder. Mother?"

MJ followed in the role of Lady MacBeth,
"Come you spirits
That tend on mortal thought, use me here
And fill me from the crown to the toe top full
Of direst cruelty! Make thick my blood!"

The crowd applauded as Queenie walked up.

MJ pointed at Queenie and cackled, *"Fair is fair, and foul is foul."*

Queenie asked, "Did I miss something?"

Cora didn't know what to think after that little performance and didn't say much the rest of the evening.

• • •

I enjoyed the wedding, but the specter of the return trip hung over my head the whole time. We stayed an extra week and saw a great deal of the San Francisco area. It has to be one of the most beautiful places on earth. Against Reyburn's wishes, I paid for our trip to San Francisco. It was the least I could do. He spent a small fortune on the wedding.

On our return trip, we traveled in a larger coach, an eight-seater. Some of the newer coaches were capable of carrying sixteen passengers inside and another eight to ten up top.

In Oklahoma, we were joined by Ward Lamon, U.S. Marshal, and his prisoner, a young fellow who wished to remain anonymous. Marshal Lamon was taking him to Washington, D.C., to testify for the prosecution in a Federal case. I looked at the handcuffs his witness was wearing and felt a little sorry for him. This was going to be a long, uncomfortable trip for him.

Before he boarded the stage, Marshal Lamon warned the dispatcher, "Tell your driver not to stop the coach for anyone. I'll plug anyone who violates this procedure."

The dispatcher knew his teamsters occasionally made

exceptions to this rule, so he warned them, "You got a federal marshal on board. You better go by the book. When you get to your transfer point, tell the new drivers."

During the trip, the Marshal told us, "It's a good thing we're taking the southern route. There's some serious border business between Missouri and Kansas again. Looks like bad blood between those two states will never end."

I responded, "You got that right. Those hard-headed Kansans just won't listen to reason."

MJ was sitting across from me. She kicked me in the shin.

We stopped at the last way station in Oklahoma, where we changed horses and drivers. The old driver told his replacement, "You got a U.S. Marshall on board and he means business. Don't stop the coach for anybody."

The relief driver said, "I'll keep it in mind. Looks like y'all have to scrounge a meal for yourselves. Charlie Patch took sick and went home." *(Later, Charlie's body was found in the well.)*

I thought it odd that the new stagecoach driver and guard looked familiar to me. Obviously, they were brothers. I swear I saw them somewhere before but just couldn't remember where. I asked the driver his name and he brushed me off with, "You writing a book?"

I didn't think much of it. Some people are just plain unsociable. I met the guard as I entered the station. I asked him, "What's your name, son?"

He growled, "People get hurt sticking their noses in places they don't belong, old man."

What the hell was going on here?

We were halfway to the last way station before you get to Springfield, Missouri, when it dawned on me just where I had seen these two—on the wanted posters Queenie kept in her room. I couldn't remember their first names, but they were the Jackson brothers, members of a gang wanted for robbing mail coaches in Illinois. The Marshal and his witness were sitting right across from me. It didn't take me long to put two and two together.

I waited until we came to a wooded area, thickets of trees on both sides of the road. I leaned over to the Marshall and said, "We need to stop."

He started to protest but I didn't give him the chance to speak. I repeated, "Marshall, we need to stop."

He sighed and hollered out the window, "Pull over."

The driver cursed, but his brother, riding shotgun, said, "Pull over. I gotta go, too."

The driver spit out a big chaw of tobacco and stopped the stage.

It was hot and dusty and we had consumed a lot of water. We stopped several times a day to take Taylor into the brush to relieve himself. I would apologize and say things like, "Sorry, the little guy just can't hold his water as well as big fellows."

I'd never admit it, but I was glad for every stop myself. The man riding shotgun was drinking something other than water and needed the comfort stops just as much as we did. The driver was a better man than all of us. He didn't run into the bushes once; he just stayed on the shady side of the stage, rolled himself a cigarette, and smoked. How he could smoke and chew tobacco was beyond me.

I whispered to Marshal Lamon, "Come with me and bring your witness. It's an emergency."

As we alighted, his prisoner started to gripe. The Marshal pulled his pistol, stuck it in the young man's ribs, and quietly told him, "Shut up."

As we walked past some trees down into a gully, the ladies got out to stretch their legs. I'm sure that when we were out of earshot they made wisecracks about our inability to hold our water.

After Taylor relieved himself, I sent him back to MJ. When we were alone, the Marshal told his captive, "Take care of business, whether you need to or not."

As the young felon tried to pass water, I told the Marshal about our stage hands. He nodded and glanced through the trees to where the shotgun rider stood, his back to us, oblivious of transpiring events.

Marshal Lamon said, "I had a gut feeling about those two, but I couldn't get a handle on it."

He thanked me and asked me to watch his prisoner, offering me a pistol. I patted my own pistol and said, "I'll use this if absolutely necessary, but I can handle this little runt without it."

The Marshall displayed a truncheon and left.

As the prisoner turned to face me, I grabbed him by the collar and lifted him up. The young man's eyes went wide as his feet left the ground. With my free hand, I put my index finger to my lip, signaling for silence. As I turned my hand, his shirt collar tightened around his neck until he put an index finger to his own lips and nodded yes. I don't like to be cruel but my family's welfare was at risk.

I looked uphill. The chubby shotgun rider was puffing back up the steep incline out of the gully. The Marshal came up behind him and clubbed him, knocking him senseless.

I held my fist in the kid's face and whispered, "Stay quiet and I won't hurt you."

He stared at my massive fist and said in a voice so low I could barely hear him, "I promise."

I pulled my pistol and put it in his back and we headed up the hill after the Marshal, who had just finished putting a spare set of handcuffs on his new prisoner. We peeked through the trees. We could see the driver's legs by looking under the stagecoach. He was in his usual spot, most likely puffing on a coffin nail. The Marshal and I stepped out, about ten yards from the wagon. I prodded my prisoner with my gun and signaled danger to MJ.

(Families who live most of their lives on the frontier develop hand signals to speak over large distances.)

MJ signaled quiet to the kids. As she and the children joined us, I whispered to her, "Take over."

The Marshal looked on, surprised as MJ pulled her derringer from under her skirt. MJ made the young man sit on the ground and stood behind him. She placed the derringer under his ear. She whispered, "Just sit still, sweetie, and I won't add a hole to your head."

He was too frightened to even look back.

I signaled to the Marshal that I would circle around the back of the wagon. He headed for the front. I holstered my pistol and came around the side.

As I approached the driver, he became more alert and dropped his hand down near his sidearm. I asked him, "Got a chaw?"

He hesitated, then pulled out his tobacco. By then, the marshal had silently climbed into the shotgun rider's seat and picked up the shotgun. He slid into the driver's seat and coughed. When the driver looked up, he was staring at twin barrels. He put his hands up and I reached from behind and took his weapon. The Marshal told him, "Turn around," then he knocked him unconscious with the truncheon.

He flashed the truncheon at me and, with a smile reminiscent of MJ's, said, "You'd be surprised what this thing's good for. I've even used it to drive nails."

We untied the luggage and freed my rifle, placing the re-stacked luggage on top of the coach until it was as flat as we could get it. Then we placed our two new prisoners on their backs on top of the luggage and tied them down. Marshal Lamon wasn't too gentle with those boys. He placed the last length of the rope across their throats and snugged it down tight. He said, "I wouldn't try to move too much if I were you. Keep your mouths shut and I won't gag you."

The Marshal took the reins and I occupied the guard seat. MJ looked after the witness in the coach, the shotgun across her lap. The little weasel was so scared of MJ we knew he wouldn't be any trouble.

Not knowing who else and how many people would be on the stage, the Marshal figured the Jackson brothers would have help waiting somewhere with horses and gear. We figured they planned to bushwhack us at some spot near cover or make a move at a rest stop. We went off road on several occasions to avoid close quarters. It was rough, but safer. Marshal Lamon said, "Let's bypass the way station and head straight into Springfield."

It was a good thing we did.

There's a fork in the road. The trail to the left takes you down a long hill to a way station in the shelter of a cliff and then back to the main road. The right fork was the main road into Springfield, a trail first used by pioneers heading west and drovers going east to Springfield to bring cattle to market. No longer. Kansas City was now the premier cattle market.

Anyway, we took the right fork into Springfield and stopped at the sheriff's office. The Law took the Jackson brothers off our hands and rounded up a posse. We went to The Butterfield Overland Mail Service office and told our story. They were extremely apologetic and supplied us with a new driver and guard.

When we arrived in Warsaw, two telegrams awaited us. The Marshal received a telegram from the Springfield sheriff, who told us our instincts were good—the rest of the Jackson gang was waiting at the way station. The sheriff and his posse took them by surprise and captured them without firing a round.

The other telegram was from The Butterfield Overland Mail Service main office. They were grateful to get their coach and team back undamaged, and because of the tremendous inconvenience we suffered, they would refund all passengers' money for the return trip. We were astounded. I told Marshall Lamon, "Maybe Butterfield was afraid we'd sue."

Lamon replied, "Bopping those numbskulls on the head was worth it."

• • •

Crazy John, James Eads, and a group of businessmen pitched in to build the O'Fallon Polytechnical School, a place where people could be trained in manufacturing skills. After all, St. Louis was the manufacturing center of the state and skilled labor was a real boon. It took nine years to build the darn thing and Crazy John died before it was completed. In 1868, they sold the school to the St. Louis Public School System.

Our Town

1859. I turned 70 and my hair was completely white, but at least I had a full head of it. Luckily, I was in truly remarkable health. I read in the paper that Charles Darwin, an English naturalist, proposed what he called the *Theory of Evolution*.

According to Darwin, everything develops in stages. Living things change in form and ability to deal with the environment in which they exist. These changes are gradual, usually minute in nature, and the results are scarcely noticed because of the slowness of the process. Then viola! Something old becomes something new.

I wondered if that's what happened to me. Was I a—what did he call it—a mutant?

Many thought Darwin was a crackpot or a soul-less charlatan. Religious organizations denounced his ideas as heresy. I wasn't sure. It was such a common-sense idea.

MJ sided with religious authority and was reluctant to listen when I talked to her about Darwin's theory. I used myself as an example, "I'm different from many of my contemporaries. I've had my share of serious injuries but I heal more quickly than most. I seem to be immune to deadly diseases around me, like the fever that killed so many soldiers at Fort Bellefontaine, and the cholera plagues."

MJ countered, "You are blessed by God and haven't suffered such conditions because of virtuousness."

I muttered, "Oh brother."

"You work hard and never let any man do work you wouldn't or couldn't do yourself. The Lord wouldn't desert a man like that. Darwin needs to read his Bible and, it appears, so do you."

After that little lecture, I dropped the subject. I believe that trying to convince others that your belief is the be-all end-all smacks of presumption and arrogance. I took particular care not to voice this opinion around MJ. Let sleeping dogs lie.

Both Cornelia and Sophie got married in 1859. Cornie married Andrew Provine, a professional actor she met while working box office at The Old Salt Theater. Sophie married Richard Cheney, a lineman for the telegraph company.

Tom Miller was in ill health for the past few years and missed a lot of work. He finally became too sick to work at all. Sam Wiggins was semi-retired. He let his son Samson and his nephew Billy handle the ferryboats while he worked the trading post.

Occasionally, Sam joined me on the *Pole Cat.* He and I hauled Richard Cheney and his crew back and forth across the river and to several island locales. The telegraph company was still trying to figure out a way to run lines across the Mississippi River that would last for more than a couple of days. It was a tough proposition for Richard and his crew.

We held the weddings on our front lawn and receptions in our home. Many people attended both weddings.

Oddly, it was the beginning of an enlightening time for me. Influenced by Darwin's suppositions, I found myself taking a different look at everybody. My observations led me to believe that maybe Machingo and Nahaboo knew the real truth. They spoke of totems and animal spirits that guide us and how we reflect this animal spirit, and how we may even resemble this spiritual guide. The more people I saw, the more I began to see how they could hold such a belief.

I met scrawny, bespectacled men who looked like owls, huge men who resembled bears, and fierce-looking men who bore the aspect of wolves. I beheld long-necked women who looked like swans and chinless females likened to turkeys, squishy faced people with the face of ducks, and short, squat, short-nosed people with the guise of hogs.

I knew many couples who grew to resemble one another. I had to ask myself. Are we thinking animals who conjure up ideas such as spirits and immortality to assuage the fear of death, or are we spirits having a human experience?

I ferried a man across the river and we got to talking about evolution. He was an odd-looking fellow. His hair looked like it was combed by a tornado. He wore leather and had a string of nasty-looking teeth around his neck. Curiosity got the better of me so I said, "Nice necklace. Who's the original owner?"

He jangled the teeth and answered, "A dinosaur."

"A dinosaur?" I took a closer look. "What's your name?"

"Berdak. My parents named me Keith but my friends call me Bad News."

"Why's that?"

"Well, they say I'm a doom-sayer. I'm what you call a naturalist, something akin to a Native American. I study the environment and the effect we humans have on it."

"I take it you don't have a high opinion of our effect on it."

"We're like lead in the belly. We just don't belong here. Look at your city. How many cholera epidemics will it take before they stop dumping crud in the river? The buildings are black with soot and the air is foul. That's really healthy. Everyday more trees are felled and land is being cleared for expansion. Eventually there'll be no more wildlife and way too many people. Soon, pollution and disease will wipe us out. We'll be extinct, like the dinosaur."

"Soon?"

"Geologically speaking, yes. In human years, no. We probably have another 5,000 years. Maybe."

"That's a relief. Sounds like we still have time for lunch. Join me?"

He did and we discussed Darwin's theory. For a scientist, he had a funny way of looking at things. He made me laugh all through lunch.

While sitting on the porch after lunch, I posed my question to him, "Well, Bad News, what do you think? Are we just thinking animals or are we spirits?"

He scratched the back of his head and then finally answered, "We're dinosaurs."

I was sorry to see him go.

• • •

The family and I went on a riverboat excursion to visit New Madrid. The aftermath of the earthquakes was still evident. It was unbelievable. There were jumbled piles of stone and 5-mile-long fissures filled in with black rock. New Madrid had been a large city, the center of Spanish power in America. Half the city was washed away in the earthquakes as riverbanks collapsed and carried the detritus away to help form Reel Foot Lake in Kentucky. We all went away with a renewed sense of respect for the power of Mother Nature.

John Clemens and his investment group in Hannibal had a good year. The Hannibal and St. Joseph Railroad became the first railroad to be completed across the state of Missouri. The Hannibal-St. Joe would eventually have to sell their line to Kansas City to the Missouri Pacific Railroad, which had already paid for this access.

St. Louis always had its fair share of pest and rodents, like any city. We had seven-year locust plagues and brown beetle swarms. The crow population increased fivefold in 1859. For Machingo, these visitations were harbingers of ominous events.

When we first arrived in St. Louis, we saw the occasional rat. After all, we were near the river. As the city grew, so did the rat population, another tenet of civilization.

This year, there were rats everywhere. In my neighbor-hood, we joined forces to fight them. Armed with clubs, we smoked the rats out of their tunnels. When the rats emerged, we beat them to death with the clubs. Darwin called it "survival of the fittest."

I called it a dirty job.

Speaking of dirty, so many businesses and homes used coal for fuel to boil water for steam heat that the city was slowly becoming covered with soot. Some days the sky looked dirty. Crazy John thought the clouds of soot affected the weather. Maybe so. Tom Miller's lungs were befouled and he died from what the doctor called "consumption."

I read in the paper that Junior Chouteau was suffering from some sort of blood malady and his vision was failing. His New York physician called his blood condition a family trait with varying consequences. His physician even sought the advice of naturalist Charles Darwin.

Other specialists were consulted. They gave lip service to the advancement of science and the evolution of medicine. Heimdall's Horn! Junior better have his "B.S." sniffer working. With "evolutionary medicine" will come the "evolutionary snake oil salesman."

• • •

By 1860, there were three million slaves in the United States. Slavery had been outlawed in almost every other civilized country, and animosity between abolitionists and slave owners grew. There was a tension in the air. Claiborne Fox Jackson, a pro-slaver, was elected governor of Missouri.

The St. Louis economy was booming. With statewide train service and 60% of the state's industrial output, St. Louis was "the city" in Missouri.

Navigating the river was a challenge. In 1860 over 100 steamboats a day unloaded more than a million tons of cargo at St. Louis wharves. Our ferryboat business nearly doubled and we couldn't handle all the traffic. We actually welcomed competition.

Crazy John's personal economy boomed as well. According to the paper, after all his philanthropic efforts and charity donations, his net worth was $8,000,000.

Governor Fox Jackson and his compatriots worried the rising fortunes of the City of St. Louis in the national economy would solidify its ties with the industrialized North. With a little help from his friends, he initiated a state-appointed board of police commissioners for the City of St. Louis in an effort to have a large police force at his beck and call.

The crow population doubled again and crow dung was everywhere. Huge flocks flew over and temporarily blotted out the sun. Sam Wiggins took an occasional pot shot at them, an act that drew the ire of the local constabulary. Now that we were part of the City of St. Louis, discharging weapons inside city limits was prohibited.

Californians were still complaining about the amount of time it took for news from Washington, D.C., to get to the West Coast. Russell and Waddell, freight haulers since 1850, came up with the idea of The Pony Express. They received a commission from the U.S. government to carry the mail west from St. Joseph, Missouri, to Sacramento, California, by pony rider.

The ad they proffered for riders became the topic of conversation everywhere, even at our dinner table. For $25.00 a week, expert riders, 18 or under, preferably orphans, were needed to risk their lives hauling mail 75 miles a day by pony. Buffalo Bill Cody once rode 300 miles in one day. In the 18 months The Pony Express was in business, a couple of riders died but not one bag of mail was lost. By 1861, telegraph lines were completed across the country and The Pony Express went the way of the dinosaur.

• • •

DAN PATTERSON

On 29 January 1861, Kansas, the *Sunflower State,* was admitted to the Union as the 34th state.

A short time later, the St. Louis Railway Company came into existence. Its president was William Sherman. At the foot of the hill on which my mansion stood, beginning at the intersection of East Grand and North Broadway, track was laid south to downtown and then to South St. Louis. The horse-drawn railcars contained comfortable seating and affable conductors.

George and Virginia had their first child. They named my new grandson Eugene after Virginia's father. MJ voiced some displeasure, but not me. They could have named him Abe after our new President for all I cared. A name's a name.

War

*E*arly in the year, several states voted to secede from the Union and the Confederate States of America came into existence. By April, there was armed conflict and more states joined the CSA. Robert E. Lee took the reins of commanding general of the rebel army.

It seemed like only yesterday I was hauling Lee up and down the Mississippi River on a mission for the Union Army. He told me engineering was his first love. At any rate, the Civil War had begun.

Back in 1836, in an editorial in his newspaper, the *St. Louis Observer,* old Elijah Lovejoy tried to convince everyone that slavery was a sin. Good, church-going Christian slave owners debated him. Now Americans were killing Americans. There's no debate here. Fratricide may be the worst sin.

At the start of the war, there were more Union soldiers in Missouri than any state in the Union. Lincoln's first Secretary of War, Simon Cameron, sent word to John C. Fremont, who was the leader of the Union Army in Missouri and T.H. Benton's son-in-law, to cease building forts around the city of St. Louis. The city was so divided Cameron thought the effort was a waste of time. He figured there would be as much fighting inside the forts as outside.

Fremont disobeyed this directive. He was certain St. Louis would be attacked from the west by rebels intent on raiding the huge arsenal just south of downtown. So he built ten forts around the city, star-shaped like French garrisons, with lines of sight that could catch the enemy in a deadly crossfire.

Fremont set up an artillery battery around Bissell Point because of its elevation. My family and I tried to help by doing things like providing cold water on hot days or using my keelboat to fetch more rounds from the downtown arsenal for their cannons.

The artillerymen respected the fact that I was an old soldier and they seemed to enjoy my war stories. They warned me before they fired their cannons so I could open the doors and windows to my house. Otherwise, the explosive concussions would blow out my windows. They "forgot" to warn the people they didn't like.

The Army had a limited number of horses and cavalry at the beginning of the war and they wanted to increase the size of the U.S. Cavalry. They established two U.S. Corrals, huge holding pens for horses. The eastern corral was just outside of Baltimore, Maryland, and the western corral was here in St. Louis, not far from St. Louis University.

The corral could hold close to 10,000 horses, but the most it ever held was about half that amount. I can attest that's a lot of horses. We hauled more horses across the river than I can count.

All four regiments of the Missouri Dragoons *(the name comes from the way their muskets spat fire like a dragon)* consolidated with the U.S. Cavalry in 1861. Two dragoon regiments equaled one cavalry regiment.

I knew several dragoons from the days they worked for Marshal Henry Dodge. They thought the Army was in for a rude awakening. Putting inexperienced riders on horses going into battle for the first time would only result in panic and slaughter. They were right.

Fox Jackson, the Governor of Missouri, called a session of the Missouri legislature at Neosho and they passed a secession order.

A state convention was held in Jefferson City to unseat Jackson. Hamilton R. Gamble was a law partner and brother-in-law of Edward Bates, President Lincoln's Attorney General.

Gamble was elected governor of the pro-Union provisional government to replace Jackson. Fox Jackson claimed he was still the governor and his "government in absentia" spent the Civil War years trying to avoid capture.

Two governors? One is bad enough.

• • •

The Missouri Militia, which always looked very smart in their gray uniforms, became a part of the Confederate forces. They mustered in Lindell Grove *(Camp Jackson)* to honor Elihu Shepard, a militia member and a veteran of the War of 1812 and the Mexican War.

Out of curiosity, James and I went to the ceremony. Larry let us use his carriage, but he stayed home for obvious reasons. I couldn't believe the size of the crowd. Just about everyone in St. Louis was there.

Captain Nathaniel Lyon, the commandant of the U.S. Arsenal in St. Louis, thought the Militia was using the ceremony as an excuse, that they really came to town to raid the arsenal. Union soldiers, mostly volunteers, surrounded Camp Jackson and took the Militia prisoner. Major Bernard Farrar, Doc Bernie's son, delivered the demand to surrender to General Frost, the Missouri Militia leader.

After the Union Army moved in, the crowd outside the grove, a nasty mix of abolitionists and southern sympathizers, turned ugly. James and I decided it was best to head home.

We were just a few blocks away when we heard a single gun shot. Then we heard a thunderous volley. A few minutes later, we heard another gunshot, followed by another volley, more gunfire, and another volley. Then silence.

James turned the carriage around and we made our way back to the site of the fracas. I've seen Indian massacres and battlefields soaked with the blood of my companions in arms. This "slaughter of the innocents" was the most compellingly gruesome sight of all. Civilians and soldiers were dead. The wounded, writhing on the ground in pain, cried for help. The bullets didn't discriminate—age, sex, or color didn't matter.

A soldier, Corporal Adolphus Busch, asked us if we would

transport wounded in our carriage. Of course we agreed. As he
and his father-in-law, Private Eberhard Anheuser, helped us put
wounded in the carriage, they told us what happened.

As the last few soldiers left the grove, bayonets fixed,
people shouted insults and hurled stones. Someone fired a shot
and the volunteers fired a volley above the heads of the crowd.
The person who fired the shot tried shooting again but his gun
misfired. A soldier bayoneted him in the belly. A shot rang out
from elsewhere. This time the volunteers fired into the crowd,
killing over three dozen people and wounding many others.
There were more gunshots and Union soldiers and Missouri
Militiamen alike fell to the ground. After the next volley, the
gunfire stopped.

William Sherman and his son, who were in the crowd,
escaped serious injury. Sherman had just arrived after
receiving word the Militia had surrendered without a fight. The
event inspired Sherman to retake his commission. If he was
going to be shot, it might as well be in uniform.

James and I hauled wounded people to the medical
facilities at the Marine Hospital, a medical clinic set up for
sick or disabled boatmen. Part of the boatmen's fees collected
by the City Port Authority paid for this facility. It was just
south of downtown.

Other wounded were taken to the McDowell School of
Medicine, the medical department of the University of
Missouri until 1857, when it came under the sole proprietor-
ship of its founder and director, Doctor Joseph McDowell.

Located at 12th & Gratiot, it was one of the first schools in
the United States to use cadavers to teach medicine. This upset
many people. Mad Joe, as he was called behind his back, was
eccentric and many likened him to Mary Shelley's Doctor
Frankenstein.

A known southern sympathizer, he later fled to the South.
His college was confiscated by the Union and transformed into
the infamous Gratiot Street Prison for Confederate P.O.W.s.

• • •

Troops poured into St. Louis from neighboring states east of the Mississippi. John C. Fremont rented 150 acres of land just west of the fairgrounds from *(guess who?)* Crazy John O'Fallon and established Camp Benton, named in honor of T.H. Benton. The name was eventually changed to Benton Barracks. Late in 1861, General William Sherman was considered unfit for combat duty and was relegated to commander of this post.

Larry heard that the U.S. Corral was over half full, housing over 5,000 horses. We rode over to witness the spectacle. We could hear the thunder of hooves as we approached—a sound that struck a chord deep within me. The cadence rose and fell and I imagined the horses were tapping out a message, "Free us, free us!"

Darwin would probably tell me I'm evolving into a Native American!

In the crowd gathered at the corral, I met an amusing sort of braggart from Hannibal, Sam Clemens. He told me he came to St. Louis to visit his uncle and to write an article about the horses. Sam was a reporter and he wrote controversial articles under the pseudonym, Mark Twain.

I asked him, "Why not use your given name?"

He replied, "I don't want my father to suffer embarrassment from something I write. I'll take my own lumps."

"Are you joining up to fight?"

"Oh, I reckon not." He looked at the horses. "I spent two weeks in the Missouri Militia, but when it became part of the Confederate Army, I decided it wasn't for me."

He spent the rest of the Civil War as an observer.

• • •

In August, Gideon Weeks, Secretary of the Navy, visited the St. Louis shipyards at the suggestion of Edward Bates. Impressed by the engine-building capability of St. Louis foundries and the ship-building ability of the dock yards, the Carondelet Marine Railway and Dock Company, under the supervision of James Eads, was awarded a contract to build ironclads for the U.S. Navy.

These fine St. Louis shipbuilders completed the first
ironclad for the Navy, the *St. Louis,* on my 72nd birthday,
12 October 1861. In 1862, the U.S. Navy renamed it the *Baron
DeKalb* because they already had commissioned a ship
christened *St. Louis.*

The Carondelet Marine Railway and Dock Company
continued to build ironclads, mortar rafts, and gunboats for the
Navy. The boat builders earned the admiration of many top
military men, Ulysses Grant included.

1861 witnessed battles in Missouri at Wilson's Creek,
Salem, Springfield, and Lexington. The mind-boggling number
of men who fought and died in these battles and the utter
destruction of small towns like Athens and Belmont brought
home the price many paid in this war.

The Battle of Shawnee Mound, the site of a sacred Indian
burial ground, infuriated not just the Shawnee but all Native
Americans. I knew my old friend, Machingo, would find such
barbaric behavior an offense to the spirit world.

Speaking of the spirit world, I haven't seen any of their
"messengers to the dead" lately. Good riddance. I was sick of
cleaning up after them. I don't even want to think about where
they've gone. You know. The crows.

• • •

1862. War or no war, Cupid stays busy. We had another
quick romance, quick engagement, and quick wedding. Ludy
married Samuel May, a dry goods salesman, who had just
joined the 3rd Home Guard. I still don't know what all the fuss
was about. It wasn't like Samuel was going anywhere.

Bernie Farrar, Jr, was appointed Provost Marshall General,
a post that gives wartime authority to the appointee to take
whatever police action necessary to insure the peace of a
region. It was a tough position that called for tough decisions
about issues such as escaped slaves and censorship.

I'm not sure his father would agree with some of Bernie's
decisions. Crazy John and I didn't. Bernie ordered several
"disloyal" newspapers closed, in effect, withdrawing the right
of free speech. Many people sitting on the fence or just out and

out indifferent were so enraged they cast their lot with the South.

Jefferson Barracks was converted into a medical facility. Wounded soldiers, from battles as far away as Tennessee, were sent here for treatment, enhancing its reputation as a major military hospital. People told me the crows were back and lining the trees near the barracks.

Battles at Pea Ridge, Kirksville, and Lone Jack indicated there was no real line between the two sides in this war in Missouri. The citizens of St. Louis and its volunteer troops were forever vigilant, still expecting an attack from the west. The massacres at Macon and Palmyra reminded us that "civilization" is an illusory concept.

Jefferson Davis became the President of the Confederate States of America. I had trouble envisioning him in that role. The images of him etched in my memory as a young and happy-go-lucky soldier were strong. The hours we spent on the river were spent in spirited and humorous discussions. The people around here, myself included, were grateful for his diligence in routing his patrols so he and his troops could check on the welfare of the settlers in this vicinity. I knew he was a good man. History will probably portray him as a villain.

War is a game of waiting and worrying. Humans are resilient. To relieve psychological distress, soldiers need outlets. During my time at Fort Bellefontaine, soldiers gambled or took part in contests of skill. In the midst of all the turmoil and grief of the Civil War, I watched an interesting phenomenon develop.

New troops joined the artillery unit surrounding my house. A couple of New Englanders who had served under General Abner Doubleday brought with them a new game, baseball.

Baseball was originally called "rounders" by the British, then "Indian ball" by Americans. The game was altered when Alexander Cartwright developed a new set of rules. Baseball was further refined by Abner Doubleday.

The game was a popular off-duty activity with the soldiers.

They went to an open field by the river and played. My family and I sat up on the widow's walk and watched.

MJ didn't want me to go near the field. She knew I wanted to play and, at my age, I would get hurt. I wished I were younger. I'd like to see if I had what it took to hit a baseball, and as strong as I still was I felt I could hit it a long way.

The wooden clubs the players used to hit the baseball were called bats. Bremen had several fine mills and lumberyards. White pine was used to manufacture bats. It was floated down the river from Wisconsin and Minnesota forests in the form of log rafts. The millers formed teams and played against each other.

Barrel makers from the new Union Cooperage Company and local furniture makers also got in on the action and formed baseball teams as well. They also competed to see who could produce the finest bat.

I think this game may have a future here.

Colors

1863. On January 1st, President Lincoln issued his *Emancipation Proclamation.* This decree declared freedom for all Negro slaves in all States, including territories still in rebellion against the Union. The Dutch followed suit and abolished slavery in their country.

Some slaves were able to escape their owners and they headed north. There was still no bridge across the Mississippi River so Missouri slaves needed a way to get over to Illinois, a "free" state. Finders started hanging out at the ferry landing.

Larry spent one morning helping Sam Wiggins at the trading post. Lunch was ready and MJ asked me to fetch him. We left the trading post and headed up the hill. Some ornery slave stalker stepped in front of us. He had waist-length silver hair and bad breath.

He asked me, "This your nigger?"

"No, this is Larry."

"He got papers?"

"He's got 'em. You'll have to take my word for it."

"Mister, I usually don't pistol-whip old men, but in your case, I'll make an exception."

He had his pistol halfway out of the holster when I smacked him flush on the chin. He went up and then he went down, out cold before he hit the ground. I kicked his gun away and Larry picked it up.

"Remove the bullets, Larry, and give me the gun."

Sam threw a bucket of water on the slave chaser and he woke up sputtering. I grabbed him by the front of his shirt and jerked him up, holding him a couple of inches off the ground. I stuffed his pistol in his holster and told him, "Hit the road."

When he came back with friends, Union troops operating the artillery batteries surrounding my house helped Larry, Sam, and me run them off. These flesh traders claimed their rights were being violated! Can you imagine that?

We hid escaped slaves in the cavern below our house. When the river was low, Larry would lead them through the maze to the river and onto the *Pole Cat.* It was tougher to get them down to the boat when the river was high. Too many prying eyes.

One night, James came back with a crease in his skull. Larry said finders would try to track them on the river from the Illinois side and sometimes they'd take a pot shot at them. Tonight one of them got lucky. Larry said it was getting harder and harder to find a safe place to put in.

There was another battle at Springfield this year and hundreds of skirmishes over the rest of the state. In fact, during the Civil War, 1,162 engagements took place in Missouri, 11% of the total.

• • •

I'll bet the crows gathered in Lawrence, Kansas. There had been animosity between Kansas and Missouri for years. Boundary disputes led to lawsuits. The Jayhawks thought everyone in Missouri was a secessionist. Any Missourian claiming otherwise was a liar. Madness!

Over 115,000 Missourians served in the Union Army while only 30,000 men fought for the Confederacy. The total of 145,000 Missourians, 60% of men of military age, made Missouri first in proportion to population. I reiterate. Seventy-five percent of these Missourians fought for the Union. I guess they don't teach math in Kansas.

John Brown got himself hanged over the slavery issue. Kansas "Redlegs" would swoop into Missouri, shoot up a place and everyone in it, then go back to Kansas to brag about it. Their favorite gathering place was Lawrence.

Claiming to be an agent of retribution, Billy Quantrill

gathered a force of 450 Missourians and rode into Lawrence. His raiders shot and killed every man they saw and burned Lawrence to the ground. Then they looted the place.

Some Missourians saw Quantrill as a hero. I didn't, and most people agreed with my assessment. Murder and robbery aren't heroic deeds. The horrific raid on Lawrence guaranteed bad blood between these two states forever. All those men killed in cold blood. Now there was a feast for the crows with a very bitter taste to it.

Gangs of outlaws abounded. They called themselves Redlegs, Confederates, irregulars, or even abolitionists, but they were really just bushwhackers and guerillas who attacked and robbed people all over the states of Missouri and Kansas. Local lawmen didn't have the resources or resolve to deal with these bands of cutthroats. Many people left their farms and moved to cities like St. Louis and Kansas City.

Some people learn early that using anger gets them what they want. Their anger becomes a nasty habit. Lucky people come to realize that the continued practice of an "eye for an eye" leaves you blind and totally bereft of feeling and spirit.

The Kansas "Redlegs" and Quantrill's "Raiders" fell prey to what we Norse call the "cold anger," the desire for revenge. These men committed acts that dishonored them, unlike the "battle lust" or "berserker rage" that allowed my Norse heroes to commit great feats of strength and overcome superior enemies in the "heat" of battle.

A Norse warrior dying in honorable battle earns a place in Valhalla, where he'll engage in combat for all eternity. As a boy, I dreamed of such a death, but not anymore. Valhalla is not the place for me. I like the occasional day off.

• • •

I read in the paper there was a tremendous battle at a little town in southern Pennsylvania called Gettysburg. A certain Confederate victory was turned into a defeat for Lee and his troops. It was probably the turning point of the war. It was also a tragic day for parents, since over 100,000 of them lost sons that day.

After reading of this disaster, I climbed up to the widow's walk, wishing for the thousandth time I had made the entrance to the roof a little wider. I sat in my favorite chair, as was my wont these days. I watched the sky, and napped, woke up and watched the sky, and napped.

I dreamed more and more of people who had passed on—my father, my uncles, other loved ones, and old friends. Mary visited me often. Sometimes my visitors talked to me.

This day, I dreamed about little Lewis. I was standing in the downstairs hallway. The front door to my house was open and brilliant light flooded through it. In the midst of this glimmer stood my little Lewis. He extended his hand to me and said, "It's okay. You can come out and play now."

I awoke with a start and my heart fluttered. For a moment, I thought my old ticker was going to give out. I felt weak and it was a while before I could go back into the house. I truly felt mortal.

Let me tell you the family war story that occurred at a 4th of July celebration in Hyde Park.

The Farrar Mansion had been converted into a beer garden downstairs and a hotel upstairs. The park was jammed with people. Newspaper accounts of what happened this day would say nearly 10,000 people were in attendance, including close to 100 Union soldiers from Benton Barracks. Many of these soldiers were in the Army on the "go to prison or serve" option. They weren't our finest citizens. Also in the crowd were people who wore colored ribbons to identify themselves as southern sympathizers.

A large balloon hung over the park and a band was playing. Supposedly, a horse would be attached to the balloon. The balloon would be cut free and lift the horse into the sky. People paid a pretty penny to see this event, extra for a place down close. Some of the Benton Barracks soldiers tried to force their way forward to get a better view of the "flying" horse.

The southern sympathizers in the crowd took exception to these Yankee usurpers and a brawl broke out. The balloon was destroyed. The fight carried into the beer garden and Farrar Mansion was badly damaged. Soldiers called to the scene from Benton Barracks fired "rubber" bullets into the crowd. Some of those rubber bullets had metal jackets *(were real)* and six people were killed and a dozen wounded.

(An investigation failed to produce the culprits who fired live ammo at the crowd.)

Luckily, MJ, the kids, and I were at the watermelon stand near the gate when the fight erupted. We exited immediately and watched from the other side of the fence. There was a police station nearby and the police responded quickly. Men, women, and children rushed the gate in an attempt to escape the park. Some people would have been trampled if the police hadn't seized control of the crowd.

The balloon was ripped to shreds and the fire that was used to keep the balloon inflated set off all the fireworks. The party was over.

Hero

$\mathcal{I}$t was the last night in October. James' knee was acting up again, swollen to twice its normal size. So I took his place when Larry needed help to haul a couple of fugitive slaves across the river, a woman and her son. I was only too glad to volunteer. Old folks usually get to do only the boring stuff. We stowed the fugitives below and headed toward Cahokia.

There was a full moon, but we couldn't see it. Dark clouds raced above us, too high to drop rain, but thick enough to blot out the stars and the sky. There was just enough fog to bounce our voices back to us. It was eerie and slow going.

I throttled back and we cut through the water slowly until we got to the Illinois side. We came out of the fog, so I cut the engine and let the swift current take us. About a mile from Cahokia, we hit a snag. We could see that a snarl of limbs from a sunken tree was caught in our paddle wheel.

I didn't want to start the engine for fear of making matters worse, so we attempted to pole our way loose. No luck. I started the engine after all, putting it in reverse at its lowest speed. Nothing! I tried forward. Still nothing! We were dead in the water and there was nothing we could do about it.

No one goes into the water this time of year, day or night. Too cold! I told Larry we'd just have to wait until morning, when Sam Wiggins would send one of his boys out to look for us. How stupid of me! The only thing worse than a fool is an old fool.

One of us would have to keep watch while the other slept. The words were no sooner out of my mouth when the first round whistled past my ear. We hit the deck. Larry crawled aft to grab our rifles. A few minutes later, the next round tore through the side of the boat just above the water line. Great Odin! Someone was shooting at us with a buffalo rifle. Judging by the time lapse between rounds, I figured it was a lone shooter. Hell, he could take his time. We weren't going anywhere.

My passengers in the hold were shouting. I yelled to them to get behind a crate, lie as flat as they could, and cover their heads. I tried to remember what I had stored in the hold, but my memory slipped on me. I hoped there was nothing explosive.

Larry handed me a box of shells and my new rifle, a .44 Henry, a prototype of a repeating rifle made by Henry Arms that held ten rounds. I started loading shells.

(The following year, Henry Arms would come out with a better version that held 14 rounds.)

John O'Fallon gave me the Henry earlier this month for my *(ugh)* 75th birthday. Like most prototypes of repeating weapons, it had a tendency to jam, usually the result of improper spring tension. I discovered that if I put only eight rounds in the chamber instead of ten, my Henry fired freely. I just had to reload a little sooner.

(Oliver Winchester bought Revolvolonic Rifle and Henry Arms in 1864. By 1866, they started mass production of a much better repeating rifle called the Winchester.)

I yelled, "Larry, get below. Ask our guests to man the bilge pump."

I peeked through the gun port and the lone gunman fired again, ripping a hole below the water line. I saw the muzzle flash. I fired my rifle in that vicinity until the rifle was empty. I pulled a box of shells from my pocket and reloaded. I aimed through the gun port and emptied the Winchester again.

There was another muzzle flash and the railing to my left exploded, sending splinters into my arm and face. Damn, it hurt. While I reloaded, I wondered what other senior citizens did with their nights.

Larry came back on deck, took one look at my bloodied face and arm, and crawled to what he thought was the safe side of the boat. A .50-caliber round tore a hole in the boat right next to his head. Now he had splinters in his face as well. Before I could protest, he scampered over the side and into the cold, dark river.

I headed for the stern, trying to keep low. It wasn't easy keeping my big old rump down. I heard splashing and peeked over the back of the boat, just in time to see Larry duck under the water. I caught the muzzle flash from the corner of my eye and jerked my head down as another round took off a belaying pin. It hit the deck with a dull thud. The son of a gun had climbed a tree. The skunk already had the high ground on us. I returned fire, emptying my rifle again.

Larry came up for air. He shouted, "Cap'n, my tomahawk."

I yelled, "It's coming." I crawled midship, fetched the tomahawk and a crowbar from the footlocker, and returned. The tomahawk was sharp. Larry passed a lot of time on this boat honing it.

I knew exactly where Larry was, on the leeward side of the paddle wheel. I stuck my hand over the rail and Larry took the tomahawk. Another shot rang out and I heard Larry yelp, and then a splash. I reloaded as I repeatedly called his name. Silence. My heart sank.

I heard the water break and a gasp for air. "Larry," I yelled again, breathing a sigh of relief when he answered. "You all right?"

"Just a flesh wound. I can free us, Cap'n, but I dropped the tomahawk on the paddle wheel. Gotta get it."

Damn! If the gunman didn't get him, the freezing water surely would. I had to keep the sniper occupied. I picked my hat up off the deck and told Larry, "Get ready."

I stuck the hat on the end of the crowbar and poked it over the rail. It's a good thing my head wasn't in it because a .50-caliber round whizzed through it, destroying the hat and knocking the crowbar from my hand.

As if in answer to a prayer, the clouds slid by and the full moon lit the night. I yelled "Now, Larry," and stuck my rifle through the gun port and fired at the bushwhacker. I snapped off seven rounds as rapidly as possible, leaving one in the chamber.

I could make out a silhouette on a high limb, a man hugging the side of a tree. He was close. By Loki's magic! I was lucky to be alive.

Shortly, the shadow relaxed and leaned away from the trunk to reload his buffalo rifle. I took careful aim and squeezed. The man flew backward out of the tree and into another. The tree snagged him and he hung upside down, his head about a couple of feet from the ground. His long silver hair brushed the grass and glistened in the moonlight. He didn't move.

I looked into the water. With the moon out, I could see the tangle more clearly. It was there one minute; then it was gone. In an instant, we were free. The boat started to float away. I grabbed a pole and stuck it in the river, slowing our motion until we stopped. I called, "Help."

Nothing happened. "You in the hold. It's safe. Come help. It's safe."

The woman and her boy climbed out of the hold, hesitating at first, and then came to my aid. The mother wasn't big, but her arms were well muscled from daily labor. She took the pole and held firm. I went to the stern and looked in the water.

I didn't see anybody. The moonlight was gleaming off the water now and visibility was good. Where was Larry?

The seconds ticked away. Still no Larry. Maybe he was carried past us. I ran forward to look. Nothing! I looked into the dark water of the river and my stomach dropped. What should I do? I wanted to jump in to see if I could find him, save him. Either my courage failed me or my brain was working. Anyway, I didn't make the futile gesture.

As I watched the river flow by, I felt the same dread sense of helplessness that I experienced when little Lewis was in his death throes from cholera. I shivered and realized it was a miracle Larry lasted as long as he did in the freezing water. I wondered if the river would give him back to us.

The boy tugged on my sleeve. He pointed at his mother who was near tears. "There's something down there," she said, "wrapped on the pole."

We both knew what it was.

I took my gaff and ran it into the water alongside the pole until I struck something. I wriggled it around until I snagged the object. Object! It wasn't an object! It was Larry! I yanked with all my strength and pulled his body out of the water and up the side of the boat. The woman and I got him into the boat.

Resuscitation, maybe? I gasped when I saw the big hole in his back. I turned him over. The entry wound wasn't much smaller. Flesh wound, hell! A .50-caliber round had passed completely through his body.

There would be no last minute rescue for Larry.

• • •

As I sat there in shock, the swift current carried us downriver and the boat was running free. Realizing our peril, the woman yelled at me, "The boat! Do something!"

She finally got through to me. I grabbed the wheel and regained control of the boat. I took the woman and boy to the drop off point. Larry had planned to lead them to the Richardson farm while I waited on the boat. They would have to go it alone. I couldn't leave Larry and, truth be told, I just wasn't up to it.

The woman understood, "We've traveled alone before. We'll be all right."

I gave them directions on how to get to the farm and watched them until they were out of sight. I shivered, either from the cool night air or from the feeling of helplessness that swept over me. I went below, hammered a temporary patch over that hole below the water line, and headed home. I tied up the *Pole Cat* but I didn't leave the ship. MJ came down at dawn and found us.

I told MJ, "I promised Larry a Viking funeral and, come hell or high water, I will give him one."

MJ didn't utter a word. She went to the house to tell Taylor and James what had happened, then to Larry's tepee to fetch one of Nahaboo's old blankets. James and Taylor followed her on to the boat. James was limping badly. The sight of Larry lying so still on the deck was too much. James said, "I should have been there," and started to weep.

Then we all broke down.

Silently, we wrapped Larry in the blanket. MJ stitched up the blanket, while my boys and I went to the bunkhouse to get Stumpy Fredericks' old bunk bed to use for a funeral bier. James wrestled with the straw mattresses while Taylor and I carried the bunk bed to the trading post.

During the trip, I saw my sons' names where Stumpy had carved them on the footboard. I knew what I had to do.

I was carving Larry's name next to Taylor's when Sam Wiggins arrived to open the trading post. Curious, he asked, "What's with the bunk bed?"

When I told him what happened, he went white and his knees buckled. He'd been having fainting spells lately, so I put out my hand to steady him. I said, "Sam, sit down before you fall down. Put your head between your legs."

When I knew he was okay, I went back to my carving. It wasn't easy. I had to stand a step back from the bunk bed to see what I was doing. God, it's hell getting old!

I turned back to Sam, "Don't mention the bushwhacker. Just tell people Larry drowned while freeing the *Pole Cat* from a tangle."

Sam got up and walked over to the boat. I followed. He let out a long whistle when he saw the damage done by that buffalo gun. He said, "That was one hell of a snag."

He fell silent when he spotted MJ working on Larry's shroud. I said, "Sam, we need to build a raft." No reply. "Sam!"

He snapped to and said, "What? Oh, sorry, I, uh, . . . we already got one. Billy snagged a stray yesterday."

He pointed to *Sea Serpent*. On the deck was a white pine raft. It had seen better days, but it would do.

(Occasionally, some river rat failed to secure their raft and it'd break free and come down the river unattended. We called them strays. They were a hazard and any riverman worth his salt would retrieve them from the river to keep them from doing any damage.)

We needed to re-secure the logs on that raft. I sent James and Taylor to do the job. Sam played straw boss. They boarded the ferry, Sam grabbed some hemp from the boat locker, and they went to work.

I was just putting the finishing touches on my wood-carving when Machingo showed up. I wasn't surprised to see him. Nor was he surprised to see us working on a funeral bier. He came beside me and admired my handiwork. He said, "It is right."

He went to his pony and retrieved his paints from the sled. When he returned, I asked him, "How did you know?"

He started painting next to Larry's name. While he worked, he answered my query, "In dream, I see Larry's tomahawk in mouth of great northern pike. Nasty looking fish. Have long silver hair. Tomahawk bleed and river not wash blood away. I ride with The Late Moon on my shoulder."

He finished his artwork. Next to Larry's name, he had painted a beaver, "Now The Maker cannot be sad when he meets Larry."

Seeing that beaver brought back a jumble of memories—Crazy John and Larry at the beaver dam trying to hold back their laughter; my first meeting with Larry, a brave little boy wrestling with his fears; Larry jumping around with my battle-axe, playing Viking; Larry tossing a burning spar into the river and being shot for it; Larry never failing to laugh at Sam's bad jokes. The memories overwhelmed me. I nearly broke down.

Machingo attempted to ease my sorrow, "He lives in my heart, too."

I took a deep breath and relaxed. Then I told Machingo the story of Larry's bravery and I added, "It was a million to one shot that pole snagged him."

Machingo was silent a moment, "No, Captain. Not chance at all."

The boys finished repairing the raft and we secured the funeral bier to it. Then we piled firewood around the bunk and spread a bale of hay underneath. The bier was ready.

We laid Larry's body on the bier and waited for sundown, as was the Viking custom. Machingo assented, "Viking funeral good. Larry travel by The Evening Star."

I looked at the funeral bier and realized something was lacking. Then it hit me. I sent Taylor to fetch my Norse battle-axe. It would be a sin to send a warrior to Valhalla unarmed.

While up at the house, Taylor told the artillery unit about Larry and the news spread quickly through the neighborhood. By the time we commenced Larry's Viking farewell, a large crowd had gathered on the riverbank. Larry touched many lives.

Fatigue was overtaking me when Crazy John showed up just before sunset. He clambered out of his carriage and shuffled down to the raft. His eyes were red and puffy.

He looked at the funeral bier and started to speak but couldn't get the words out. It's about the only time I'd ever seen him speechless. I stepped to him and hugged him. We had a good cry. It lifted my spirits and I no longer felt exhausted.

As the light from the sun dwindled in the west, I slipped the handle of the battle-axe through a gap in the shroud near Larry's chest. We doused the raft with flammables and set it adrift.

Machingo used Nahaboo's old bow and the Shawnee arrow Nahaboo gave me to set the raft afire. The flaming arrow hit its mark and a great flame billowed toward heaven. The pyre burned for a long time. As the flames flickered out, I said, "There you go, son. A Viking and Shawnee funeral both."

No Respite

1864. George and Virginia had another baby, a boy. They named our newest grandson, Louis. It wasn't Lewis, but it was close enough for me and it made MJ happy. She sent them some of Taylor's baby clothes.

Governor Hamilton Gamble died and was replaced by his lieutenant governor, Willard Hall. Gamble had been in ill health for a while and just the year before was injured in a train wreck. People commiserated by pointing out that Gamble was old and had lived a long life. Well, that thinking may make them feel better, but not me. Gamble and I were less than a year apart in age!

Gamble's most famous decision came when he was the only one of three Missouri Supreme Court Justices to vote in favor of giving Dred Scott his freedom.

Gamble defended Machingo and me when The Great Gambini took us to civil court after the St. Louis Prosecuting Attorney refused to bring charges against us for the death of The Mongolian Mauler. The prosecuting attorney witnessed the event himself and called it justifiable homicide.

So Gambini sued us for the loss of income he would suffer because we "destroyed" his prime attraction. Gamble, who was the Missouri secretary of state in 1824, was Crazy John's lawyer. John persuaded him to defend us. We won the case.

The Grand Mississippi Valley Sanitary Fair opened in May. Its main goal was to raise money in an effort to provide aid to wounded soldiers, Union or Confederate. I took the family to the fair. They held raffles, sold food and drink, and even sold beer and wine. I had a great time and a little too much to drink, something I rarely did. MJ said I made a fool of myself. She teased me for days.

The fair raised over a half million dollars, most of which was spent on medical supplies. It was uplifting to see people come together to aid their fellow man, especially in the midst of the sordidness of war.

The war dragged on. A force of 12,000 Confederate troops under former Missouri Governor and Confederate General Sterling Price entered southeast Missouri and appeared to be working their way to St. Louis, engaging Union soldiers in skirmishes at Farmington, Ironton, and Pilot Knob. The city went on full alert but the rebel troops were repelled at Pilot Knob and turned west toward Jefferson City. Everyone was relieved—MJ and I included. We were too old to fight and too sick at heart to bury any more young men.

Taylor ran off and joined the Army. He was 13 years old but big for his age and could easily pass for 18. Besides, they were taking all able bodies, regardless of age. Talk about poetic justice. Now, I knew how my mother must have felt when I ran off and joined the Army. I was miserable.

I ran into Emil Mallinckrodt at the Broadway Market. He told me, "Otto and Edward are in Germany studying chemical analysis."

I replied, "Good for them. They're a long way from this war. Learning something new sure beats the hell out of killing your neighbor."

Conspiracy

1865. The Civil War officially ended on April 9th, a war that took the lives of over 620,000 men. MJ and I rejoiced the war's end and prayed for Taylor's return. Our joy turned to sorrow five days later when President Lincoln was assassinated in Ford's Theater. He was shot in the head by an actor of all things, John Wilkes Booth. MJ and I saw his brother Edwin trod the boards here in St. Louis.

Lincoln's death hit me hard. The papers were full of conspiracy theories. The local paper printed an article in the editorial section by Noah Brooks of the *Sacramento Union*. Brooks claimed Secretary of War Stanton and Secret Service Chief Colonel Lafayette Baker exceeded their authority. They violated the rights of hundreds of people, arresting them and charging them with crimes they could not have possibly committed. Brooks insinuated that maybe Stanton and Baker had a hand in the plotting.

Booth was shot and killed against orders. Booth's landlady, Mary Surratt, was arrested for conspiracy and thrown in prison under intolerable conditions. She was the first woman to be executed by the United States Government. Stagehand Ned Spangler was found guilty of suppressing information that might have prevented the murder. He was sentenced to five years hard labor at Fort Jefferson.

Doctor Samuel Mudd, a known Southern sympathizer, treated Booth's broken leg and was sent to prison for, as he said, "upholding my Hippocratic oath."

At the same time Lincoln was being shot, attempts were made on the lives of Vice-President Johnson and Secretary of State Seward. Seward was in critical condition for some time, but eventually recovered. Mrs. Lincoln was sure Johnson had some part in the assassination.

Andrew Johnson became our President and, drinking problem aside, made a tremendous effort to continue Abe's goal, the reunification of the country and the American people.

It was a troubling time. I wished T.H. were still alive. Maybe he could make some sense of all this.

• • •

My cousin, James, Uncle Daniel's son, returned to St. Louis from Virginia shortly after the war broke out. He was arrested by Union forces as a Confederate sympathizer and incarcerated in the Gratiot Street Prison until the end of the war. During his incarceration, his wife, Anna, had to pay huge fines for owning slaves.

After his release, MJ and I visited James. His lengthy prison stay was unkind to him. Although several years my junior, he didn't look it. He didn't talk of his tribulation and we had the good sense to avoid the issue.

James took delight in telling us how he avoided paying the "closet tax" levied by the county by installing cupboards in place of closets. It was a story we had heard before but we had the good grace to act as though we were hearing it for the first time.

Crazy John

"The Lord giveth and The Lord taketh away."

A crow said that to me. I swear. I was up on the widow's walk sitting in my chair, my usual morning routine in my later days. This old crow, which had lost an eye, was a regular visitor. Old One Eye, as I called him, landed on the fence rail. Like most mornings, he had plenty to say. I usually just nodded at his cawing, generally agreeing with him and tossing him an occasional breadcrumb. He's okay. Now, I admit I dozed off and jerked back awake quite a bit, so I'm not sure if I dreamed it or if it was real. All I know is, clear as a bell, the crow said, "The Lord giveth and The Lord taketh away."

I closed my eyes and rubbed them with my fists to test if I was awake. I heard a caw and I opened my eyes. Old One Eye was gone. I rubbed my eyes again. It must have been a dream.

Later that day, we received a telegram from George and Virginia, announcing the birth of a granddaughter. They named her Cora. I thought MJ would be upset, but she didn't say anything immediately. Later that night, she admitted she was embarrassed by the absurdity of her reaction to their naming their first-born son after Virginia's father. What's in a name? After five years of war and death—a new life, now that's important.

MJ brought the telegram up to the widow's walk and handed it to me, a grim expression accentuating her hard features. While reading the letter, I heard a crow caw. I saw

Old One Eye on the limb of a nearby tree. After reading the good news, I asked her, "Who died?"

She was taken aback, "How do you know someone died?"

"A little bird told me."

She didn't know what to say to that.

"Who died?"

"Crazy John."

The news struck me like a round from a buffalo gun. I had flashbacks of moments with him that were so vivid it was as if I actually went back to those moments in time and then returned to the present. I couldn't speak. MJ hugged me. She understood my silence and left.

I spent the afternoon and evening alone. I looked to the heavens, remembering everything I could about my friend, sometimes dozing off and dreaming of him. Just before sunset, Old One Eye swooped down and landed on the top of the trapdoor. Once again, in his strange crow way, he said, "The Lord giveth and The Lord taketh away."

He flew off, leaving me to try to make sense of a world that no longer was the one I thought I knew.

Crazy John was survived by his wife, Ruth, and four sons and a daughter. Attendance at his funeral was impressive, an eclectic mix of the rich and influential and the poor and grateful.

At his eulogy, an open forum at John's request, his business colleagues spoke of his service to the community, how he was a catalyst for ventures that helped put St. Louis on the map. They marveled at the many hats he wore—banker, broker, buyer, seller, bull, bear, financier, speculator, partner. He was the president of a couple of railroads and a philanthropist who gave liberally to schools like O'Fallon Polytechnic and Washington University.

The scions of industry were in accord that John O'Fallon was a shining example of what an ethical businessman can do for a community. They were generous in their praise of John O'Fallon and his dedication to progress, but for me they left something out.

What about the "crazy" part?

After the land sharks, it was the little guys' turn. Simple people from all walks of life agreed that Crazy John was the fairest of men, unprejudiced and accepting, a person who did not place you against a measuring stick to evaluate your worth. Many told tales of how Crazy John helped them get the start they needed to make life better for them and their families.

Bakery owner, saloon keep, maid, trash hauler, school teacher, barber, you name it, they were there to give testimony to the passing of a truly generous human being.

When it was my turn, I shuffled forward and stood in front of the casket, facing the crowd. Every seat was filled and people were standing in the back. As I stood there, I got a sense of the crowd. Their regard for the old Irishman was palpable.

I walked to the casket and put my hand under Crazy John's nostrils, then looked back at the mourners. "Just checking," I said, "making sure Crazy John's not pulling another of his practical jokes on me."

There was a buzz and someone said, "That'd be Crazy John, alright."

MJ and Ruth, sitting side by side, smiled, tears on their cheeks.

"Soldiers bond." I looked at my friend at rest in his death box. "In times of duress, one reveals his true self. Crazy John fought the good fight."

I reached inside my coat and pulled out a pistol. A ripple

went through the crowd. It ceased when I placed the pistol on Crazy John's chest. "Here you go, my friend," I said. "In case they give you trouble on the other side."

I patted his shoulder and returned to my seat.

Now I don't know if you've ever been to an Irish wake. It's actually a celebration. Crazy John used to say the only difference between an Irish wedding and an Irish wake was one less drunk.

Before the wake, we attended the last rites at the cemetery. On the way back to our carriage, I heard a woman say, "That's him."

I looked in the direction of her voice and was surprised to see Junior Chouteau sitting in a wheelchair, a nurse behind him.

"Junior," the word slipped through my lips.

"Bissell," he crowed as he pointed to his eyes. "Long time no see."

I motioned to MJ to go on. "About six years now, right?" I said, remembering the newspaper account of his misfortune.

He lifted the blanket on his lap and I could tell his legs were shriveled. "I hope you don't mind if I don't get up."

I knew nothing of the atrophy of his limbs. I mumbled, "Not at all."

Junior said, "Yes, not too much left of me," he paused for emphasis, "but I'll bet you're as big as a whale by now."

Junior laughed until he coughed.

I let the remark slide. "Nice of you to pay your respects, Ju . . . , uh, Pierre."

He grinned at my attempt at civility. "Not too many originals left, are there, Bissell?"

"If the human race is lucky, there will always be people like Crazy John."

He shook his head from side to side, "I was talking about me, you fool!"

Feeling pity for him, I said, "Good day," and walked away. He ordered his nurse to follow me. Behind me, I heard the wheelchair kick up rock on the gravel path.

"Wait, Bissell," he intoned, "Wait! Wait! Hey, where's

your famous sense of humor?" I stopped and turned. His nurse stopped his wheelchair just short of me. "I just want to ask you one more thing."

"What?"

"Do you think anyone will remember your speech at the funeral parlor?"

I didn't know and I didn't care, so I answered with a question of my own, "What does it matter?"

"It doesn't, Bissell." His sightless eyes bore into me. "That's the point."

If he expected a reply, I had none. I waited.

He continued, "I've had nothing on my hands but time to think, Mon Capitaine." He fixed his empty eyes on me and continued, "I'm loaded, Bissell, filthy rich. If I wanted, I could have all records of your existence erased. When all is said and done, you won't even be a footnote in history, while my exploits and the exploits of my family will be regaled far and wide."

"So?"

"So? That's all you have to say?" He shook his head, "You're a real throwback, Bissell, a dip in the evolutionary curve, just a bump in the road." He laughed at his own joke. "You fool," he said and began to choke. As his nursed rolled him away, he recovered enough to say, "See you in hell, Bissell."

He died a short time later.

Junior claimed he could deny me my legacy. How? My legacy rests in the hearts and minds of the people I met in the daily routine of my life. History records the deeds of the builders and shakers of societies. Families, neighbors, friends, and co-workers record the truth of a person.

● ● ●

A new Missouri constitution was adopted and ratified by the citizens of Missouri. They finally abolished slavery two years after the *Emancipation Proclamation*. I thought it would

be the end of finders, but they just started calling themselves
bounty hunters and hunted criminals instead of slaves.

Tom Fletcher was elected governor. He rode the first passenger train from St. Louis to Kansas City and declared that
Missouri was the most "progressive" state in the Union.

That was good for a laugh.

Changes

1866. I now have a 40-year-old son. What does that make me? Old, old, old!

Alleluia! We received word from Taylor. He was alive and living in Staunton, Virginia. He volunteered to fight but, because he could read, the Army made him a mail clerk. Everyone called him lucky. He didn't think so. This is Taylor's war story.

Taylor was a few miles away in Lynchburg when Lee surrendered to Grant at Appomattox. That night, some diehard Confederate sniper bounced a bullet off his head, putting him in a coma for a while. When he came to, he couldn't remember a thing. He was just another nameless face to the people tending to him. They were so busy taking care of wounded from both sides, record keeping went by the boards.

A nurse took an interest in him and visited him daily, even on her off days. The patient next to him repeatedly told him he was sure lucky to have such a lovely girl fretting over him. Being called lucky awoke something in Taylor. He started to think that might have been his name.

He had a recurring dream about being on a riverboat with two giants who stood taller than the mast. In his dream, he was filled with dread, fearing the ship would sink under their mighty weight. They passed a castle on a tall hill and he thought, "The king needs me. I must wake up."

During the day, his memory returned in bits and pieces. He had the dream again. This time the giants were just large people, and when the boat passed the castle a name popped into his head, Picot. Immediately, he put names to the faces. He awoke with a start and his memories flooded back, as if the dam holding them at bay had burst.

He mustered out of the Army, took his pay, and followed his nurse to Staunton. After a brief, uh, courtship, they wed. He's working for her father's newspaper.

• • •

MJ and I were overjoyed to hear Taylor was alive. She joked about his amnesia, saying it's the poorest excuse she ever heard someone make up to get out of writing to his mother. We laughed until we cried.

Anne married a leather goods maker, George F. Wilson. George had been married before. His first wife died in child-birth, as well as the baby. We held a small wedding service and reception at our home.

They finally built a railroad bridge across the Mississippi River, running from Quincy, Illinois, to Hannibal. Life on the Mississippi was going to change.

A group of scholars and businessmen created the Missouri Historical Society. This organization's goal was to preserve the history of Missouri.

A salesman for Lincoln Insurance came to my door. Oops, sorry, not salesman—he called himself an agent *(just like a minion of Satan)*.

I was polite but refused to invite him inside. He wouldn't take "no" for an answer. Finally, I had to suggest to him that he was going to need some life insurance for himself if he didn't leave.

Door-to-door salesman—now that's a dangerous job.

A fire destroyed most of Primus Emerson's boatyard in Carondelet. Arson was suspected because of a labor dispute. Some thought it was some Yankee taking a measure of revenge against the former Confederate.

The business was uninsured and his loss was estimated at over $60,000. I should have sent that Lincoln Insurance agent to his house.

In what some felt was retaliation for Henry Picot's Confederate loyalties, the city of Carondelet, as a part of their road building project, razed the hills next to the ground that supported Picot Castle. This action resulted in the castle's eventual deconstruction.

• • •

1867. Population growth and the memory of cholera epidemics associated with this phenomenon led the City of St. Louis to hire Thomas Whitman, an engineer, to build a water treatment plant. I couldn't agree more. Clean water is paramount to good health. *(Thomas was a brother of the poet Walt Whitman.)*

The upper waterworks was built on the Chain of Rocks. Franklinville Farm was about two miles due west of the site. The lower works was built at the foot of Bissell Street.

(The city named a street after me. So did Madison County in Illinois. Straight across the Mississippi River, Bissell Street continues on the Illinois side.)

They started building water towers on Bissell Street and Grand Avenue to assure water pressure and named the lower water processing plant, the Bissell Point Waterworks.

The widow's walk became my roosting spot. I could watch the construction, listen to my birds, breathe in the change of the seasons (especially autumn, when people burned their leaves in ash pits, a marvelous aroma), but mostly, I could nap and dream.

I found myself dreaming more and more of departed friends and loved ones. One day, I started feeling a little poorly. My chest was tight and my fingers were numb. I thought I'd better go inside and lie down. When I stood, the world started to spin, so I sat back down. Maybe I passed out. I don't remember.

I dreamed I was fishing, sitting in a canoe. While my line

lay unmoving in the water, the fish leapt out of the water and laughed at me. Then the fish changed.

Suddenly they had human faces, the faces of people that I knew—Crazy John, Uncle Dan, Nahaboo, Larry, little Lewis. They would leap up and flick their tails under them and somehow balance themselves on the top of the water. They urged me to join them in their frolicking. Crazy John shouted, "Jump on in, you old fart. The water's fine."

Larry swam by and poked his head up, "Join us, Cap'n."

Little Lewis piped, "Come out and play, Daddy."

Nahaboo challenged, "Come, Captain. We will wrestle the stars."

I heard the sweetest voice behind me and turned to look. Mary, as beautiful a mermaid as you would ever want to see, called, "Husband, I await you. Do not be afraid."

I plunged into the water, only now it wasn't water, it was a billowy cloud. For a moment, I floated on the surface, light as a feather. Mary, who now lay on her side on the cloud, patted the place in front of her. As I swam through the mist toward her, I heard a familiar voice far off, yelling, "Lewis! Lewis!"

A disembodied voice whispered, "You have to go back now."

Suddenly, I plummeted through the cloud, heading for the earth below. I started to spin in a circle until I felt as if I were water going down a drain. Wham! I landed inside my self and gravity regained its hold on me.

I felt heavy, very heavy. I also felt someone shaking my arm and patting my hand. I raised my arm. It was weighted like a fallen oak. I dropped it back down and forced my eyes open. MJ's face was about an inch from mine. James was standing behind her. She said, "Thank the Lord! I've been trying to wake you for ten minutes. Are you all right?"

It took me a second to clear the fog that filled my head. I told her, "Yes. No. I don't know."

She and James helped me down the steep and narrow stairs into the house. MJ sent James for a doctor. His diagnosis was a mild heart attack. He said I needed to get more rest. I thought,

"More rest. That's what got me into this trouble in the first place."

The doc also told me, "Stay off the widow's walk, Lewis. It's dangerous for an old timer like you to be up there. At your size, if anything serious happened, they'd have one hell of a time getting you down from the roof."

For the most part, I stayed off the widow's walk. Oh, I'd steal up there when MJ wasn't around. I figured I'd see her returning in plenty of time to get back down before she saw me. I didn't count on falling asleep and getting caught red-handed.

After one of MJ's patented tongue-lashings, I started going down to the *Pole Cat* instead. I sat on the deck, watched river traffic, and occasionally fished.

People heard I was unwell and came to visit. One of my well-wishers was Emil Mallinckrodt. He brought me some apples, claiming, "Eating fresh fruit is the key to good health and a long life."

Emil certainly looked healthy. I agreed, "And it keeps the scurvy away."

"Edward and Otto have returned from Germany." His voice was filled with pride. "With Gustav as director, they have formed their own company, G. Mallinckrodt & Company, Manufacturing Chemists."

I had heard Gustav was a shrewd businessman. I said, "Tell your boys I wish them well. If this blasted war's taught us anything, it's that we need better medicines."

"No doubt. Fare well now."

Another of my visitors was Machingo. His hair was white and his skin was leathered but his eyes still held the sparkle of youth. We reminisced for hours, mostly about those who were no longer here. Machingo told me he was returning to his tribe for a final visit. Thick-headed as usual, I didn't realize he was going home to die.

We took down the tepee and packed it on his sled. The last thing he said to me was, "Stay the course, riverman. It has been a good dream."

MJ joined something called the Missouri Women's Suffrage Club. It sounded like trouble to me. Kansas City was growing. I read in the paper that they established their first high school.

• • •

1868. Secretary of War Stanton led an effort to have President Andrew Johnson impeached, an act that furthered my suspicion that Stanton had something to do with Lincoln's death. Johnson remained in office by a single vote. Ulysses S. Grant was next in line.

(The following year, Grant was elected President and appointed Stanton a Supreme Court Justice. Stanton died before taking his seat on the bench.)

They built a railroad bridge across the Missouri River. The country was connected.

The first St. Louis Insane Asylum was erected. On October 13th, Bremen Bank opened, with a lot of fanfare. I don't think the two events are related, but who knows?

Taps

It was 26 November 1868. I dozed while sitting on the deck of the *Pole Cat* underneath the wooden awning over the pilot's seat. I was taking advantage of the shade, sitting in my favorite chair, my back to the sun. I woke up, or rather, I thought I woke up because there was a bright light in my eyes. I shielded my eyes with my arm, but to no avail. The light shone through my arm like it was glass. I felt a pull, a gentle tug, and I found myself heading toward the light.

As I neared, I could make out a group of people clustered in the center of the radiance. They called to me with voices I knew, separate but one. The veil of brilliance lifted and I was in the presence of everyone I missed so dearly after they exited the mortal coil. They exuded warmth and affection and I basked in this shower of love. I didn't want to wake up from this dream. So, I didn't.

October 12, 1789–November 28, 1868

Epilogue

2002. Change is inevitable and often dramatic. Bremen is now called Hyde Park. Some of the neighborhood is blighted, but the architecture is still marvelous. Urban blight happens to all communities. It's called getting old. Area businesses, coupled with the desire by the City of St. Louis to restore this historical area, have given rise to a spirit of hope for revival.

In 1874, the Union Stockyards opened at the foot of Bremen Street. The Union Stockyards gave way to the Krey Meat Packing Company, which was founded in 1882. The Hermann Oak Leather Company, a related industry, was founded in 1881. The Union Stockyards, Hyde Park Brewery (later *Carling Brewery),* and the Krey Meat Packing Company are no more, but the Hermann Oak Leather Company is still a thriving business.

The Mallinckrodt Chemical Company, led by the innovative Edward Mallinckrodt, became an industry giant and is still flourishing. The Mallinckrodts were pioneers in the packaging of pharmaceuticals, the production of lubricating gels for Model-T Fords, and the development of chemicals for enhancing x-ray development.

Mallinckrodt played a huge role in bringing WWII to a close by developing high-grade uranium compounds for the atomic bomb. The flexibility and risk-taking nature of this company is a fine example of what we Americans are proud to call "Yankee Ingenuity."

Bremen Bank, which opened in 1868, about the same time Captain Lewis Bissell died, is still a prosperous institution. Just down the street, the Broadway Market thrives as well, its success contributing to traffic congestion caused by the steady flow of trucks to this area. East of Bissell Point, halfway to the river, lies the Proctor & Gamble Company, a fixture near the top of the Fortune 500 list of the top businesses in the world.

Trains and trucks are some of the most common sights in the area as the transportation industry goes about its daily routine. Machine companies, warehouses, and manufacturing plants dot the landscape from Highway 70 to the river. The buildings are old, but the ideas are new.

Thousands of people pass through Captain Bissell's home every year. Sitting in the Bissell Mansion, at what is truly the heart of this community, one can feel the presence of those who have gone before. Renewal is a matter of trust and hope. I'm sure Captain Lewis Bissell, John O'Fallon, and the many others who where here at the beginning would see the problems of today as a challenge and an opportunity to make a better tomorrow.